For Jea ~ this
I hope you
St. Clair tale ♥

DEFENDING THE DUKE

The St. Clairs
Book 4

Alexa Aston

Love,
Alexa Aston

DRAGONBLADE PUBLISHING, INC.

Additional Dragonblade books by Author Alexa Aston

King's Cousins Series
The Pawn
The Heir
The Bastard

Knights of Honor Series
Word of Honor
Marked by Honor
Code of Honor
Journey to Honor
Heart of Honor
Bold in Honor
Love and Honor
Gift of Honor
Path to Honor
Return to Honor

The St. Clairs Series
Devoted to the Duke
Midnight with the Marquess
Embracing the Earl
Defending the Duke

*** Please visit Dragonblade's website for a full list of books and authors. Sign up for Dragonblade's blog for sneak peeks, interviews, and more: ***
www.dragonbladepublishing.com

PROLOGUE

Ridingham Academy—1795

ANTHONY GODWIN STOOD in the headmaster's office, having been summoned an hour earlier. He'd been told his father would soon arrive to take him away. Fear curled around his heart, almost choking the breath from him. But he wouldn't apologize for fighting. It had been Rinson's fault. Anthony merely defended himself.

A discreet knock sounded on the door and the secretary entered, saying, "His Grace, the Duke of Linfield, has arrived."

The headmaster rose. Anthony saw nerves flit through the man as he put on a mask of bravado.

"Send in His Grace."

Moments later, the Duke of Linfield entered. The room—and the headmaster—seemed to shrink in his presence.

"Good afternoon, Your Grace. Would you care for—"

"Is the boy staying at Ridingham or not?"

Anthony took note that his father referred to him as the boy.

Not *his* boy.

The headmaster flushed a dull red. "I believe it is in the best interest of the other boys at Ridingham Academy if Mr. Godwin finds another place in which to continue his education."

"I'll see him alone."

Anthony swallowed. He locked his knees to keep from swaying. His father rarely spent any time with him. In fact, he couldn't remember the last time they had been alone.

The door closed and the duke finally turned his attention to his son. His eyes narrowed.

"Fighting? Again?"

"Yes, sir."

"Do you have anything to say for yourself?"

He wished he could tell his father about the circumstances. How Rinson had bullied him relentlessly ever since he'd arrived at the school. The older boy taunted and belittled him. Stolen from him. Lied about him. Anthony had taken it, knowing older boys always did so to younger ones. Finally, though, Rinson had used his fists and Anthony had retaliated. He couldn't help being a better fighter. None of that mattered, though. He already knew whatever he said would be met with hostility—or worse.

Indifference.

"No, sir."

The duke sighed. "This will be the third school that has requested you leave."

"I know," he said sullenly.

"Belligerence doesn't suit you," his father noted.

His hands balled into fists.

"Anger can be an effective weapon," the duke said, glancing at his son's hands. "You are angry. Learning to harness anger is difficult but it's a lesson you need to learn."

Anthony had no idea how to do so. It seemed he had been born angry. Or made that way. His mother had died in childbirth after producing him. His father paid scant attention to him. His brother made his life miserable.

Craving his father's attention, he bravely asked, "Could you teach me that lesson? How to rein in my anger?"

The duke looked at him as if he'd grown three heads. "Why on earth would I care to do so?" he asked, clearly baffled by the request.

"Because I am your son?" he offered, hoping for a scrap of recognition as to their relationship.

The duke's jaw tightened. "I already have a son I teach everything to. My heir."

"Theodore is nothing but a bully," Anthony blurted out. "He's bullied me ever since I can remember. You favor him."

The duke's eyes gleamed. "Of course, I favor him. And rightfully so. Theodore is a marquess. Heir to a dukedom. Most every man in England will be subservient to him one day. Only a handful of men will be his peer or outrank him. He's been *bred* to bully others. To stand above all. To use the power he has now, power which will grow once I am gone and he becomes Linfield." He paused. "I'll always favor him over you. There's never been any question in that regard."

Anthony had always known his father preferred his brother but hearing the words spoken aloud hurt more than he could have imagined.

"But I'm his brother," he protested. "Surely, he could be nice to me. I'm family."

The duke snorted. "Theodore will never be nice to you. He's scared to death of you." ·

The remark puzzled him. "He's four years older than me."

His father assessed him. "He has good reason to fear you, Boy. You're already far more clever than Theodore ever will be. Before long, you'll physically catch him in height and weight and then surpass him. You're even better looking. His ears stick out and with his thin hair, he'll go bald by the time he's thirty."

The duke flicked a piece of lint from his coat. "He's jealous of you and always will be. If he can bend you to his will, he'll be able to do so with others."

"I know he'll be Linfield someday," Anthony protested. "I never will. Can't you make him—"

"Make him what?" the duke interrupted. "Like you? *Love* you?" He laughed. "Theodore will never have any kind feelings for you. Where you're concerned, it's pure jealousy. And hatred. He knows you killed his beloved mother."

Anthony's fists tightened.

"You want to strike me. I know. It's written all over you. You'll need to learn to mask your emotions as well as manage your anger. The military will do that for you."

He frowned. "What if I don't want to be in the army?" he challenged.

"Second sons go into the military," his father said, his tone revealing that Anthony would have no other option. "It will give you discipline. You're a bright boy. If you could stop leading with your fists and think before you strike someone, you have the makings of being a leader."

The duke turned and went to the door. "We'll leave now. Your things have been collected."

He followed his father to the carriage waiting outside. They climbed in and the duke immediately closed his eyes. Obviously, their conversation was over for now. For several hours, Anthony stared out the window. Wondering where his next school would be. If he would learn to control his temper. What life in the army would be like one day.

The carriage turned and he realized where they headed. He looked and saw his father's eyes opened.

"We're stopping to visit Aunt Constance?" he asked.

"More than that," the duke revealed. "You'll be living with her. She will manage everything. Find you a new school. That sort of thing."

An uneasy feeling settled over him. "For how long?"

"Until you finish your education," the duke said crisply. "You'll spend your holidays with her. I'll purchase your military commission once you've turned eighteen. Then you'll be on your own."

The duke's words stunned him. "You're . . . cutting me loose?"

"I have the son I need. I plan to spend all my time molding him into being the perfect Duke of Linfield. It's going to take a huge amount of effort to do so. You've been far more trouble than I'd expected. I don't wish to bother with you in the future."

The carriage came to a halt. The door opened. His father gave him a pointed look so he rose unsteadily and moved toward the door, where he was hoisted to the ground by the footman. The door closed and Anthony looked inside the carriage. His father stared straight ahead. He realized he wouldn't get a word of goodbye, much less any encouragement. His gut told Anthony he would never see his father again.

Good . . .

The driver set his trunk next to him. He caught the look of sympathy in the man's eyes and quickly lowered his own, fighting back the tears that stung his eyes. The driver returned to his seat and, with a flick of the reins, the carriage set off again down the lane. Slowly, Anthony raised his eyes, watching it depart. As it rolled away, the anger that had existed within him exploded, burning as a roaring furnace, the blazing heat sweeping through him, claiming his soul. He no longer existed to his father, if he ever had. He silently cursed the man who'd played a part in giving him life, as well as his worthless brother. He didn't need them. He would never think about them.

An arm went about his shoulders. He glanced up and saw Aunt Constance standing next to him. Tears brimmed in her eyes but she gave him a brave smile.

"I'm so glad you've come to stay with me, Anthony. I always wanted to have children. Now, I'll have my own little boy to love."

"Father never loved me, did he, Aunt Constance?"

She smoothed his hair. "He's never loved anyone but himself. Not even your mother. And certainly not Theodore. I don't think Linfield is capable of love." She smiled brightly. "I think you'll be better off without him."

Anthony was eight years old.

CHAPTER ONE

London—January 1816

L AUREL WRIGHT RECORDED each item and its price before placing it in the basket. She provided the total and waited expectantly for payment, knowing Mrs. Jones wouldn't have enough money to pay the entire bill. She wished she could allow the woman to take all of the goods anyway but Mr. Cole had expressly forbidden her from doing so, stepping away from his policy of giving customers the privilege to purchase goods on credit and allowing them to pay at the end of each month. As of last week, everyone who entered the chandler's store, whether they purchased cheese, bacon, or any other groceries, had to pay for all items bought before they left the premises. She feared too many people had taken advantage of Mr. Cole's generosity and that was why he had to insist on payment in full. Since she managed his ledgers, she understood why he'd made the drastic change. It had cost them a few customers since the policy had gone into effect but at least there was coin in the till and Mr. Cole could pay his own suppliers in full for once.

The woman shook her head and took two items out of the basket. After contemplating for a few moments, a third joined the two on the counter. Laurel deducted the cost from the total bill and struck the goods from her list. The longtime customer nodded and painstakingly counted out what was due.

"Thank you, Mrs. Jones," she said, smiling kindly. "I'll see you next time."

Mrs. Jones shrugged and shuffled from the store. Laurel replaced the withdrawn items on the various shelves and returned behind the counter. She closed the ledger, placing it and the till on the shelf beneath the counter.

The bell tinkled as the door opened again and she saw Mr. Cole had returned.

With Julius Farmon.

She suppressed a shudder and kept a bland expression on her face. Laurel hated Mr. Farmon with a passion. He had bought up much of the neighborhood and raised rents, including the tenement where she lived with her mother and brother. Their small abode barely was large enough for the three of them yet they paid the bulk of what they earned in rent. It had helped when Mama held a job but after her heart attack several months ago, the doctor had wanted Dinah Wright off her feet and out of the workforce. Her mother's heart condition had weakened her to the point where she could no longer even sew on the side, which had supplemented the Wright family's income. Now, Laurel and Hudson scraped together what they could to replace the missing income. She not only worked as a clerk at Mr. Cole's but since she was good with numbers, she kept the chandler's books for him, staying late after the store closed to work on them. The additional sewing her mother used to take on had now fallen to Laurel and she completed those projects late into the night.

Her brother had quit school last month in order to contribute more to the family's income. Hudson had been a mudlark for many years while attending school, scrounging the Thames at low tide for things that might have washed ashore. He'd collected anything of value and sold it. Now, Hudson worked two jobs. During the day he was a coal porter, unloading coal from ships along the wharf and delivering it to customers. At night, he was a waterman, watering horses at cab stands. Laurel only saw him for a few minutes late at night before he fell into bed and occasionally in the morning before they both left for work. She kept telling herself this wouldn't last forever. That Hudson would sit for the upcoming university exam and earn a scholarship and become someone important. His teachers had called him nothing short of brilliant and she was determined that he would make a better life for himself.

If her brother did win a place at university, she would be thrilled—but she worried about replacing his portion of their income when he left London. They barely managed as it was, with rent so expensive. Fortunately, Mr. Cole let Laurel take home some items that were just this side of going bad. If eaten right away, they didn't usually cause any stomach problems. As far as clothing went, Laurel was able to sew the few things they needed. The modiste where Mrs. Wright used to work for many years still gave Laurel scraps to use for patching elbows and knees on her brother's clothing. Or she had until her death two weeks ago. The shop had now closed.

Mr. Cole surprised her by turning the sign hanging from the door, indicating they were closed. It was only two in the afternoon. She couldn't imagine why he would be closing at such an early hour. As he came toward her, she focused on her employer and not the man by his side. She could feel Mr. Farmon's eyes assessing her but she ignored him, afraid she knew the reason why he accompanied Mr. Cole.

"Is something wrong, Mr. Cole?" she asked.

"We've business to discuss," Farmon replied.

Reluctantly, Laurel looked in his direction. Farmon was a good two inches shorter than she was but she was tall for a woman. He was almost as broad as he was tall, with eyes black as night and a sour expression on his bloated face. Several rings adored his sausage-like fingers. Though he dressed as a gentleman, she knew of his immoral character and ill humor and just how dangerous he could be. Last month, the tavern owner two blocks away had balked at the increasingly large weekly payment Farmon demanded business owners pay him for the privilege of operating in this neighborhood. Farmon had visited the tavern and had his henchman hold the owner down while he cut out the man's tongue, telling him this would prevent future complaints from being aired.

She'd also witnessed firsthand the terror Farmon brought. Their neighbor across the hall had injured his back at work and lost his job. Mr. Greenley owed Farmon a small debt and worried how he was to pay it. Julius Farmon had come in person to collect what was owed him. Seeing that Mr. Greenley wouldn't be able to work anytime soon, he'd cut the man's throat and taken his screaming six-year-old daughter from the tenement as payment. When Laurel asked her mother what Farmon intended to do with the young girl, her mother explained that she would be sold into prostitution.

Because of incidents such as these, Laurel knew to keep her distance from a man as evil as Julius Farmon. If he bought Mr. Cole's chandlery, though, that would be difficult.

"Cole here tells me that you keep the books for him," Farmon continued. "I'd like to see them."

"Why would I show them to you?" she challenged.

The man's eyes narrowed and she wished she'd kept quiet. Though she did her best to be kind to all and act demurely as a young woman should, this man ruffled her feathers. Laurel tended to speak her mind, which her mother constantly rebuked her for doing. She felt she was just as smart as her twin and didn't believe she should remain quiet simply because she was a woman. Of course, society had different ideas regarding the role of women. Men ran the world and would never consider women to be their equals. She would do good to keep her thoughts to herself and watch her tongue in the future.

"Show him the ledgers, Laurel," Mr. Cole said nervously.

She studied her employer, seeing the sweat beaded along his brow, though the mid-January winter day with its blustery wind had plunged temperatures to where water froze.

"Yes, Mr. Cole."

Laurel retrieved the ledger under the counter and said, "If you'll come with me, Mr. Farmon."

She led him through the closed curtain and back to the space used as an office. It was here Mr. Cole wrote up the orders he placed and where she kept all her records—by customer, by month, and by year.

"How far back would you like to see?" she asked, keeping her voice even though her nerves were frayed.

"Three years."

"Very well."

She went to the shelves and pulled what Farmon wished to view, setting out the books in different piles and explaining to him how she accounted for various things.

When she turned to go, he said, "Stay."

It wasn't an invitation.

Laurel sat and watched as he flipped through different ledgers. He nodded to himself sometimes and clucked his tongue in disapproval twice. Every now and then, he would ask her a question and she was thankful she was able to answer it to his satisfaction.

Finally, Farmon closed what he perused and studied her. She felt herself grow warm under his intense scrutiny.

"You know numbers, I'll give you that."

"Women can add, you know," she snapped, once again regretting her flare of temper.

His hand shot out and grasped her wrist. She froze. Her eyes met his and she saw he wanted to intimidate her. She swallowed and took a deep breath, trying to keep her fear locked away.

"How would you like to run this store?" he casually asked.

It would be a wonderful opportunity—if Julius Farmon wasn't her employer.

"What about Mr. Cole?" she countered.

"I'm buying the chandlery from Cole," he replied. "Since you're familiar with everything and have a good system in place, you would be his natural replacement. I wouldn't have to train anyone else."

Excitement mixed with disgust. Laurel didn't want to work for this man but if she ran the shop, it would mean more money. If Hudson did leave, she would be able to care for Mama.

Cautiously, she said, "I earn money both as a clerk and for keeping the books. What would my salary be if I managed the store?"

Farmon smiled, his teeth yellow and crooked. She shivered, sensing evil within him.

"The same."

His answer startled her. Maybe he hadn't understood her question and so she decided to clarify things for him.

"If I gained more responsibility by managing the place, I should be fairly compensated," she pointed out.

"You would run it. And continue to serve as both clerk and bookkeeper."

"Then why wouldn't I receive more salary?" she asked, her voice rising in anger. "Because I am a woman?"

"Your salary remains the same." An odd glow entered his eyes. "But I do have a way you could earn more. If you'd like to take advantage of a . . . unique opportunity."

Her stomach twisted. "What would it involve?"

"Making me happy."

She might be a young woman of eighteen but she'd grown up just the other side of poverty—and knew exactly what Farmon meant.

"I'm afraid that won't be possible," she said stiffly. She rose, hoping to throw off his fingers, but they still held her wrist firmly.

Farmon also came to his feet. "You are exactly who I want to service me. You will accept my offer. You'll run the store by day and keep me happy at night. Both will keep you plenty busy."

"No!" she said, jerking her arm away. "I am not that kind of woman."

He laughed. "Every woman in your position is that kind of woman, Miss Wright. Despite your haughty airs and skill with numbers, look at you. That threadbare gown. The drawn look to your cheeks. Being too thin from not eating enough. And I hear that pretty mother of yours is doing poorly. Surely, you want to make sure she's taken care of properly?"

His fingers slid to grip her forearm. His touch repulsed her. She took a step back, freeing herself.

"I repeat. I am not that kind of woman, Mr. Farmon."

"You're saving yourself for marriage?" he asked, a sly look in his eyes. "Too bad your mother didn't."

"Leave my mother out of it," she snapped. "She is the best person I know. You aren't fit to even mention her name."

He took a threatening step toward her. "I've made my offer. The shop by day and me by night. I'll even put you up somewhere so your so-called sainted mother won't have to listen to your cries of ecstasy." He paused. "It's both, Miss Wright. Or no employment at all. My reach is far. I can make sure no one else hires you."

Fury filled her. "My answer is no. I'll never work for you or pleasure you. You're a loathsome, disgusting fool."

Laurel wheeled and before she could take a step, he was on her. Spinning her around. Shoving her against the wall. Pressing his body against hers. Forcing his tongue into her mouth. Nausea rose in her as violent shudders caused her to tremble uncontrollably. With all the strength she could manage, she boxed his ears and thrust her knee into his bollocks at the same time, just as Hudson had taught her to do. Farmon cried out and stumbled from her, murder in his eyes.

"You'll regret what you've done, you little bitch. I'll see you and your family evicted. Your sick mother dead in a ditch. That brother of yours transported to Australia. No one crosses Julius Farmon. No one!"

Laurel fled, her heart pounding violently. She ran down the corridor and threw the curtains aside, crashing into Mr. Cole.

He caught her before she fell. Sympathy filled his eyes.

"I'm sorry, Laurel." He thought a moment. "Take whatever cash is in the till. Go," he urged.

She grabbed the box and opened it, scooping out what she could and dumping it into her reticule, which sat next to the till. She hated to leave Mr. Cole but was afraid if she didn't, something awful would happen to her. As it was, she'd made a target of her family with her refusal to become Julius Farmon's mistress.

She left the store, blindly running, trying to put distance between her and that horrible monster.

But Farmon knew where she lived. Nothing happened in this neighborhood without him knowing about it. How long could she avoid him?

Finally, she slowed and took in her surroundings. She was only a few blocks from their tenement. She picked up her pace and reached home. What was she going to tell her mother and Hudson? Where would they go? How would they live?

She walked up the three flights of stairs and unlocked the door, her hands shaking, and locked it again before leaning against the door for support. She took several long, deep breaths, trying to clear her mind. She would figure a way out of the mess she'd created. She had all afternoon and evening to think about it before Hudson arrived home, tired and hungry. She had a brain, one as good as any man's. She could do this.

Gradually, her racing heart slowed and Laurel stepped away from the door. She crossed the tiny room and stood before the closed bedroom door, the only other room. Her mother had been bedridden since the heart attack. She'd grown weaker and weaker and eaten less and less. Laurel feared her mother would waste away. Every night when she arrived home, Laurel feared she would find Dinah dead in her bed.

She pushed open the door without knocking, knowing if her mother slept that she wouldn't hear the knock anyway. Her eyes adjusted to the dim room and she went and sat on the edge of the bed. Her mother's labored breathing gave her pause.

"Mama?" she asked softly.

Dinah Wright's eyes fluttered open. She smiled and for a moment, Laurel could see the great beauty Mama must have been years ago before poverty etched the lines into her worn face.

"Hello, baby," her mother rasped. "How . . . was . . . your day?"

Tears filled Laurel's eyes, thinking how Farmon's offer had angered and humiliated her. "It was fine, Mama. How was yours?"

She couldn't tell her mother that she'd been propositioned to become their landlord's mistress, much less that she'd lost her job because she'd refused Farmon's advances. Her head spun with worry, wondering how they would manage. Farmon's words regarding her mother also bothered Laurel. She wanted to ask what he'd meant but her mother had long ago firmly closed the door to discussing the past. With the way Dinah Wright looked, Laurel didn't have the heart to pursue the matter.

"I'm so tired," Mama said, new lines creasing her brow.

"Can I warm some broth for you?"

"No. Just sit with me, Laurel."

She slipped her hands around one of her mother's cold ones, hoping to warm it.

"You're so beautiful," her mother said.

"No, you're the beautiful one, Mama."

"You look like . . . him."

Laurel went still. Her mother had never spoken of their father. Never. When she and Hudson were young, they had asked why other children had a father when they didn't. Her mother refused to speak about it, telling them they had her and each other and that was what mattered. As she matured, Laurel came to believe that her and

14

Hudson's father hadn't wanted them. Or her mother. She didn't know the circumstances of her and Hudson's birth, only that their mother had raised them with an abundance of love and no help from the man who'd impregnated her. Despite Mama's silence, Laurel had often wondered who her father might be. If he'd forced himself on Dinah. Or if he'd already had a wife. Sometimes, she pretended that he'd been the great love of her mother's life but he'd been killed tragically. She wondered if her mother had given herself freely to him, only to never see him again. It was a mystery she'd thought would never be solved.

Until now.

"What did he look like, Mama?" she asked softly.

Mama sighed. "Like you. And Hudson. Hair black as midnight. Dark brows. And those eyes."

Laurel knew how unique her eyes were because she saw them in Hudson every day. Both twins possessed eyes which were a brilliant emerald color. Though she'd seen a few others with green eyes over the years, none resembled the dazzling green the twins possessed.

"What was his name, Mama?"

"Not Wright." Her mother grimaced. "I called myself that when I found I was with child. Hoping others would think I'd wed and that my baby would be legitimate."

Mama had told them Hudson was her maiden name and that's why she'd called her boy that. This was the first Laurel had heard, though, about her mother taking a name that wasn't hers.

"Who was he, Mama?" Laurel asked. A part of her believed if she didn't learn now, Mama might never reveal his identity.

Dinah's hand went to her chest and she groaned. "It hurts. So much."

"Your heart?"

Mama nodded.

She stood. "I'll fetch the doctor." Though what she would pay him with, she didn't know.

"No. No doctor. It wouldn't do any good. This is the end, my sweet child. Don't go throw good money after bad."

Laurel dropped to her knees, tears spilling down her cheeks as she gripped her mother's hands.

"He's dead. I read about it. I'm glad."

She held her breath, afraid to urge her mother on. Afraid to finally hear the truth she'd longed to know.

"He hurt me." Her mother's voice trembled. "I didn't want him. He came with his mistress but he wanted me instead. He took me in a back room while she was being fitted for a new gown."

A wave of pain flooded her. "I'm sorry, Mama."

Dinah smiled weakly. "It wasn't your fault, my sweet. It was a few minutes that I've tried to forget but it gave me you and Hudson. I wouldn't trade my two darlings for anything in this world."

Her mother's eyes closed. Laurel thought about what she'd learned. Her mother had worked for the same modiste from the time she was fourteen. If only she'd known, she might have gone to Madame and asked her if she knew anything about that long-ago day.

Dinah's eyes opened again, this time wild with pain. She jerked her hands from Laurel's and pressed them against her chest as she sat up, gasping.

"Mama!" Laurel cried. "No!"

She watched her mother collapse again into the pillow and grow still.

"Mama? Oh, Mama. No, no, no . . ."

Dinah Wright was gone—and Laurel still had no idea who her father had been.

CHAPTER TWO

February 1816

L AUREL HANDED HUDSON their last apple. "Take it," she ordered. He started to argue and thought better of it. Ever since Mama's death, things had gone from bad to worse. A man had showed up, demanding triple the rent they were used to paying. She knew Farmon had sent him and it was only the beginning of the harassment. When Laurel told the man she would need more time, he'd slapped her hard. Bruising had occurred around her eye and her face swelled on the side the blow landed. He'd laughed and told her he would return tomorrow and that she better have payment in full.

Or else.

Thank goodness Hudson hadn't been home at the time. Her brother's temper flared even more swiftly than Laurel's did. He would have killed the man for touching her. She'd lied and told her twin that she'd slipped on the ice, causing the injuries to her face. As it was, Hudson wanted to murder Julius Farmon. After their mother's burial, Laurel had confessed to her brother that she had no job to return to—and why. Her brother had cursed loud and long, telling her exactly what he would do to the man. She'd convinced him to stay far away from Farmon, explaining how Farmon had threatened to fabricate charges to be brought against Hudson so that he would branded a criminal and be transported halfway around the world. All the poor in London knew being sent to Australia was a fate worse than death.

Only that knowledge had kept Hudson from finding Farmon and beating him senseless.

"I can't lose you," she'd told him. "Not after losing Mama."

Knowing the danger they both faced, they'd moved their few possessions and taken a room in a boardinghouse miles away, hoping to hide from Farmon. Hudson continued to work his two jobs but Laurel hadn't been able to find employment. She'd left without references and with Farmon buying out Mr. Cole, she had no idea where her former employer might have gone. She wouldn't chance returning to the old neighborhood to ask anyone because she didn't want informers to detain her.

"I'll see you tonight," her twin said. He squeezed her shoulder reassuringly. "I'm sure you'll find something today, Laurel."

With that, he left the room.

She waited a few minutes, making sure he was gone, and then went to the bed. Reaching her hand under the thin mattress, she withdrew a folded piece of parchment, the seal on it broken long ago. She sat on the bed, the only piece of furniture in the tiny room, and opened it. She'd read the brief letter so many times, the brutal lines were emblazoned in her mind.

Do not contact me again or you will regret it. It is your word against mine. I am a duke, a peer of the realm. You are a slut toiling in a shop. No one cares what you say and would never believe you over me.

My solicitor will be waiting for you tomorrow afternoon three blocks to the west of the dress shop. Make sure what he gives you lasts. No more will be forthcoming.

Everton

Her heart told her the terse message came from her father. No, the man who had violated her mother. Laurel supposed once Dinah found herself with child, she must have tried to get in touch with her attacker, telling him of her circumstances and asking for monetary help. Though she must have received some compensation, based upon the contents of the letter, it was obvious this Duke of Everton chose not to take responsibility for forcing himself on a young girl. Laurel had never given any thought to the men and woman of the *ton*. They moved in a world of their own making, their lives never touching someone like her. Now, though, since she'd found this letter Mama had hidden for so many years, resentment filtered through her, eating away, knowing this lord had ravished her mother and never given a second thought to the offspring he'd created, much less claimed responsibility. She wouldn't have expected a duke to give them his name but the aristocrat could at least have seen they were fed and clothed properly.

Desperation now forced her to act in an unsavory manner. She couldn't find work. She wanted Hudson to have the chance to attend university. Though her mother had raised her to know right from wrong, hatred burned brightly inside Laurel for Everton and all those like him who took advantage of the less fortunate and tossed them away as if they were rubbish. Her mother had said the man who had hurt her was dead but there would be a new Everton. Most likely, her father's son had taken his place in the House of Lords and assumed the title of duke.

Her half-brother . . .

A duke would have money. Lots of it.

And Laurel planned to blackmail him into giving her enough to ensure her and Hudson's survival.

With a bit of money, Hudson could sit for the upcoming exams. Win a place at Oxford or Cambridge. They could leave London and take a room near the university. Her twin could attend classes. She would find work and keep house for them. The money she would ask Everton for would be a pittance to a man in his position—but it would help change the course of the twins' lives. By leaving London, it would also guarantee that Farmon would never find them. He'd never be able to accuse either of them of wrongdoing. Once Hudson graduated, they could go anywhere in England. York. Canterbury. Leeds. They could make a new life for themselves—with just a little money from Everton to tide them over until they could stand on their own two feet again. It wouldn't do for two bastards to make themselves known to Polite Society. Surely, a duke would part with a few pounds in order to avoid such a scandal.

Laurel was counting on it.

She folded the letter and slipped it into her reticule. Smoothed her skirts and pulled on Mama's cloak, which was over two decades old. It didn't matter that she didn't cut a fashionable figure. What counted was that she would carry out her scheme without Hudson being any the wiser. She would get the money from this duke and they would escape the city and begin a new life.

If she could go through with blackmailing a peer of the realm.

She hated it had come to this. That Farmon drove her to do something she never would have done if she hadn't lost her job. If Mama hadn't died. Drawing on the little courage she had, Laurel left the room. She descended the stairs, wavering for a moment with dizziness. She hadn't eaten in two days and the smell of the morning meal their landlady provided as an extra for the tenants who paid for it wafted through the air. Clutching the banister, she closed her eyes, steadying herself. After a moment, she'd recovered and continued down the staircase.

Laurel left the boardinghouse and headed for Mayfair, the winter wind biting her cheeks and numbing her fingers. She knew the area to be the most fashionable part of town. Somewhere, a servant or hansom cab driver would be able to tell her exactly which house belonged to the Duke of Everton. She would show him the letter the previous duke had written and threaten to reveal the existence of his bastard children unless this duke gave her ample payment. Then she would give him the letter and disappear. His reputation—and the dead duke's—would remain intact.

She only hoped her plan succeeded.

JEREMY ST. CLAIR, Duke of Everton, listened carefully to Matthew Proctor. His former tutor, who'd escorted Jeremy on his Grand Tour years before, had become estate manager of Eversleigh, the Everton country seat, and now functioned as Jeremy's man of business.

While most of the *ton* didn't bother to dirty their hands with matters of business, he thrived on it. His father, the previous duke, had squandered most of the St. Clair fortune. Jeremy had learned upon his father's death how little was actually left. It had taken several years but he was blessed with a keen business acumen and patience. He'd restored the family's wealth and hired Matthew to manage much of it on a daily basis. Still, he liked having his hand in all matters and made critical decisions when necessary.

"I think it is a wise investment, Matthew," he said when his friend finished speaking. "Go ahead."

"Thank you, Your Grace." Matthew rose. "I'll see you next week with my new report."

"I'm looking forward to it," Jeremy replied as he rose and the two men shook hands.

As Matthew left the large study, he was replaced by Jeremy's favorite person in the world.

His duchess.

He'd wed Catherine four years ago but he'd been in love with her long before that. Circumstances beyond their control had separated them for several years. Jeremy had even married and had a daughter. After his wife passed, Catherine Crawford came back into his life—and everything from that moment on had been right. He loved her with a passion that could not be put into words. Catherine and their children were everything to him.

She crossed the room, as graceful as any duchess ever had been. His wife was beautiful and gifted.

Most of all, she was his. And he was hers.

His arms went about her. "Have I told you today that I love you, Duchess?"

It was a game they'd played since their marriage and he never tired of telling her those words.

Catherine's eyes lit up. "I believe you did, Duke. Once when you woke me from a very deep sleep. Again, after you made love to me. Twice as we breakfasted. And when—"

He silenced her with a lingering kiss. He felt her melting into him and his arms tightened around her as he deepened the kiss. Her fingers kneaded his shoulders.

"Did you lock the door?" he murmured against her mouth.

"No. Because it's almost time for tea."

"Tea can wait," he growled, kissing her again. He'd thought his hunger for her would end but it had only grown stronger over the years.

Catherine broke the kiss. "We have guests coming. Luke and Caroline."

"They can wait."

She laughed. "No, they can't."

"Then we can be late," he suggested, kissing the tip of her beautiful nose.

"No, we can't."

"They're newlyweds," he protested. "They're probably doing what we're doing right now and will be late themselves."

Her throaty chuckle made him want to gobble her up.

"A compromise," he offered. "Shall we continue this after teatime, Duchess?"

She kissed him soundly. "Oh, I do like the idea of that, Duke."

Jeremy released her but took her hand, entwining their fingers, the need to touch her too great. He led her upstairs to the drawing room.

"Can we at least kiss until they arrive?" he pleaded, bringing her hand to his lips and pressing a tender kiss upon her fingers.

"I thought you'd never ask." She wrapped her arms around his waist and they lost themselves in one another.

After some minutes, he sensed the door opening and eased Catherine from him, turning his head and seeing his brother and sister-in-law had arrived. From the look of Caroline's swollen lips, they'd done their share of kissing in the carriage on the way over.

"Good afternoon," he said pleasantly and kissed Caroline's cheek before giving his brother a bear hug.

"We're the newlyweds," Luke teased. "You'd think we'd have cornered the market regarding kissing."

"Rachel and Evan have tried to keep up with us," Jeremy said, referring to their sister and her husband. "You might be able to surpass them but my duchess and I are years of kisses ahead of you."

They all laughed and seated themselves. Luke handed Catherine a box.

"I stopped at Evie's Tearoom for a few treats," he said. "Caroline had business with Mr. Walton. I made good use of my time and visited Mrs. Baker and Mrs. Stinch. When they learned we were headed to see you, they insisted on sending along something."

Catherine opened the box. "Oh, you brought scones. How lovely."

Luke took his wife's hand and kissed it, then rubbed it against his cheek. "Caroline is still mad for their scones. It was the only thing she could keep down for a few months."

Catherine smiled at her sister-in-law. "I've had the same problem. Especially with the twins. You are glowing, though, Caroline."

Luke smiled. "She is radiant, isn't she?"

"I don't always feel radiant," Caroline grumbled good-naturedly.

"My ankles are thickening as fast as my waist. I'm more than ready for June to arrive."

"So am I," declared Luke. "Our first baby. Of many."

Jeremy smiled. His brother had always been wild about children. For a few years, Jeremy had wondered if Luke would ever come to his senses and settle down. He'd been one of London's most famous rogues, bedding women left and right. Thank goodness, Caroline had come into his life. Luke was positively batty for his wife.

As he should be.

"Do I have time to pop up to the nursery before tea?" Luke asked.

Catherine nodded. "You better make the time. The children would be positively crushed if their Uncle Luke didn't visit them."

"I'll be right back," he promised and left the drawing room.

Caroline patted her belly. "I can't wait for Luke to see this little one. I've never known a man who adores children as much as he does. I think I fell in love with him as I watched Delia make him her own personal pony. He wrestled with Timothy. Read to Jenny." She smiled at the memory. "He will be a wonderful father."

Cor entered the room at that moment and Jeremy rushed to her. His grandmother had raised him and his siblings since each of the three had lost their mothers in childbirth. Now seventy-six, Cor was moving a little more slowly than in past years but her mind was still as sharp as a razor and her tongue could slice a man to pieces with little effort.

"How is my favorite grandmother doing?" he asked, taking her arm and leading her to a seat.

"Better now that I can visit with these two lovely ladies," Cor replied. "How are you feeling, Caroline, dear?"

The women began talking and Jeremy's mind wandered. The teacart arrived and Catherine busied herself pouring out tea.

"Shall I go drag Luke from the nursery?" he asked. "If I don't, Caroline might gobble up all of the scones and he'll have none."

"Go ahead, Duke," his wife encouraged, her eyes bright.

He knew she was thinking of what they'd be doing after teatime and winked at her.

"I'll be back shortly," he promised.

As Jeremy left the drawing room and closed the door, he went to the staircase and found Barton ascending it. He'd never seen the butler ruffled in all his years of service.

Until now.

"Barton? What's wrong?"

"Your Grace . . ." The man's voice faded. He shook his head. "I always feared this day would come."

"You're worrying me, Barton. Spit it out."

"It's the young lady, Your Grace."

"What young lady?" he demanded.

"The young lady that wishes to see you."

"Do you have her card?"

Barton grimaced. "She's not that kind of young lady, Your Grace."

By now, Luke descended the stairs from the nursery above. "What's going on?" he asked.

"Barton is tongue-tied," Jeremy complained. "About some young lady." He faced the butler. "What does she want? And who is she, a woman without a calling card, and apparently no chaperone accompanying her?"

"I need to speak with you on an urgent matter, Your Grace," a voice said.

Jeremy glanced to the stairs and saw the young woman in question marching up them. She reached the top and his heart began pounding rapidly as she approached.

"We have business to discuss," she said crisply.

He hadn't a doubt in his mind as he took in her appearance but it was Luke who found his voice first.

"My God—you're a St. Clair!"

Chapter Three

AUREL HADN'T KNOWN how to address a duke until she heard the butler speak to the tall, dark-haired man. And then another man just as tall and broad and dark-haired appeared as she moved up the staircase. She'd been afraid if she continued waiting downstairs that the servant would return and either say the duke wasn't in—or he'd refused to see her. She thought she better take the initiative and seek out Everton.

Before she was thrown out.

He could still do that, she knew. Desperation had pushed her to this peer's doorstep and up his staircase into the sanctity of his home. The next few moments would be critical, though.

"I need to speak with you on an urgent matter, Your Grace," Laurel said, pleased that her voice was firm and even. "We have business to discuss."

The butler had already eyed her oddly when he'd opened the door but now both these powerful men looked at her in astonishment. Her confidence began to falter. Then one of them spoke.

"My God—you're a St. Clair!"

Her chin raised a notch as she studied them and they her. She immediately knew why the man knew who she was. Both he and the duke he stood next to possessed the same, vivid emerald eyes that she and Hudson did. It was as if she wore a banner proclaiming she was a bastard daughter of the family. No wonder the butler had seemed flustered when she appeared at the duke's door. He had known exactly where she came from, if not her name.

The slightly older one, the duke, looked to the butler. "Thank you, Barton," he said, dismissing the man. Obviously, he didn't want a servant to overhear their conversation. The butler nodded and slipped away.

The duke turned to her. "I am Jeremy St. Clair, Duke of Everton." He indicated the man on his left. "This is my brother, Luke, Earl of Mayfield."

Laurel didn't know how to react. The duke waited for something which she didn't know to do. Finally, he reached for her hand and clasped it, bowing to her. Releasing it, the earl did the same. She found herself flustered. Looking into these men's faces was like seeing a different, older version of Hudson. It rattled her—and she couldn't afford to lose her wits. Not when she was about to propose blackmail.

But how exactly was she to bring up such a sordid matter?

"Our grandmother is in the drawing room down the hall, along with our wives, taking tea. Would you care to join us?" the duke asked pleasantly, as if bastards dropped by on a weekly basis.

"Very well," she said curtly, trying to hide the nerves that were causing her legs to go wobbly.

The duke offered his arm. "May I escort you there?" he asked politely.

"Of course," Laurel replied.

She lifted her hand, not exactly sure where she was supposed to put it. The duke placed it on his forearm and led her down the hall, the earl trailing after them. They arrived at a door and the earl hurried to open it and ushered them in.

As they entered, she saw the room was enormous. Ten families could live within it. Thick rugs covered the floors. Plush furniture placed in groupings for conversation filled the spaces. Artwork on the walls showed lush landscapes. Laughter came from the far side and she observed three women engaged in conversation. When they drew near, all talking ceased. The younger two women, both in their twenties, smiled tentatively at her.

But it was the older woman, the duke's grandmother, who commanded Laurel's attention.

Her grandmother . . .

"You're a St. Clair," she proclaimed. "What's your name, Child?"

"Miss Wright," she managed to get out.

"I suppose my son was your father."

She stiffened her spine. "I don't know, my lady. I never knew anything about him. I only recently discovered his name to be Everton and that he was a duke."

Curiosity filled the old woman's face. "How did you learn of him? Did your mother finally tell you?"

"My mother is dead," she said flatly. "I discovered a note in her belongings after she passed."

"Might I see this note?" the duke asked.

"Let Miss Wright sit first and take a cup of tea," the beautiful woman with abundant auburn hair said, giving Laurel a warm smile. "She looks as if she could use one. I am Catherine St. Clair, Miss Wright, the Duchess of Everton. Won't you please join us?"

Laurel knees were quaking now. Sitting sounded like a very good idea. Suddenly, nausea and dizziness filled her as these strangers all stared at her. She started to speak and then felt herself go limp. The last thing she heard was someone shouting to catch her.

When she came to, she was lying on a settee. The duchess and the other woman, whom she assumed was the earl's wife, hovered nearby. She could tell the younger woman was with child.

"She's coming around," the duchess said and knelt beside her. "Miss Wright, are you better now? Were you overwarm?"

"Yes," she said, sitting up, her head woozy.

The duke pressed a cup into his wife's hands and she held it out to

Laurel. "Here. Drink this. It's strong and sweet."

Laurel did as she was told, the hot brew coursing down her throat, warming her as it traveled to her belly.

"Duke, do bring her a biscuit. I fear she's still a tad lightheaded," the duchess commanded.

Her husband retrieved a biscuit and brought it over. The duchess offered it and Laurel nibbled at it, trying not to eat it too quickly.

The duchess studied her. It was as if she could see down to Laurel's soul.

"You're hungry, aren't you?"

"Yes, my lady."

The earl quickly filled a plate and rushed it to her. The five anxiously watched as Laurel ate everything. Food had never tasted so good.

"More tea," the duchess said and soon another cup was given to her.

Laurel sipped it, feeling terribly guilty about what she was going to do to these lovely people.

Finally, she finished the tea and handed the cup to the duchess, who placed it on a nearby table.

"Do you feel like talking with us?" the duke asked gently.

"Yes." Laurel tried to rein in her galloping thoughts, wondering where she should begin.

The five all took seats near her, concern apparent on every face. Before she could speak, the old woman, who'd taken the place on the settee next to her, took her hand.

"You are my granddaughter. My son's child. I am sorry it has taken so long to meet you."

"May we see the note?" the duke asked again.

When she hesitated, he said, "We've no doubt you're a St. Clair, Miss Wright. One look at your hair, eyes, and cheekbones and it's obvious to us all. I know my father's handwriting. Would you mind sharing the note with us?"

"What if I hand it over and you tear it up?" she boldly asked.

The duke looked taken aback. "I would never damage something that was yours, Miss Wright." His mouth set and she knew he was angry with her because she'd seen the same look cross Hudson's face many a time.

Reluctantly, she removed the reticule still attached to her wrist and opened it, retrieving the note and handing it to the duke. As he read it, his eyes grew hard. He passed it to his brother, who looked just as grim. The earl gave it to his grandmother, who read it aloud.

Hearing the words spoken in front of these people cut Laurel to the quick.

"I shouldn't have come," she said quickly. "I'm a by-blow. I have no right—"

The duke came to his feet and then knelt before her. Taking her hand, he said, "You have every right to be here, Miss Wright. You are a St. Clair—and St. Clairs take care of one another. I apologize for my father's crass behavior. That he took advantage of your mother and refused to claim responsibility. I know her death and discovering this letter has affected you deeply but I want you to know, we are here for you. Me. Luke. Catherine. Caroline." He paused, smiling at the woman seated next to her. "And Cor, most of all."

The duke rose. "You see, our father was a bitter man. A wastrel. He drank too much and gambled away most of the St. Clair fortune and unentailed properties. It surprises none of us that he acted in such a reprehensible manner." He paused. "But you have family, Miss Wright. Two brothers and a sister. Rachel isn't here today. She is Marchioness of Merrick."

The duchess chuckled. "She'll be furious that we got to meet you first. Our Rachel is very possessive when it comes to family. You will have a fierce ally in her." She smiled at Laurel. "In all of us. Jeremy is right. Since you are alone now, we want to be your family and help you in any way we can."

Laurel burst out into tears. She had never cried so long or hard as guilt washed over her. She'd come to blackmail the duke and instead, he and his family had welcomed her with open arms. Various St. Clairs took turns embracing her. Stroking her hair. Patting her back. Murmuring words she didn't even understand but somehow they soothed her. Finally, she composed herself and straightened her spine.

"You've all been lovely," she declared. "I came here today because I was desperate. I have lost my position in the chandler's shop where I was employed. My mother died. We can't pay the rent. I was hoping . . . somehow . . . to . . ."

She couldn't finish the words. Couldn't tell them she was going to try and force their hand to give her money.

Her grandmother wrapped an arm about Laurel. "You have a home now, Miss Wright. You are a St. Clair. You will never lack for anything ever again. You will live with us and come to know everyone." The old woman stroked her cheek. "What is your Christian name, Child?"

"Laurel," she said shakily.

"Oh, that's a lovely name."

"But I'm not a true St. Clair," she protested. "Not a real brother and sister. Only a half-sister, I suppose."

The earl roared with laughter. "We're all halves around here, Laurel."

His words confused her.

"My mother was the first duchess," the duke explained. "When she died in childbirth, Father wed again."

"That would be my mother, the old sod's second wife," the earl continued. "When my mother died in childbirth, Father married again, Rachel's mother. She, too, died in childbirth. So you see, Laurel, we're all half-brothers and half-sisters." He looked to the duke. "Long ago, though, when our Father died, Jeremy became as a father to Rachel and me. He decided that it was ridiculous to think in halves. We became full brothers and a sister at that point."

"And we have remained that way ever since," the duke proclaimed, "adding more to the fold with our two wives and Rachel's husband. They are also siblings to us, as is Catherine's sister, Leah, and her husband, Alex." He beamed at her. "Today, we add another St. Clair to our family. I feel I should call for champagne."

"I've never had champagne," she blurted out. "I didn't come here today to ask you to take me in, Your Grace."

"You need a place to live," the duchess said, clasping Laurel's hand gently. "We want you here. Not only for you to get to know your brothers and sister, but you also have nieces and nephews, as well. Please say you'll come live with us, Laurel. You are wanted—and loved."

Tears streamed down her cheeks again. "That would be lovely. But . . . I haven't told you everything, Your Grace," she protested.

"We have the rest of our lives to hear everything," the duke proclaimed. "Besides, enough of this Your Gracing. I am Jeremy."

"I still have to tell you something," Laurel said. "It's not only me."

The room fell silent as everyone stared at her.

"I have a twin brother. Hudson." The rest came out in a rush. "We're eighteen. Nineteen come October. Hudson is very, very smart. So smart that we've hoped he could win a place at university. On scholarship."

"Where is Hudson now?" her grandmother asked, her eyes bright with interest.

"At work. Days he's a coal porter and nights he's a waterman. He doesn't even know I'm here. I didn't tell him about finding the duke's note to Mama."

The duke—Jeremy—took Laurel's hands and brought her to her feet.

"Hudson will be as welcomed as you are, Laurel. I'll send for him now. Is he at the docks?"

She nodded.

"He'll be here in an hour's time," the duke promised. "Excuse me." He signaled his brother and the two men left the room.

Everton returned a few minutes later. "Don't despair, Laurel. All will be well."

They talked for half an hour, Laurel learning small things about this new family of hers, glad they didn't press her for more details of her life. Then the door flew open and a woman with raven hair and St. Clair eyes burst into the room, followed by a quiet blond and two other men. Luke St. Clair trailed behind them and she decided the duke must have sent his brother to retrieve the rest of the family and explain the situation to them.

The woman dashed across the room and pulled Laurel to her feet and then hugged her so tightly Laurel feared she might never let go. Finally, she released Laurel.

Smiling, the woman said, "I am Rachel, your sister." She gestured for the others to join them. "My husband, Evan. My best friend and Catherine's sister, Leah. And this is Alex, Leah's husband." Rachel beamed. "Oh, we have so much to talk about!"

Suddenly, a familiar voice said, "What in the bloody hell is going on?"

She turned and saw Hudson standing in the doorway. He looked very out of place in such an elegant room, his face and hands smudged with coal, his workingman's clothes rumpled and stained. She also knew he was angry and bewildered at being summoned to an elegant Mayfair townhouse and finding her there.

Laurel went to him and sensed others following at a distance. She reached her twin but his eyes looked past her. She glanced over her shoulder and saw the three St. Clair siblings had joined her in a show of support.

Looking back at her brother, she saw his jaw had dropped. No words emerged until he finally said, "They look like us, Laurel. They all have our eyes. It's . . . like looking in a mirror."

The duke stepped forward and offered Hudson his hand. "That's because we're all St. Clairs, Hudson." With a broad smile, he added, "Welcome to the family."

CHAPTER FOUR

"HIT HIM AGAIN, Linfield!"

"Throw another right, Linfield!"

"Pummel the bastard, Linfield!"

Linfield . . .

Every time Anthony heard the name shouted at him, he smashed his fists into his sparring opponent. The man now wavered, swaying from side to side.

"Finish him off, Linfield!"

He threw once last punch, an uppercut to Martin's jaw, lifting him off his feet. Then his opponent went down with a thud.

Cheers erupted throughout Gentleman Jack's. The red field that had blurred Anthony's vision subsided as his anger cooled. A calm flooded him. He turned to the crowd, his face its usual mask. Someone doused him with water and the liquid spilled down his bare chest. Another man handed him a tin cup and he drank the cold ale, relishing it. He wiped his forearm across his brow, mopping away the sweat, and stepped from the marked-off ring.

Gentlemen of the *ton* slapped his back as he walked through the crowd. He heard the name again, over and over. His bloody name.

Because *he* was the Duke of Linfield.

He reached the edge of the crowd and Gentleman Jack himself took Anthony's elbow, guiding him through a door and down a corridor to an empty room. He collapsed onto a stool. The Gentleman tossed him a towel and he wiped the sweat from his face, arms, and chest before rubbing it through his thick hair and throwing it aside.

"One of these days you're going to kill someone, Your Grace."

He glared at the former boxer, who shrugged and added, "What drives you?"

Gentleman Jack had never asked him that question. No one had since his return to London.

And he would never answer it truthfully. Because the truth hurt too much.

"I no longer have any French bastards to direct my anger toward," he said lightly.

The owner of the boxing club chuckled. "You're probably the only gent in London who would've cared to see the war continue." He shook his head. "I'll leave you to clean up and dress."

Anthony nodded. Once Gentleman Jack vacated the room, he stood and began pacing, trying to manage the heightened rush of energy. The excitement that boxing brought eventually resulted in complete exhaustion, as if he'd been thrown from a horse and had the wind knocked from him. His racing pulse slowed. The awareness and sensitivity to every detail began to blur. His strength waned as his pounding heart began to return to normal. His dry mouth longed for strong drink.

He wished he could crawl into a hole and let the earth swallow him whole.

The Gentleman was wrong. Anthony had never liked war. The things he'd seen and done over the last decade had scarred him emotionally, as much as the physical wounds he'd suffered from a bullet hole and slices from a sword. At least on the battlefield, though, he'd had a place to bring his seething rage. To direct it against an enemy who threatened not only England but all of Europe.

Bonaparte was in exile once more, however. His escape from Elba Island and the resounding defeat at the Battle of Waterloo last summer had once more seen the dictator locked away, this time on St. Helena. Anthony would have liked to remain as a guard to make sure the Gallic bastard never darkened the shores of Europe again. Fate, though, had led him home. He was no longer one of Wellington's trusted staff members. He wasn't even in the army. He'd been forced to sell out.

Because he was the Duke of Linfield.

He spat on the ground, disgusted with the moniker that now hung about his neck. Everywhere he went, people addressed him as Your Grace, fawning over him. Or if they imagined themselves friends to him, they called him Linfield. In truth, he was close to no one and pushed the world away.

Except for Aunt Constance, and even she was wearing on him. She'd come to town late last night. He'd learned of her and Hannah's arrival once he came home from the latest gaming hell he frequented. He'd left early this morning, first to ride and then come to Bond Street so he could box all his emotions out. It was time to face the music, though. He would return to the Linfield London townhouse. He didn't think of it as home because it never had been. He and Theodore had been left in the country as children any time the duke traveled to the city. And then Anthony had gone to his aunt's country estate to live, one left to her by her father. She abhorred town life so he'd never had the opportunity to see London.

Things were different now. Aunt Constance had brought Hannah with her, according to his valet. He'd never laid eyes on his half-sister. It shocked him when his aunt wrote to him at school when he was ten, telling him of Linfield's marriage and the subsequent arrival of a baby. Hannah held to family tradition and killed her mother in childbirth— just as he had. He had an inkling why they'd come to town. He was twenty-eight. That made Hannah eighteen—and the perfect age for her come-out.

Would his aunt expect him to escort them to *ton* affairs? Without a doubt. That was the last thing Anthony intended to do. War had been brutal—but real. The gaiety of empty society events held no meaning for him. Yet he was now at the top of that society, cream who had risen to the top, thanks to the deaths of his father and brother. Only a handful of dukes existed in England. Dread filled him, knowing every mama would push their daughters at him. He didn't care to wed. He didn't care to do anything other than ride. Box. Drink.

And forget.

A brief flush of guilt ran through him. As Linfield, he had numerous properties. He'd visited none since his return. Estate managers had sent letters to him without receiving any replies. The same had been true for solicitors. He cursed aloud. He didn't want to be the bloody Duke of Linfield. He didn't want the responsibility. The estates.

He sure as hell didn't want to be known by a name that he'd loathed from the time he was young.

Anthony slipped his shirt over his head and then dressed as best as he could without the help of a valet. He supposed he should start bringing Monkton with him to Gentleman Jack's establishment. His valet tried to hide his look of horror every time his master returned from a bout of boxing. Bloody hell. How was he supposed to know how to tie a cravat? He was a soldier. His talent was for strategizing— and killing Frenchmen.

He claimed Bucephalus from a stable hand and rode to his Mayfair townhouse. It was one of the largest in London, or so he was told by his valet, who seemed to know everything about the *ton*. He left his horse with a groom, wishing he could rub Bucephalus down himself but dukes weren't supposed to do that kind of thing. Wanting to avoid his aunt for as long as he could, he entered through the kitchen, causing the scullery maids to titter, and made it to his rooms safely. Monkton awaited him. The valet quickly hid his disappointment and said he would see to a bath.

An hour later, Anthony was bathed and dressed to perfection. He'd told Monkton to let his aunt know he would receive her in the library and made his way there now. Entering, he saw her seated in a large chair, a glass of sherry next to her as she read. She had always been a great reader and anytime he thought of her, it was with a book in her hand. She looked up and smiled.

The invisible wall he surrounded himself with, keeping out others, began to crumble. This woman had been a mother to him. Confidant. Godsend. He went to her, kneeling and kissing her hand.

"Aunt Constance. It's so good to see you."

Her mouth twisted wryly. "If it is so good, then why did it take until almost three in the afternoon before you greeted me?"

"I had things to attend to," Anthony said, rising and taking a seat in a nearby chair.

"I know what you've been up to," she said knowingly. "Servants talk. Especially when someone my age demands answers." Her brow creased. She reached and took his hand. "Oh, Anthony. I know how hard this has been for you. Why didn't you come to me when you returned to England?"

He smiled evenly and withdrew his hand. No show of weakness. Not even before her.

"You say it's been hard. It hasn't. After all, who doesn't want to be a duke?"

Yet even he heard the bitterness in his words.

"I am one of the wealthiest men in England now. I own multiple estates. Everyone wants to be my friend. Ask my advice. Hear of my exploits on the battlefield. I am sought after because of my title. A title I never wanted. I would renounce it if I could."

Her eyes narrowed. "I've gotten here just in time, it seems." She stood, leaned over, and slapped him.

He looked up at her, stunned.

"You will stop acting like a petulant child who hasn't gotten his way. You are Linfield now, whether you like it or not." She softened her tone. "I know you associate the title with your father and brother. It's just a name, Anthony. You will bring yourself to it. You will be the duke neither of them could ever be." She seated herself.

"I hate it," he admitted. "Every time someone calls me Linfield. It's as if bugs are crawling along my flesh."

"You'll get used to it. The day will come when it won't matter anymore. Then another day will arrive and you won't associate it with anyone but yourself."

"I hope so," he said. "I would ask that you always call me Anthony, Aunt." He knew once a man inherited a title, especially a duke, that even his close family members referred to him by it. He couldn't stand the thought of her using the name Linfield when she spoke to him.

"Of course." She paused. "I assume you know why I came to town."

"Because my half-sister needs a come-out, I'll daresay. I suppose she's of that age."

"Correct. And you need a wife."

He shot to his feet. "What? No, Aunt Constance."

She rose and clasped his shoulders. "What better way of starting a new life than with a bride, Anthony? You realize you will need an heir?"

"I don't want children," he said. "I certainly don't want sons. Pitting them against each other." He shuddered.

She squeezed him gently. "You would never be like that. You are not the man your father was. *You* will be a good father. You will love your children. Spend time with them." She smiled gently. "I think having a family is what might save you."

He'd never thought of taking a wife. He'd assumed his entire adult life would belong to the army. It rankled him that the very thing he loved had been taken from him. But marriage? He didn't know the first thing about it. Or women.

"I know what you're thinking. You don't even know how to

dance. I've arranged for a dancing master to come teach Hannah all she needs to know. The two of you can practice together. At least Monkton got you to a tailor. You're dressed decently enough now but you'll need much more than what's in your wardrobe come the Season. All kinds of evening clothes. Clothes to drive through the park in. Ones to attend routs and balls. Garden parties."

"I'd rather the enemy have gutted me than attend a garden party, Aunt."

She smiled. "You will go. You may even learn to like it. Especially if you find a nice young lady to make an offer to. Somewhere out there is the perfect woman for you, Anthony. We'll find her for you. It may not be this Season but you'll be thirty soon. I expect you to wed by then."

He couldn't help but laugh. "You sound like Wellington, drawing up battle plans. Ready to attack the enemy head on."

Aunt Constance smiled. "I always did think women would make better commanders than men." Taking his arm, she said, "Come to the drawing room. I've arranged for us to have tea with Hannah. It's about time you met your sister."

"Half-sister."

She clucked her tongue. "Hannah is a sweet girl. A bit naïve but she'll make a good wife. Of course, she is dying to get to know her mysterious older brother and thrilled to be in London for the first time after a lifetime in the country."

Anthony escorted her to the drawing room, where a young girl came to her feet. As he crossed the room, he saw a mixture of hesitancy and eagerness on her pretty face. Unfortunately, she closely resembled the man who had sired her. She had light brown hair and soulful brown eyes and barely came to his shoulder. Looking at her filled him with distaste.

She curtseyed. "Good afternoon, Your Grace."

He took her hand and tried to put aside his instant dislike. "There'll be none of that. We are family. Call me by my name."

41

She smiled. "Oh! Thank you, Linfield."

He winced. "No," he said firmly. "My Christian name. Anthony."

She looked puzzled. "Is that allowed?" she asked her aunt.

He released her hand. "I'm a duke and head of this family. You will respect my wishes."

Hurt crossed her face. She lowered her eyes. "Yes, Anthony."

"Shall we sit?" his aunt asked, shooting him an intimidating look.

The tea cart arrived and Aunt Constance asked Hannah to pour. He supposed this was part of learning the social graces. He hadn't sat down to tea in a very long time.

"Our aunt tells me you're to make your come-out this Season," he said, trying to make conversation.

Hannah's face lit up. "Yes. I'm going to a modiste tomorrow. That is, if you . . ." Her voice faltered.

He realized what troubled her. "You are my responsibility, Hannah. Buy whatever Aunt and the modiste say you need. What good is all this money I have if I can't spend it the way I choose?"

She worried her bottom lip. "You would choose to spend it on me?"

"Yes. I expect to see you in very many pretty dresses. A different one each time we attend a new event."

Her smile touched his heart for a moment and Anthony realized he didn't want to get close to this girl. He needed to marry her off and let her be someone else's responsibility.

"We should address what happens," he began. "You are an innocent. Aunt tells me you've been raised in the country and that this is your first time in London."

Hannah nodded.

"Many young ladies will want to become close to you. Try to be your friend. Gentlemen will flock to you because you are the daughter of a duke and the sister to one. You possess an enormous dowry. You must watch your behavior. Never be alone with any man. In fact, if any wish to court you, they must first ask for my permission."

"Yes, Your Grace," she said demurely.

"Anthony," he corrected. "Also, do not accept any offers of marriage. I'll make it known that all offers are to come to me. I will thoroughly scrutinize any suitors and their backgrounds. I don't want you being taken advantage of and wedding someone who is down on his luck. You will marry a man who doesn't need your dowry. One who will respect you."

"Yes, Anthony."

"Most importantly, Hannah, you are never to be alone with a gentleman. Men want very different things than women. For the most part, men are not to be trusted. You are never to go anywhere with a man unless you have proper supervision. Is that understood?"

Her cheeks pinkened. "Aunt Constance has spoken to me about my reputation. How I am to always be chaperoned. That I do not want to find myself compromised."

"Listen to her advice. She is a very wise woman."

Hannah studied him. "Will I be the only one seeking to wed, Anthony? Will you also do so?"

"Aunt informs me it is my duty to carry on the line and wed," he said. "I will do so in good time."

Anthony supposed he might as well find a bride since he was being forced to attend the Season. If he did find one, he would never have to be dragged through another Season again. He decided to look for a woman who had no opinions of her own. One who would keep his house and bear an heir and expect nothing from him. Once he had his heir, he would give his wife the freedom to live her life as she chose. He knew it was the way of the *ton*. He thought no woman should be saddled with him. Anthony knew something was broken inside him, something that would never be able to be repaired. This way, the dukedom would have a successor—and he could retain his own liberty. Be his own man without dragging down his wife or child into the abyss of anger that constantly raged in his soul.

CHAPTER FIVE

"**I** LOVE THAT you are so knowledgeable about current events, Laurel," Rachel said with enthusiasm. "You have strong opinions on everything. That's very refreshing."

Laurel took a sip of her tea as Kitty brought them a new pot, along with a second plate of macaroons. Caroline's eyes lit up as she took the first one.

"Mr. Cole always bought a newspaper each day. He allowed me to read it after him, usually when things slowed down at the store. I was drawn mostly to politics and economic issues."

"You're the first person who has explained the Corn Laws to me in a way I can understand," Catherine said. "And I find this new Davy lamp for coal mining quite interesting. I wonder if Jeremy knows about it."

"He does," Laurel said. "We even discussed the first test of it underground at Hebburn Colliery. Jeremy told me he has already invested in Davy lamps."

"I'm just delighted you've joined our book club," Leah said. "Already, your contributions to our discussions have made us a much livelier group."

Leah had encouraged Laurel to join the subscription service at Evie's Bookstore and become a member of the book club that the store sponsored. Though Laurel had never read a book before, she had finished three now and enjoyed getting together to discuss it with other females.

"But you never read any of the gossip in the newspaper?" Leah asked. "You know Lord Byron is experiencing difficulties. His debts are growing and his marriage is teetering on failure. I've read he's thinking of fleeing London to escape the growing scandal."

Laurel shrugged. "Society news didn't seem important to me. I knew none of the people the papers discussed. Frankly, I never thought I would meet any of them."

"Oh, you will," Rachel promised. "You should start reading about the *ton* immediately. Don't worry. We'll catch you up on the gossip you need to know, as well as make sure you know which men to avoid. We don't want you compromised by some scoundrel."

Mr. Walton approached their table. "Lady Mayfield, do you have time to discuss the new shipment that has come in?"

"Of course," Caroline replied and then looked to her companions. "If you'll excuse me, ladies. I believe I'll be tied up for a few hours so feel free to leave without me."

After Caroline left the table, suddenly Leah turned white as a sheet and gagged.

"Oh, no," she murmured, holding her hands to her mouth.

"I've got you," Rachel said, swiftly getting her friend to her feet and leading Leah from the table.

"Is she ill?" Laurel asked, confused. "She was fine just a moment ago."

Catherine grinned. "I believe my sister will have good news to share with us. From the look on her face, I'm going to guess we'll have a new niece or nephew come autumn." She paused. "Have you been around women who are ready to bear a child?"

"Not really," Laurel admitted. "Only the ones who came into Mr. Cole's chandlery to shop. I worked long hours and then went straight home. Mama didn't socialize or have friends." She smiled. "That's why I've enjoyed spending time each day in the nursery with your children,

Catherine. They are delightful."

She had never thought she might one day marry. Just existing from day to day had been all she could think of. The idea of a husband or children had never been something she'd contemplated. Being around her new nieces and nephews, though, brought a deep yearning for babies. A maternal spark she'd never been aware of had been lit within her.

"I hope to have children of my own one day," she shared.

"I'm sure you will. You'll meet many people during the upcoming Season."

Laurel worried about that. Catherine had taken her to a modiste for an entire wardrobe, including countless gowns to be worn to Season events. Over the last six weeks she'd been given lessons in dance and Luke had taught her to ride. She'd taken to both. She'd never known such joy as when she moved to music. Catherine had said at some point Laurel might want to take up music lessons and learn an instrument, such as the pianoforte, but there was plenty of time for that in the future.

"I'm anxious about it," she said. "I'm afraid I'll make a mistake—many of them—and embarrass you and Jeremy."

"You aren't to worry about that," her sister-in-law said. "Just be yourself." Catherine hesitated a moment. "There will be some who think you are a bit too outspoken and opinionated. Don't let them change anything about you, Laurel. Too many young women making their come-out act alike. Sound alike. Dress alike. You will be a breath of fresh air."

Since they were alone, Laurel found the courage to ask, "Are you having me make my come-out so I will leave the household?"

"What? Of course not. We are delighted to have you. Let me say this, which I hope will relieve you of your worries. My father told me this at my own debut years ago. He said to enjoy the Season and all the people I would meet and the activities I would participate in. If I found a man to my liking and thought we would suit, then by all means, marry him. If I didn't, I could have as many Seasons as I wanted." She smiled wistfully. "Papa gave me the gift of time. We want you to have that same choice, Laurel. I know this is a new world to you, one you never dreamed you'd participate in. Don't force yourself to find a husband. We would be happy to keep you with us forever. If you do find someone you like, though, remember that we will always be your family. You and your new husband will be welcomed at Eversleigh or any St. Clair home."

"Or Edgemere," Rachel said, sliding into her chair.

"The same at Fairhaven or Fairfield," added Leah, color back in her face as she took her seat.

"I assume you're speaking of marriage," Rachel said. "I hope you will wed someday, Laurel. You are a natural with children. Every time you come into the room, Seth holds his arms out to you."

"My Rose is the same way. She's quite taken with you," Leah said. Blushing, she added, "And I'm sure the new baby will also love his or her Aunt Laurel."

They congratulated Leah, learning the baby would come in October.

"Back to marriage," Rachel said. "Don't rush into anything. I didn't. My first Season, I danced more than any girl ever had. I went to concerts and the opera. Routs and musicales. I thoroughly enjoyed myself—and didn't find one man who interested me in the least."

"Rachel was the most beautiful girl of that Season," Leah said. "We made our come-out together. I was lucky enough to find Alex."

"I was lucky enough not to settle for anyone because Evan waited for me. I didn't even know who he was that year. He was still fighting in Spain at the time but fate has a way of working things out for us." She grinned. "Besides, you'll need to marry for love. All St. Clairs do."

Laurel had already observed how love matches seemed to run in the St. Clair family. She was a practical person, however, and the idea of love and romance didn't really appeal to her. She wanted a husband who would respect her and her opinions and be a good father to the children they had. She also had been secretly reading the gossip columns in the newspapers without telling anyone. From what they told, a love match was a rare thing in Polite Society. Most married for status or wealth, trying to join great families together. She may be part of a great family—but she was from the wrong side of the blanket. Despite Jeremy telling her that she was his sister and providing her with a generous dowry, Laurel knew not many men would be interested in wedding a duke's illegitimate daughter. Her only hope was that whomever she wed, he would not mind her seeing her St. Clair relatives often. She smiled to herself, wondering if any girl making her come-out had ever thought of selecting a husband based upon where he lived. Since Jeremy and Luke had country estates in Kent and Rachel and Leah had husbands with their country seats in East Essex, Laurel hoped if she did have a man interested in marrying her that he would live somewhere near them so they could visit her relatives often.

"Enough talk of marriage," Catherine said. "We need to finish our tea. I must get home and write more. Mr. Bellows is eager for my next book."

They finished the plate Kitty had brought and then left the tea-room. Laurel remained quiet, pondering how quickly her life had changed in a few short weeks—and how the Season might bring the biggest change of all.

LAUREL SAT PERFECTLY still, allowing the maid to fuss with her hair. She'd never dreamed of the number of servants members of the *ton* employed. It had been hard to break many ingrained habits since she'd been living in the Everton townhome. She'd tried to make her bed only to be stopped from doing so by two maids. She asked for a needle and thread to sew on a loose button and had the garment in question taken from her. She was bathed and dressed and even had someone style her hair for her as if she were a helpless child who couldn't hold a brush.

When she'd talked with Hudson about it, he'd told her to let the servants do their jobs. He explained they were paid to do those things and if Laurel took tasks away from them, they might not be needed and lose their positions. She'd never thought of it like that and appreciated Hudson's advice. She only saw her brother at meals and when she practiced dancing because he was preparing day and night for the upcoming university entrance exams. Mr. Proctor, Jeremy's former tutor, was preparing Hudson and told Laurel he believed her twin would sail through anything tossed his way. Her brother would not participate in the Season until after he finished his education. Already, Jeremy and Hudson discussed the role the youngest St. Clair would play in family business affairs. After his initial shock at learning of his parentage, Hudson had calmed down and now seemed happy with the changes brought to his life.

"There, Lady Laurel. You're all set." The maid smiled. "You'll be the prettiest young lady at the ball."

Laurel still didn't think of herself as a lady and found it odd being addressed by a title. Catherine had explained that any daughter of a duke would be referred to in that manner. They'd spent endless hours discussing the correct way to address others in society. How Rachel had been Lady Rachel until she wed and then she was known as Lady Merrick. How dukes and duchesses were called Your Grace. That a woman whose husband died became known as a dowager, even if she were quite young. The endless rules proved confusing and were another reason Laurel worried about making an error tonight as she met so many new people.

She rose and thanked the maid. Her stomach flipped and flopped every which way, nerves eating away at her. There was simply so much to remember besides how to address people. What conversation was deemed appropriate. Which fork to use and even how much to eat. That she should only dance with a man once or gossip would swell about her. It surprised her if she danced with a gentleman twice that it meant he was revealing his interest in her to the entire *ton*. She had so much jammed into her brain that it threatened to spill out, leaving her as an empty featherhead.

A knock sounded at the door and she answered it, surprised to find Jeremy and Catherine standing there together. Her brother looked devastatingly handsome in his black evening clothes, while Catherine was the picture of a perfect duchess in shades of blue silk, her auburn hair piled high upon her head. Diamonds glittered at her ears and throat.

"May we come in?" Jeremy asked.

"I was about to join you downstairs," Laurel said, her voice trembling.

"This won't take long," her brother assured her.

She allowed them to enter her bedchamber and saw Jeremy had something in his hand. An almost flat box. Curiosity filled her. He opened it and she gasped. A pearl necklace and bracelet rested against black velvet, the creamy white elegant against the dark background.

"This is for you," Jeremy revealed. "Others making their come-out will be wearing jewelry. Catherine and I wanted you to have something simple and tasteful."

Laurel began shaking her head. "No. I can't accept something so valuable," she protested.

His emerald St. Clair eyes held hers. "I'll never be able to make up for the lost years when our father cast aside your mother. I can only hope we move forward, in love and trust. Please, Laurel. We want you to have this. Please accept it."

Tears filled her eyes. "You've already done so much for me. Gifted me with countless gowns. Taken Hudson under your wing and promised to educate him and then teach him about business. You have offered us friendship—and love."

By now, Catherine lifted the necklace from its case and moved behind Laurel, fastening the clasp. Jeremy took the bracelet and secured it on her wrist. She gazed down, speechless at the beauty of the pair.

"Thank you," she finally managed. "I will wear the set always and treasure who it came from." Laurel fingered the necklace, amazed she now possessed something so incredible.

Catherine laughed. "Pearls are for any occasion but you'll receive other jewels, I'm sure."

"From whom?" she asked. "Luke?"

Jeremy roared with laughter. "Luke would certainly gift you with some if he thought it would please you. No, Laurel, Catherine means your future husband. You'll receive various gifts from him. For your wedding. The birth of your children. Perhaps on your birthday."

"This is such a different life," she said softly. "I may never get used to it."

Catherine embraced her and then Jeremy did the same, kissing her cheek.

"It's time to make our way to the Rutherfords' ball," he declared.

As they went downstairs and climbed into the carriage, he reminded Laurel that the Rutherfords had been childhood friends of the St. Clairs. Amanda was now Lady Stanley and her brother, Lord Aubrey, was a viscount and would one day become the Earl of Rutherford.

"Aubrey is quite handsome and polished," Catherine said. "He's also intelligent. And an eligible bachelor."

"He wanted my duchess but I was determined she would be mine." Jeremy lifted his wife's gloved hand and kissed her fingers.

"Lord Aubrey is a good man," Catherine said, her eyes twinkling at her husband. "I'm sure he will want to get to know you. Many people will."

"That's what I'm afraid of," Laurel admitted. "I know there's been gossip about me and more will come tonight."

"We St. Clairs can be unconventional sometimes but you are beautiful, graceful, and intelligent, Laurel. Ignore the gossip. You'll make good friends over the next few months and I'm sure I'll have to fight through a long line of suitors who will call upon you every afternoon." He sighed. "It will be just like with Rachel and Leah. All those damned flowers filling the house."

"Men will send me flowers?" she asked.

"They will," Catherine said. "They'll call and have tea. Ask you to ride in the park. Wish to escort you to the theater or opera. Exciting times are ahead. Just remember, it's important to always have someone with you. Being properly chaperoned is something I know you're not used to but it's very important."

Laurel nodded. "Rachel has talked to me about it. She's explained how I don't want to be ruined. I promise you both that's the last thing that will ever happen to me."

CHAPTER SIX

A
S THEY LEFT the carriage, Laurel saw Rachel and Evan waiting for them. She was glad to have more of her family by her side as she embarked upon her first ball. Caroline and Luke had decided not to attend any events this Season, retreating to Fairhaven to await the birth of their first child in two months. Laurel would miss chatting with Caroline because she enjoyed her fiery spirit. Luke blamed his wife's independence on the three years she'd spent in America, claiming its citizens had rubbed off on her. He did so with a fond look in his eye, though, and Laurel knew her new brother appreciated his wife because of her experiences there.

"Are you ready for the ball?" Rachel asked, slipping her arm through Laurel's. "I love the pearls."

"They were a gift from Jeremy and Catherine."

"That was thoughtful of them. Evan and I should have done something for you, as well."

"You have done more than enough, Rachel. You've introduced me to family friends. Lord and Lady Morefield. Lord Merrifield. At least I'm going into tonight knowing others. I also met a young woman at Madame Toufour's shop last week when I went for my final fittings, a Lady Hannah. She's also making her come-out this Season. She has never been to London and had never even met her half-brother since he was in the army the last decade. He is now her guardian. She is a bundle of nerves, worried about meeting people and remembering names."

"You like her?" Rachel asked as they entered the Rutherfords' townhouse.

"Very much."

"I had Leah to share my come-out year. It's good you'll have Lady Hannah. I'll make sure she is invited to our upcoming musicale."

"That is kind of you. Catherine has already sent an invitation for the ball she and Jeremy are hosting tomorrow night."

"Be sure to introduce me to her and this half-brother tonight," her sister said.

The rest in their party caught up to them and they joined the receiving line. Laurel tried not to seem wide-eyed as she took in the magnificent gowns other women wore and the elegance of their surroundings.

They reached their hosts and Lord and Lady Rutherford welcomed them. She moved along the line, where Rachel had already pointed out the Rutherfords' two grown children also stood.

"This is Lord and Lady Stanley," Rachel said. "My sister, Lady Laurel."

Lady Stanley gave her a warm smile. "I am delighted to meet you, Lady Laurel. My brother and I have been friends with the St. Clair family since we were children. I do hope to get to know you better. Would you be available to come to tea tomorrow?"

"I could escort you to my sister's home," said the handsome man to her right.

"Oh, this is Viscount Aubrey, my brother," Lady Stanley said.

Laurel took in the tall, quite nice-looking gentleman. "That would be lovely, my lord. However, I will require a chaperone."

His brows arched. "Oh, so you've heard I'm a rogue?" he teased.

"Admitting to a new female acquaintance that you are a rogue might not be the best way to start a friendship," Laurel told him.

He smiled. "So, we're to have a friendship? Of course, Amanda and

I are already friends with your St. Clair siblings. I am glad we also will become friends with you." He paused. "Might you save the first dance for me?"

She nodded. "If you'd like. That's very kind of you, my lord."

"Come along," Rachel said, tugging on her arm. "Else Aubrey won't have time to flirt with the rest of the pretty girls coming through the line."

The viscount laughed heartily as they moved away.

Her family stood together in the ballroom and Laurel noted while others circulated, greeting old friends, everyone went out of their way to come to the Evertons. Jeremy had warned her that while there would inevitably be some gossip about her birth, she was a St. Clair and should ignore people who disparaged her. He'd also told her he'd make sure her dance card was filled with friends of his and other suitable gentlemen. As he promised, her programme began filling quickly, though she made sure to note Lord Aubrey as her first partner.

Then she saw Lady Hannah and her aunt and waved to them. The pair made their way over and Catherine greeted them, having previous made their acquaintance at the modiste's shop the previous week.

"Thank you for the invitation to your ball, Your Grace," Lady Constance said. "With my nephew only recently returned from war and myself having spent my entire life in the country, we haven't had many invitations come in."

"That will change," Catherine assured the older woman. "My sister and Lady Hannah seem to have already become fast friends. It will be good for them to attend events together and have one another's support."

"Yes," Rachel said. "Merrick and I will be hosting a musicale next week and you're certainly expected to attend it. Lady Alford, my closest friend, is known for her garden parties. You'll come to that, of course."

Lady Constance smiled. "I appreciate that and believe with invitations from St. Clairs coming our way, it will be only natural for more to pour in."

As the others talked, Laurel turned to her new friend. "Are you as nervous as I am?"

"Probably more so," Lady Hannah admitted. "At least you have a large family supporting you."

Laurel hadn't told the young woman she'd only known about—and lived with—this family for six weeks. She supposed Lady Hannah would hear the gossip and make up her own mind whether she wanted their friendship to continue or put it by the wayside.

Several men approached them, signing their dance cards, and Lady Hannah asked, "Who is your first dance partner? My half-brother will be mine. Thank goodness we've practiced dancing together. I won't feel so odd attempting to do so since I know him."

"Lord Aubrey asked me for the first dance," she replied.

"Oh, here's Anthony. You must meet him."

Laurel turned and saw a man striding in their direction. For a moment, she thought a golden god had come to life. His hair seemed kissed by the afternoon sun. He was as tall as her new brothers, with broad shoulders that nicely filled out his dark coat. His chiseled cheekbones seemed able to cut glass and his strong jaw marked him as a man who would tolerate no nonsense. But what caught her breath were his crystal-blue eyes.

"Godwin!" called Jeremy. "It's good to see you."

The two men shook hands and Jeremy said, "Godwin and I were at school together. He was a few years behind me. I've followed your career under Wellington. Well done. I hear you're the new Duke of Linfield. I'm Everton now." He paused. "Let me introduce you to my family."

Jeremy made the introductions, ending with Laurel. She curtseyed to the duke and he took her hand. For a moment, she forgot to breathe as those intense blue eyes took her in.

"Your Grace," she managed.

"It is a pleasure, Lady Laurel. Hannah mentioned meeting you at the dressmaker's."

He finally released her hand and Laurel told herself to breathe. "Yes, we met at Madame Toufour's shop. My sister-in-law, Her Grace, said Madame is the best in all of London."

"I am dancing with my sister this first time but might you care to do so with me?" he asked.

Laurel had one opening left on her card. The supper dance. Rachel and Leah had told her to save it for someone special. Without a doubt, the duke was the man who'd most impressed her this evening.

She offered him her programme and he signed his name to the final spot. The musicians began tuning their instruments and a hush went over the crowd as they anticipated the start of the first ball.

Suddenly, Lord Aubrey appeared at her elbow. He bowed. "Are you ready to help open a new Season, Lady Laurel?"

She wasn't quite sure what he meant but accepted his proffered arm. She fought the urge to turn back and look at Linfield, knowing she needed to concentrate on her first partner. When she saw only the Rutherford family take the floor, she looked around, baffled.

"Why aren't any others coming out?" she whispered, seeing a sea of faces watching but no one following them, only Lord and Lady Rutherford and Lord and Lady Stanley on the dance floor.

"We have a tradition of only Rutherfords dancing the first measures of the opening song which is played. Have no fear, Lady Laurel. Others will join us soon. After all, it is a ball. Dancing is expected."

Panic filled her. "No one else is out here but us?"

Aubrey grinned. "Exactly."

With that, the music began and he swept her into his arms before she could protest. Or faint. Thank goodness Catherine had insisted she have a dance master. Laurel had practiced many hours, learning all kinds of dances and taking to them with ease. Her brothers, Hudson included, had been drawn into partnering with her through hours of endless practice, though Hudson had protested, saying he needed to concentrate on his studies. Jeremy had told Hudson even the best, most serious scholars took time for a little fun every now and then. Her twin had obviously not agreed but had been smart enough to keep his mouth closed, knowing it was through Jeremy's influence that Hudson even had a chance at university and a much different life from the one he'd left behind.

As they moved to the rhythm of the beat, Laurel relaxed.

"You enjoy dancing," Lord Aubrey observed.

"I do," she admitted. "I haven't done it for very long, though. I'm sure you've danced with women much more accomplished."

"I beg to differ. You're marvelous at it," he complimented. "I believe you're talented at a good many things, my lady."

She didn't know how to respond and murmured a thank you to his compliment. Catherine had told her gentlemen would flatter her and the best response was a simple one.

The music continued and other couples began flooding the dance floor. When the music ended, the viscount squeezed her hand and led her back to where Jeremy and Catherine had been standing before he claimed her. The couple joined them, Catherine's eyes shining at her husband.

"Thank you for the dance, Lady Laurel," Lord Aubrey said. He turned to Catherine. "My sister has invited Lady Laurel to tea tomorrow. Would you and Everton care to act as chaperones for us?"

Catherine looked to Laurel and she nodded that she was in agreement with the arrangement.

"We would be happy to do so, my lord."

"Then I will call for you at a quarter past three." Aubrey bowed and left them.

Jeremy had a disgruntled look on his face. "I'm already having to beat off suitors, I see."

"Do you not approve of Lord Aubrey?" Laurel asked.

"We were close growing up. Then he thought to steal my duchess." He slipped an arm about his wife's waist. "Fortunately, she had the good sense to know I was the only man for her."

"Everything is fine, Laurel," Catherine assured her. "Lord Aubrey merely likes to tease Jeremy about it every now and then." She turned to her husband. "Go and dance with your sister now, Duke. I'll be waiting right here for you."

Laurel's eyes went wide, seeing the heat flare in Jeremy's eyes as he looked at his wife.

"You better be, Duchess."

He led Laurel back to the middle of the floor. "You did very well with your first dance. Aubrey is a good man. Don't give our little rivalry a second thought."

They danced without conversation. Jeremy had been the best of her practice partners, gliding with smooth grace. Rachel had shared that he never danced with anyone but Catherine and that by partnering with her at the opening ball of the Season, he was declaring to all Polite Society his approval—and acceptance—of her.

After their dance, she had a variety of partners and finally found a moment to slip away to the retiring room. Lady Hannah was leaving as she approached, her cheeks flushed.

"Are you enjoying yourself?" Laurel asked.

"Very much so. I never knew I could have such fun. When are you dancing with Anthony?"

She realized that Anthony was the Duke of Linfield. "Soon. For the supper dance."

They parted ways and she went inside. A bevy of women filled the room, gossiping and primping their hair. Laurel stepped behind one of the vacant screens to relieve herself, thankful for a brief moment alone. Then she heard her name.

"She's called Laurel. What kind of name is that?"

"You know those St. Clairs. They say and do whatever they want."

"She's not really one of them, though, is she? The Duke of Everton can foist her onto Polite Society and call her *Lady* Laurel—but those of quality know exactly what she is."

A sinking feeling came over her. She reminded herself that she'd been warned of gossip and not to listen to it.

She came out from behind the screen and washed her hands. A servant handed her a towel. She followed the two older women that she suspected had been speaking about her, wondering if she should ignore them—or confront them.

The pair paused and the taller one said, "I can't believe Aubrey thought to partner with her. And for the first dance of the evening! He must not have heard about her being a by-blow. I'm surprised the Rutherfords even invited her."

"She's got the St. Clair looks, though," her companion noted. "Aubrey has a thing for pretty girls. Even if they are baseborn. I heard she was a shop girl or something of that nature."

"I'm sure her morals are as loose as her mother's were. The poor woman thought she could land a duke. If this chit thinks she will find a gentleman to wed, she's sadly mistaken. Even if Everton supports her. When no gentleman offers for her, I'm sure Everton will scuttle her back to the country. No one of good standing in London will want her."

Laurel's anger had grown as she'd eavesdropped and she now cleared her throat. The two women turned, both their mouths forming perfect *O's* as they saw the object of their conversation standing before them.

"My mother was a better woman than either of you could ever dream of being," she said, her voice low but distinct. "*She* was a true lady and would never have disparaged someone with such ugly words as you have used. You may be dressed in your finery and jewels but you will never be a true lady as she was."

Before either of them could reply, someone took her arm.

"There you are, Lady Laurel. It's time for our dance."

The Duke of Linfield led her away.

Chapter Seven

Anthony had been right. He'd rather be surrounded on a battlefield by a thousand French soldiers rather than in the midst of a *ton* ball. He'd danced with Hannah and then forced himself to do the same with three other young ladies making their come-out. He could remember nothing about them, from their names to what they wore. Their conversations had been stilted and his time wasted. Retreating to the card room, he indulged in a couple of brandies as he skirted the edge of the room.

Thinking to find a bride on the Marriage Mart was a mistake. In the future, he would escort Hannah and his aunt to whatever event they decided to attend and then he'd either make himself scarce or leave and return for them later. He wasn't ready for a wife. Or a family. Already, he was bored. Perhaps he could wait till the end of the Season and see which debutantes hadn't formed an attachment. He'd simply pick one of them and make an offer. That way he'd still have accomplished Aunt Constance's goal. A leftover wallflower would fit the bill. She would be bland. Amenable. Her parents would be thrilled that a duke offered for her. That way, he would get a wife without having to take the time to woo one. A wallflower would be forever grateful and adhere to any rules he put forth. He would continue to live his own life and never need be challenged at home.

Leaving the card room, he lurked in the hall outside the ballroom, not ready to go inside again. He knew the supper dance drew near and had made a commitment to Hannah's new friend, though he couldn't remember her name. She was a St. Clair, though. It was obvious from her height to her hair and eye color. Jeremy St. Clair had been ahead of him in school, while Luke St. Clair had been behind Anthony. He knew neither well but did respect the new duke. Jeremy had a reputation of defending younger boys from bullies. Bullying younger students was the way of English schoolboys but Jeremy had wanted no part in it. Anthony was certain that St. Clair had a hand in keeping the older boys from harassing Eric Saunders, whom he'd learned was now Lord Morefield.

He supposed he should return to the ballroom and look for the St. Clair girl. Then he saw her trailing two women, their heads bent together. From the look on her face, the women were up to no good. They came to stand near him and he shrank behind a tall, potted plant, curious as to their conversation.

What he overheard appalled him.

Then before he could step forth and put an end to their wickedness, the object of their gossip did so herself. She reprimanded them quietly and swiftly, looking as brave and bold as Queen Boadicea as she rebelled against the Romans. Anthony had never been one to be easily impressed but her courage bowled him over. If what these women said was true, the young woman was a bastard of the previous Duke of Everton, though it seemed the current one didn't care and accepted her as a full member of the family.

Though this St. Clair didn't need saving, he stepped in. "There you are, Lady Laurel. It's time for our dance."

He took her arm and steered her toward the ballroom. They reached it just as the strains of the supper dance began and he led her onto the floor. As they danced, he noticed how anger only added to her good looks. Her emerald eyes were stormy and the splash of color on her cheeks made her even more attractive.

"I must thank you, Your Grace," she finally said halfway through the dance. "I have a temper and I let it get the better of me. Jeremy and Catherine warned me that others would belittle me. I told myself I wouldn't let it affect me if I heard any gossip."

"But they spoke ill of your mother," he said. "You needed to defend her."

"I did." She gazed into his eyes. "You must have heard what they said, Your Grace. While it was kind of you to keep to our dance, I will understand if you wish to avoid my company and sup with someone else."

His gaze met hers. "I can think of no better person to share the midnight buffet, my lady. You showed both poise and mettle as you addressed those rumormongers."

Anthony still couldn't remember her name but he was fascinated by her.

"They weren't rumors, Your Grace. I am a bastard. A half-sister to Everton. In fact, I've only known him a few weeks. My mother was quite ill and recently passed away. I discovered among her things the true origin of mine and my brother's birth."

"You're a twin?" he asked, his interest growing.

"Yes. My brother is not present tonight. He is preparing to enter university."

"I knew Everton in school. He is a fine man."

"His Grace has proven himself to be most kind to Hudson and me, considering the circumstances. I apologize again for you having to hear me confront those women but my mother told me to always stand up for myself—even if my legs were shaking."

He chuckled. "That's how I felt most of the time when fighting the French."

The music ended and he found himself reluctant to release her. Suddenly, the evening had proved far more interesting than he ever thought it would be as he led the St. Clair girl in to supper. He spied Hannah and saw a gentleman in his mid-twenties seating her with several others. Relief filled him that she had found someone to spend this meal with.

Because Anthony didn't want anything interrupting his time with the woman on his arm.

"May we join my family?" she asked. "I see Catherine has saved us a place."

He would have preferred to sit only with her but saw the arrangement of the room had no tables for two.

"Of course. It is your very first ball," he noted. "I'm sure the Evertons are anxious to hear how things are progressing."

"Progressing?" she asked, a slight frown on her face.

As he guided her across the room, he said, "It's no secret that a come-out is simply another name for placing young ladies on the Marriage Mart."

He felt her stiffen and regretted his words.

"I am not for sale, Your Grace. My family has assured me that I don't have to select any man as a husband this Season. Or any other. Who knows? I may simply choose to remain unwed. After all, what man wants a duke's bastard as the mother of his children?"

Her tone was light but Anthony knew the gossip of the previous encounter had wounded her. He thought it interesting, though, that Everton had said this illegitimate half-sister needn't wed. Perhaps he was just being kind, knowing that most men of the *ton* would not be interested in taking on a woman with a certain reputation and background, even if she were the daughter of a duke.

"Then you may enjoy your Season without any constraints," he replied smoothly.

"Or expectations?" she asked.

By now, they had arrived at the table and the Duchess of Everton indicated where they should sit. The table included the duke and duchess and her sister, Lady Alford, and her husband. The conversation proved lively and Anthony finally was reminded that his companion was named Laurel. She certainly didn't hold back her opinions and seemed quite well-informed about many topics, especially for an illegitimate shop girl.

Eventually, the topic turned to the recent war and he was asked to give a brief summary of his activities, which meant recounting what Wellington had done and where, since he'd been on the commander's staff.

Lady Laurel turned to him as the others moved on to new topics.

"Do you feel the war was a waste?"

Her question startled him. "Not at all. Someone had to stop Bonaparte. It was left to England to see him defeated once and for all, especially after he escaped captivity."

"I agree that Europe didn't need to be under a dictator's dark cloud but isn't war itself asinine? The tremendous cost, not only financially but in terms of human life."

He actually agreed with her but refrained from speaking his mind. It wouldn't do for that opinion to get out. A duke and former aide to the greatest military hero in English history severely criticizing the very act of war wouldn't sit well with any patriotic citizen.

"Take America, for instance," Lady Laurel continued. "Why did we have to fight there not once—but twice?"

"The first time was to end a rebellion," he said, his position that of any Englishman loyal to his king and country.

"But didn't they, as citizens, have rights?" she pressed. "They were being made to observe all kinds of laws, including those of taxation, without any type of representation in Parliament."

"The colonies were a part of the British Empire," he said stiffly. "We offered them our protection."

"Without any say whatsoever in government," she challenged. "And then when we couldn't defeat them, we abandoned their shores, only to intervene again."

"The Americans almost cost us our own freedom," he said. "England was trying to defend not only herself but Europe against Bonaparte. Having to deal with our bastard cousins only drew troops and monies away."

"They already had fought—and won—their political independence but England still repressed them economically," she said. "The Americans were fighting for their very livelihood, Your Grace. Fortunately, enough of the fat, rich, old men who run the War Office decided they would be better suited as allies and economic partners with us and ended that foolish conflict."

Her opinions enraged him. Yet for the first time, he'd heard an argument different from any he'd ever been exposed to previously.

Ready to end this discussion, Anthony firmly said, "We will have to agree to disagree on matters of war, Lady Laurel."

This woman was dangerous. Not only was she quite beautiful, but she was as sharp as any man of his acquaintance. He didn't need a woman who would constantly challenge him. He sought a pliant, unassuming wife he could order about. This fiery, passionate St. Clair would never go quietly into any marriage, much less remain a silent partner within the union. Though Anthony felt a strong attraction to her, he would tamp it down. Lady Laurel St. Clair was not the woman for him.

Supper ended and he escorted her to the ballroom once again.

"Thank you for our dance and an interesting supper," he said before bowing and retreating to the card room once more.

When the ball ended, he found his aunt and half-sister and led them to their waiting carriage. Heavy traffic prevented them from moving for quite a while. Hannah filled the time, prattling on about the evening and her many dance partners. Finally, the vehicle began to move and Anthony relaxed.

Until the conversation turned to Lady Laurel.

"Thank you, Anthony, for dancing with my friend. Lady Laurel is very interesting, isn't she?"

"I quite like her," Aunt Constance remarked. "She isn't the typical boring young miss that I remember from my come-out Season."

"You had a come-out?" Hannah asked, surprise evident in her voice.

Anthony hadn't known this, either, and listened with interest.

"Of course, I did. I was the daughter of a duke," his aunt said haughtily. "As such, I was courted by many young men, some of the most handsome and eligible bachelors of the day."

"Why didn't you wed then?" Hannah asked, perplexed.

He felt the atmosphere in the carriage change, as if a blanket of sadness descended.

"I was engaged to be married," she said quietly. "My fiancé had business for his father in the Caribbean. In fact, we were to live in Jamaica after our wedding. Edmund went there to prepare a home for us on the plantation and complete a business transaction."

She fell silent and Anthony wondered if she would continue.

Finally, Aunt Constance said, "Edmund's ship went down on its return to England. Two sailors survived. Both revealed too many goods had been placed aboard the ship. When it reached rough seas and a violent storm struck, the ship hadn't a chance with such a heavy load of cargo and sank." Her voice broke. "The idea of wedding anyone but Edmund was distasteful. We were in love and no man appealed to me after that. I chose to remain a spinster to honor his memory."

"Oh, Aunt Constance," Hannah said, her voice wavering. "I'm so sorry."

She patted her niece's hand. "It's all right, dear. My father gave me my own residence in the country. The gay, carefree life in London held no interest for me. And I was able to have children of my own, first with Anthony and now you."

Hearing his aunt's tale of heartbreak confirmed in Anthony's mind that love matches were wasteful and would harm a soul as much as the anger that he carried in his own heart. He doubled his resolve to find a silent wallflower who would give him no trouble.

He also decided to address Hannah regarding the situation.

"Hannah, I wish to speak to you about Lady Laurel. I don't think she is an appropriate person for you to befriend."

His sister scowled. "You heard the gossip about her tonight. That she is the duke's illegitimate half-sister."

"I did," he confirmed. "An association with her would hurt your chances in making a good match."

"But she's my friend, Anthony. I cannot abandon her."

"You barely know her," he said, his patience thinning.

"Well, I'm not going to listen to you," she said stubbornly. "Why should I? You didn't even bother to come to see Aunt Constance or me when you returned from the war. You don't even like the fact that you are my guardian. Family means nothing to you. At least Lady Laurel, though illegitimate, has been warmly accepted by the St. Clairs. They have taken her in and made her one of them. Tomorrow night's ball is even in her honor. I don't care what you say. Lady Laurel is a good, kind person. Many of the women I met tonight are not. They were vicious gossips and not the kind I would care to extend the hand of friendship."

The vehicle slowed and came to a stop. The carriage door opened and Hannah sprang up and took the footman's hand and exited.

Aunt Constance shook her head. "She has a point, you know. I approve of Lady Laurel and her loving family. I will allow Hannah to continue the acquaintance. I hope that they grow to be fast friends. And any man who would judge Lady Laurel harshly for her birth father's appalling behavior isn't one good enough to court Hannah, much less wed my niece." With that, she also left the carriage.

He climbed from the vehicle, frustration building. He was a bloody duke—and his own family wouldn't even listen to him. He strode into the townhouse, angry because his own heart was trying to make room for Lady Laurel.

Anthony refused to open it to Laurel St. Clair—or any other woman.

CHAPTER EIGHT

THE NUMBER OF bouquets that arrived startled Laurel. She read through the attached cards, recognizing some of the names but having no recollection of meeting many of the others. Catherine told her that not all the flowers came from men she'd met. Some might be from those who wanted to make her acquaintance. Sending an arrangement was a way to garner favor with her.

"They'll be calling on you, too, in droves," her sister-in-law assured her. "We won't receive any visitors today, though. I need to make sure everything is ready for your ball this evening and we also are taking tea at the Stanleys'."

"I didn't even think about all you would have to do today, Catherine. I never should have accepted Lady Stanley's invitation. Do you think we should postpone the outing?"

"Most everything is taken care of, Laurel. I will meet with Barton and Mrs. Talley to make a few adjustments but I think leaving and taking tea will be a nice respite from all of the activity around here. Besides, we will arrive home in plenty of time to attend to your toilette."

Laurel spent time writing thank you notes for the flowers she'd received and then talked with Hudson, telling him about her first ball. Her twin asked a few questions but she could see he wasn't truly interested in the men she'd danced with and what food was served.

He shrugged. "I don't see the point of it, Laurel. Getting all dressed up in fancy clothes, night after night. Seeing the same people you saw the day before. What do you talk about? What do you do other than dance?"

"It's meant as a way of socializing," she explained. "Also, it gives eligible bachelors the chance to meet their future spouses. It's jokingly referred to as the Marriage Mart."

A blank look appeared on his face, as if the idea had never occurred to him. "Why, that's bloody awful."

She laughed. "It's not as if they line up all the unmarried females and have the men inspect our teeth as they would a horse."

"Still, you're basically on display." He frowned. "Do you even want to get married, Laurel?"

"At some point. I've grown very fond of our nieces and nephews and spend time in the nursery with them each day. I would like to marry and have children of my own."

Her words affected Hudson deeply. "I guess I never thought of us being apart. Other than when I go to university." He sighed. "We really are going to lead separate lives in the future, aren't we?"

She leaned over and hugged him. "We are family, Hudson. Closer than most siblings because we are twins. The fact that we were raised in humble circumstances drew us together. That bond will never be broken. But as we've added to our family, or rather the St. Clairs have added us to theirs, one day I will marry and have children. You will, too."

"Me? Never," he proclaimed. "Women don't interest me. Neither do children. Don't get me wrong. I like women. I like our nieces and nephews. Having my own family isn't a priority for me, however. I have you and all these St. Clairs and their spouses and children. That's more than enough. I want to pursue my education and then go to work for Jeremy. He has so many varying business interests. Shipping. Mining. Transportation. I want to learn about them all. That will consume my time. It wouldn't be fair to leave my wife alone while I devoted all of my time to business."

Laurel thought one day Hudson might change his mind. He was still young. Besides, being around all these love matches in the St. Clair circle might rub off on him. Not her, though. She still wanted a husband and children but her practical nature told her love wasn't in the cards for her. Despite the attention she'd received last night, she knew tongues wagged today over her status. She might be a novelty within the *ton* now but the interest in her—both good and bad—would soon wear off. She was still a wrong side of the blanket St. Clair and doubted few men would become interested enough in her in order to woo her. She only hoped there was some man out there who might disregard all the gossip and give her a chance. If not a member of the *ton*, then perhaps a doctor or solicitor. She didn't need a husband with a fancy title.

Lord Aubrey arrived right on time and she, Jeremy, and Catherine joined him in his carriage. The ride to the Stanleys' residence took very little time and she thought they should have walked the short distance. Hudson's words echoed in her mind, though. She knew it had taken grooms to ready the horses and carriage. A driver to deliver them. Footmen to assist them from the vehicle. That employed a good number of people. Laurel wouldn't begrudge anyone the chance to make a steady living. She'd also noted how considerately her relatives treated their servants and knew they were happy to be employed in such a good household.

A pleasant hour passed as she got to know Lord and Lady Stanley over tea. Lord Aubrey proved to be very amusing and seemed truly interested in her opinions. When he dropped them at the Everton townhouse, he escorted her to the door.

"Would you reserve a dance for me tonight, Lady Laurel?" he asked.

"The first one again?"

"No. I'd rather spend more time with you. I think the supper dance will do."

"I will mark your name beside it," she promised.

Laurel went inside and, at Catherine's suggestion, lay down for an hour. Surprisingly, she fell asleep and her maid had to awaken her. The family had a very light dinner in a small dining room, consisting of cold meats and cheese, since nearly every servant was involved in preparations for the ball and the large midnight buffet.

Afterward, Laurel bathed and then her maid dressed her. They had tried several different hairstyles and she was glad at the one they'd settled upon. It was a simple chignon with a few loose tendrils surrounding her face. Her gown was the palest of lilacs, with satin shoes dyed to match the luxurious silk dress. Her new pearls were the perfect accessory and she was glad to have them. She'd taken note of every girl making her come-out last night. All of them wore some type of jewelry. She was grateful Jeremy and Catherine had thought to gift her with some so she wouldn't feel so out of place.

Catherine had pulled her aside and asked how things had gone last night. Laurel omitted mentioning the gossip she had heard—and the Duke of Linfield's rescue of her. She still didn't know what to think of him. He seemed interested in her one minute and then distant the next. She found him unbelievably handsome but she knew the attraction to be one-sided. After all, he was a duke, one of a select few in all of England. He would never wed someone with her background. He'd been polite enough to dance with her, thanks to her budding friendship with his half-sister, but Laurel didn't expect anything beyond that. Especially after she'd expressed her frank opinions regarding England's war with the Americans. The former army officer had visibly bristled at her comments.

In a way, she felt a kinship with America. It was a part of England and yet the colonies had been outsiders. England had treated them unkindly, milking them for what she could get without regard to their welfare. It was comparable to the *ton* and how they expected the rest of England's citizens to be at their beck and call, always subservient, never expressing an opinion.

It didn't matter. She would continue her friendship with Hannah and the two would enjoy their Season together.

Her maid finished with her hair and Laurel gazed into the mirror, pleased at her appearance.

"You look ever so beautiful, my lady. Even more so than last night. And you've got an entire ball in your honor!" the servant exclaimed. Then she gazed at Laurel a long moment and revealed, "We're all pulling for you, my lady. Every single servant. You being almost one of us, as well as one of them."

She nodded. "Thank you, Retta. I understand what you mean. Two months ago, I was waiting on customers at the chandlery and tonight? I'm dressed to the nines and a part of a world that is still confusing to me at times."

Retta grinned. "You wouldn't know it, my lady. You look every inch a St. Clair."

The maid's words gave her a confidence that she'd lacked until now. With her head held high, Laurel left her bedchamber and descended to the next floor. She went to the ballroom, which had been decorated like a forest. Rachel had a heavy hand in the design and had transformed the room. Her sister now flitted from place to place, rearranging the vines on a plant and nudging a flowerpot into place.

Laurel joined her. "This is a wonderland, Rachel. I would think I'm outdoors."

"That's the effect I was hoping for." Rachel hugged her. "I'm glad you approve. You look so lovely. Did you receive many bouquets today?"

"Too many to count. And from men I either don't remember meeting or didn't meet at all."

"Has Jeremy complained overmuch?"

She laughed. "He did a little bit. I think it was all for show."

Rachel slipped her arm through Laurel's. "I agree. He enjoys playing the protective big brother. You and Hudson arriving has given him a chance to increase his role."

They left the ballroom and Rachel and Catherine began talking about their children. Rachel's husband, Lord Merrick, drew her aside.

"How was your first *ton* event?" he asked.

"I enjoyed the dancing quite a bit. I did meet some nice people."

"But not all were kind?" he asked, his blue eyes intense.

Laurel shrugged. "I was warned there would be some gossip."

"There's always gossip. People invent stories left and right from sheer boredom." He took her hand and squeezed it. "I'm not much for being social but I have learned that you must ignore what the gossips say. About you or anyone else. I have been the subject of their interest, some of it deserved. Still, know that you have a loving family surrounding you, myself included. You will make good friends. The right man is waiting for you. Don't rush to find him. When the time is right, you'll be drawn to one another."

"As you were to Rachel? She said fate brought you together."

Merrick smiled. "I fought my attraction to her like the dickens. Even shoved her away as hard as I could. But I never stopped thinking about her—or loving her. Thank God I saw the error of my ways and she loved me enough to accept me as I am. Rachel saved me in more ways than I can ever say. She is my everything."

It touched Laurel to see how much Rachel was loved by this man.

Merrick released her hand. "Love will come, Laurel. Be open to it."

"I'm not looking for love," she revealed. "I know it's not the St. Clair way. I do hope to find a husband who will be kind to me and our children and accept me for who I am, despite my humble background."

Before he could reply, Jeremy joined them. "We need to create our receiving line. Barton tells me the first guests are arriving."

"I wish Luke and Caroline were here," Catherine said as they formed a line. "I'm so used to having them with us."

"Caroline is happy at Fairhaven, eating macaroons and walking barefoot in the grass," Jeremy replied. "I wish we could be doing the same, Duchess."

"Oh, Duke, quit grumbling. Put on your hosting smile. If you're well-behaved and pleasant to everyone tonight, I have a surprise waiting for you." Catherine's eyes gleamed with mischief.

A broad smile filled her brother's face. "I'm always eager to discover what surprise my duchess has for me. Hopefully, it includes being naked in bed—with you equally naked—when I receive it."

"Jeremy St. Clair! You are insufferable," his wife declared.

The first guests reached the top of the staircase at that moment and Laurel stifled her laughter, along with the others. Her brother could say some outrageous things at times. He also did a few outrageous things, as well. Laurel had stumbled upon him kissing Catherine numerous times since she'd moved into the Everton townhome. She'd learned to quietly slip from the room and leave them alone.

Something tugged at her heart. Did she really want a loveless marriage? Jeremy and Rachel—Luke, too—seemed so satisfied in their marriages. They were playful and loving with their spouses. Could she be wrong to deliberately avoid love?

Laurel supposed time would tell. She also knew that physical attraction could be experienced without love playing a role at all. She pushed aside these thoughts and determined she would enjoy this ball in her honor.

After half an hour, she'd met more people than a person could ever know. It would take her twenty Seasons to learn all their names and titles. She was grateful when Lady Constance and Lady Hannah reached her.

"It's good to see you," she said, glancing down the line, curious why the Duke of Linfield did not accompany them.

"If you're looking for my nephew, he bypassed the receiving line and headed straight for the card room."

Laurel heard disapproval in Lady Constance's voice.

"He is a good man but, like his father, he can be difficult at times," she continued.

"He's forbidden me to be your friend," Lady Hannah blurted out. "Aunt Constance told me to ignore him, though."

Shock filled Laurel. The duke had come to her rescue the previous evening. Yet she understood immediately.

"Your brother doesn't wish to lessen your chances at making a good match," she said. "If you are friendly with me, the stain of gossip could smear your reputation."

"He's my half-brother—and he doesn't care a thing about me," Lady Hannah said, her eyes swelling with tears. "You have half-brothers and they treat you as a whole sister."

"Now is not the time, Child," Hannah's aunt chided gently. "This is Lady Laurel's night."

"I'm sorry," the young woman said. "But you are my friend. I will not abandon you."

With that, the two women stepped aside and another introduction was pressed upon Laurel. She greeted the newcomer with a smile but her heart ached. She thought she'd made a true friend in Hannah Godwin but she would never interfere in a family matter. If the Duke of Linfield didn't wish them seeing one another socially, she must adhere to his wishes and not jeopardize Hannah's chances at finding the right husband.

The line finally emptied and she rubbed her temples, a headache forming. She saw Catherine glance at her with concern and lowered her hands, giving her sister-in-law a ready smile.

"I've so many names to remember," she said brightly. "I better go and put to use the ones I've managed to retain."

Laurel stepped away and into the ballroom. Immediately, she was surrounded by a swell of people. All men, she noted. No other women but Hannah had been overly friendly last night. Her heart told her that she would need to depend upon her St. Clair sisters as her only friends. They were all married and could weather the storm of her origin. It saddened her, though, because she had truly felt an affinity with Lady Hannah and even Lady Constance.

She also thought it downright rude for Linfield to skip the receiving line, thinking his avoidance of her proved poor manners on his part. Linfield was a guest in the Everton home and should have behaved better, especially since he was previously acquainted with Jeremy.

Her programme filled more quickly than the evening before and Laurel put aside her feelings. She let the music take her away from her troubles. Several of her partners complimented her on her graceful dancing. She smiled and thanked them. None of them said much more than that. She doubted any of them wished to know her. She was merely an object of curiosity. A sudden, overwhelming loneliness filled her.

"You seem pensive," a voice said.

Laurel turned and found Lord Aubrey standing before her, looking splendid in his evening wear.

"It's a busy night," she said vaguely as he led her to the center of the room.

As they danced, she decided to speak frankly to him and said, "I know you are a great friend of the St. Clair family and have been for many years."

"Amanda and I spent many hours playing with them."

"Just because there is a longstanding friendship between the two families, please don't feel obligated to act friendly with me."

He frowned. "Are you not pleased to dance with me, my lady?"

"You are a marvelous dancer and you know it, my lord. I merely am letting you know that you don't have to pay special attention to me, merely because of the connection you feel with the other St. Clairs."

He stopped moving his feet, bringing them to a standstill. Laurel panicked because she knew it would draw attention.

"Please. Keep dancing," she whispered, not disguising the urgency in her request.

"As you wish."

He continued and she hoped their brief pause went unnoticed. Already, she had enough gossip surrounding her and didn't need more fuel added to that fire.

As the music died away, Aubrey said, "Let me make one thing clear. I asked you to dance because I wanted to. Not out of any sense of obligation."

With that, he took her arm and led her from the ballroom to where the buffet had been set up. Tables with varying sizes had been brought in and Lord Aubrey led her to one which only seated two.

"I believe Catherine wanted—"

"I want to sit with you. Alone," the viscount said firmly.

"I see."

He moved the chair out and seated her before sitting himself and said, "I'll let the line die down a bit before filling our plates if you don't mind."

She started to reply and saw Barton headed their way. She supposed the butler would ask her and Aubrey to move to Jeremy and Catherine's table.

Instead, he brought a silver tray to the viscount. "For you, Lord Aubrey."

"Hmm." Aubrey took the folded page atop it and Barton stepped aside, remaining close in case he was needed.

Laurel watched as her companion skimmed the contents. His face drained of color. Folding the note, he slipped it inside his coat.

"I must apologize, my lady. I must leave immediately."

"Is something wrong?" she asked.

"My father has passed away suddenly."

A lump formed in her throat. "Oh, my lord. I am so sorry for your loss. My mother passed recently. I understand how difficult this is."

He rose. "Let me escort you to your family."

The viscount led her to the Everton table. He kissed her hand. "I'm afraid I will be in mourning, Lady Laurel. I will not see you for a while."

Aubrey looked as if he had more to say and then shook his head. "I must find Amanda."

He left and she watched him cross to where Lord and Lady Stanley sat. He bent and spoke to her. She stiffened and rose, Lord Stanley doing the same. The three quit the supper room.

"Has something happened?" Jeremy asked, looking concerned.

"Yes. Lord Aubrey just received word that Lord Rutherford has passed," Laurel replied.

"Oh, no," Catherine murmured. "I received a note from Lady Rutherford, saying they would not be in attendance tonight. That the earl was feeling ill. This is terrible."

"Should we end the ball?" Laurel asked.

"No. The death will be announced soon enough," Jeremy said. "I'm sorry if this has colored your evening, Laurel. It seems you and Aubrey were getting along well."

"He is very nice," she responded. "As is Lady Stanley. They've both been very kind to me." She rose. "If you will excuse me. I need a few moments to myself."

Laurel escaped the ballroom. She'd never really grieved for her mother after Dinah had passed because of the financial difficulties she and Hudson had faced, as well as the threats hanging over them from Julius Farmon. She knew she wasn't reacting to the death of Lord Rutherford, whom she'd barely known, but to the emptiness she'd felt ever since her mother had died.

She needed to be away from the noise and slipped out a door which led to the balcony. The cool air of the April evening engulfed her. She moved to the far end of the terrace and leaned her forearms against the railing.

And cried the tears that had never been shed.

CHAPTER NINE

ANTHONY TOSSED HIS cards down and left the table, claiming another drink. A butler announced supper was now being served and the card room was quickly vacated. He didn't want to be around people, having to make pointless conversation. Cigar smoke still hung over the room so he decided to claim some fresh air and slipped out a side door to the balcony, knowing it would be deserted, thanks to the lure of food. He walked the length and went to stand at the end, shadows enveloping him.

It was a mistake, him being the Duke of Linfield. One that he had no power to correct. He felt like an imposter, everyone addressing him as Your Grace. He needed to live up to his responsibilities, though, and stop neglecting his estates. If only he could leave London now and visit them. Unfortunately, he was bound to remain a few more months, escorting his aunt and half-sister to Season events. Though he'd laid down the law with Hannah regarding her budding friendship with Laurel St. Clair, he knew she would disregard his wishes, especially with Aunt Constance encouraging them since she approved of the girl.

Regrettably, he also liked the chit. Too much. She was totally wrong for him and he was smart enough to recognize it. If he had to wed, he wanted a malleable young miss who hadn't a thought in her head, not one who could speak knowledgeably about recent laws passed by Parliament. Lady Laurel, though illegitimate, was proving to be a true St. Clair. Beautiful. Intelligent. Someone who would live life to the fullest, demanding to be let into her husband's heart.

He didn't have one. Where his heart should beat, there only existed a black hole still filled with rage. He couldn't let go of what his father had done to him. And despite being recognized as a valiant officer and superb strategist and leader, he loathed war and regretted all the men he'd lost. The fact that he'd never wanted to be a duke, much less carry the dreaded name Linfield, caused him further pain. Amidst his anger he felt emptiness engulfing him, a loneliness so deep and isolating that nothing could cure it.

He would fulfill his duty to Hannah. He knew she was hungry for his love and eager for them to act as if they were a true family. Anthony just didn't have it in him, though. That's why he needed to marry her off, so she'd be someone else's responsibility. Perhaps his aunt could even go live with Hannah and her new husband and then he wouldn't have to think of either of them.

Movement caught his eye and he groaned inwardly. It was probably some couple, thinking they were madly in love, sneaking outside for a few stolen kisses while the rest of Everton's guests ate and drank their fill. The door closed and a lone figure began walking toward him. Anthony slunk deeper into the shadows, pressing his back against the wall of the structure, not wishing to be seen and having to speak to anyone.

It was a woman. A tall one. As she drew near, moonlight fell across her face and he recognized Laurel St. Clair. Usually, she stood with perfect posture. Now, though, her shoulders slumped as she moved to the edge and braced herself against it. She was only mere feet away from him and he held his breath, willing her to go away and leave him in peace.

Then he watched as her shoulders shook and a sob broke from her.

What did the chit have to cry about? It was her come-out ball. All of London's *ton* had turned out for this night. She was like a fairy tale brought to life, elevated from the dregs of London society to the household of a wealthy and powerful duke. True, the circumstances of her birth were a strike against her in some people's eyes but Anthony knew the entire St. Clair family had taken her in wholeheartedly. Likely, Everton had set aside a huge dowry. Someone would wed the girl, if not for the money then for the social connection to a duke.

She cried, though, as if her heart were rent in two. Had some other wicked gossips confronted her? He remembered the pair from last night and how they sought to slander her.

And how Lady Laurel had bravely confronted them.

Suddenly, a fierce urge to protect her—comfort her—filled him. His feet moved without thought and he came to stand next to her.

"What ails you, my lady?" he asked softly.

Her head whipped up and Anthony saw tears glimmering on her cheeks. Most women turned ugly when they cried, their faces red and drawn. Laurel St. Clair only appeared more beautiful—and quite vulnerable.

Her lips trembled, drawing his attention to them, especially her full, bottom lip. Desire shot through him as she bit it, trying to still it.

"I was with Lord Aubrey," she began shakily. "He . . . received news . . . that his father has passed away."

Anthony knew the viscount she spoke of. He'd been at Eton with Aubrey, who was just ahead of him. Why would she be distressed about learning this, to the point of shedding tears?

Yet they continued to stream down her cheeks. His hand reached out and cradled her face, his thumb wiping away a tear as it fell. Her breath hitched and those emerald St. Clair eyes gazed into his own.

"Did you know Lord Rutherford?" he asked.

Her mouth trembled. "We had met. His family and the St. Clairs are friends." She shook her head. "My tears are not for him. They are for . . . my mother."

She swallowed, sorrow filling her face. "She was ill for several months. When she passed, I never grieved for her."

"Why not?"

She shook her head. "You would not understand. No one here tonight would."

"Try and explain it to me," he urged.

Lady Laurel shrugged. "It took everything Hudson and I had to be able to bury Mama. With her gone, I was too worried about how I would put food on the table for us. How we would pay a rent that had soared higher than the sky. I had no time to mourn when all my thoughts were consumed with survival." Anger flashed in her eyes. "How many guests tonight would have an inkling of that?"

Fresh tears spilled down her cheeks and Anthony embraced her, wrapping his arms about her and holding her close as she wept. He'd never embraced anyone before. When he'd been banished to his aunt's house, she had put an arm about him that day. She wasn't much for physical affection, though, and had never done so again, probably because he acted so stoically around her.

Lady Laurel lifted her face. "I'm sorry, Your Grace. I've probably ruined your coat with my tears."

"You haven't spoiled anything."

With that, he lowered his mouth to hers.

He meant for it to be a kiss of solace. One to ease her sadness and console her in some small way. He couldn't imagine what her life had been like before. Part of him understood that she not only grieved for her mother but possibly for her old, familiar life. She'd been thrown into something far different and while she no longer had to worry about starvation, the world she now inhabited in some ways could be as vicious and cruel as the one she'd left behind.

This kiss changed, though. Hunger for her rose, consuming him. One hand moved to the back of her neck, holding her steady so he could deepen the kiss. Immediately, he realized she'd never been kissed before. Especially like this. But she accepted his tongue stroking her, tasting her, and even tentatively answered his call. A shudder ran through him and he brought her against him, holding her more tightly, kissing her as if she were an oasis he'd discovered after many days wandering in the desert. He drank his fill, returning again and again, a secret part of him thrilled that he went where no man had ventured before.

"My stars!" a voice cried out.

Anthony tensed, angry at the interruption. Afraid to see who it was. Wondering if they'd have the decency to walk away and keep quiet. He broke the kiss and relaxed his hold on Laurel though he didn't release her completely. Turning, he cursed inwardly, seeing the pair of rumormongers who'd raked Laurel over the coals last night. Hot anger filled him, flaring. He knew they would return to the ballroom and spread the news of what they'd seen. That the Duke of Linfield had compromised Lady Laurel at her own come-out ball. Her reputation, already shaky in the eyes of many, would be ruined. She would have no chance of wedding any bachelor in Polite Society.

He couldn't do that to her. Not to this woman who appeared so strong to the world and yet was incredibly vulnerable. Though she was the total opposite of everything he would have sought in a wife, he owed it to her to save her reputation—by marrying her.

"Good evening, ladies," he said pleasantly, easing his arms from Laurel but then slipping an arm about her waist and holding her to him, afraid she'd dash off like a hare being chased by hounds. "I apologize for my rash behavior in public. My fiancée just received some news which upset her. A good friend of the St. Clair family, Lord Rutherford, has passed away."

Anthony watched the two women carefully as they took in not only news of Rutherford's death but that he and Laurel were engaged. Laurel stiffened, peering up at him. He brushed a kiss against her brow and looked back at the pair.

"The Duke of Everton will be announcing our engagement after supper this evening. Could you please refrain from discussing it until he has done so? Everton would hate for anyone to share the news before he did."

One woman nodded solemnly, her fear of Everton's reputation obvious. The other looked to him, her face showing delight in having found them in a compromising situation.

"When will you wed?" the matron challenged.

"This week," Anthony assured them. "I am not a man to wait. Once I offered for Lady Laurel, I knew we would be eager for the ceremony to take place so that we could start our lives together." He smiled graciously. "If you'll excuse us?"

He led Laurel back inside, avoiding the supper room. They came to stop just outside it.

"Are you mad?" she hissed. "We don't even know each other."

He shrugged. "Is it so different from other *ton* marriages? Couples meet. Dance a few times over the course of a few weeks. Take tea together and possibly ride in Rotten Row or take a carriage through the park. Many an engagement has occurred before a woman even knows the Christian name of her fiancé. It doesn't mean the marriage cannot be a successful one."

"What is yours? Your name?"

"Anthony." He paused. "I know you should call me Linfield in public but in private, I would prefer you use Anthony."

"Your Grace, this is not—"

"Not what you expected? I'm afraid if we don't wed, your reputation will be in tatters."

"Isn't it already, thanks to people like those two old biddies?" she asked, a touch of bitterness in her voice.

"Is it so very hard to imagine being married to me?" he asked softly.

His words startled her. "No. You are everything unmarried young ladies seek. You are handsome beyond words. A respected war hero. A wealthy duke."

"Then why your reluctance?"

Her mouth trembled. "Because I feel like a pretender. I'm not truly a part of this world. You shouldn't have to wed me merely because you offered a kiss of comfort when I was upset."

Anthony smiled. "I believe it turned into more than comfort. I enjoyed kissing you. Very much."

Her cheeks flooded with color.

"Go to the retiring room and wash your face. Join me in the supper room. I must speak to Everton."

She hesitated. "Are you certain, Your Grace?"

"Anthony," he prompted. "And yes. I'm very sure. If you aren't happy with me as a husband, at least you'll have Hannah as a sister-in-law."

For the first time, she smiled. "I do like her. Very much." Then a frown crossed her face. "Although she told me tonight that you had forbidden us to be friends. I understood why. You didn't want her chances of making a suitable match ruined by a friendship with me. Yet here you are willing to marry me." She sighed. "I don't understand society at all."

"You won't have to, Laurel. You'll be a duchess, one of a handful in all of England. Whatever rules you don't like, you can simply choose to ignore."

She grinned. "That would be an advantage."

He put his hands on her shoulders. "You'll be wife of a duke and sister to another. I believe you'll find yourself the darling of society." He kissed her brow. "Now, go."

She left and Anthony watched the gentle sway of her hips, something stirring within him. Laurel St. Clair was a mix of strength and fragility. She would certainly challenge him. He promised himself to guard his heart, though. He would give her his name. Children. But that was it. She wasn't to have even the smallest piece of him.

He spied the Duke and Duchess of Everton and went to their table, slipping into a seat next to Everton, who turned and greeted him.

"Good evening, Linfield. I haven't seen you tonight."

His voice low, Anthony said, "We've always been two men who could mask their feelings. Do so now," he commanded, leaning in. "I have offered for Laurel and she has accepted me. You're to announce our engagement after supper. We plan to wed this week."

A muscle twitched in Everton's cheek. "You've compromised her," he said flatly. "Someone saw you."

Anthony didn't want to go into explanations. "I did."

"You bastard," Everton said. Though his face appeared bland, Anthony saw murder in the duke's eyes.

"There's already been plenty of gossip about her, despite the St. Clairs closing ranks around her. By wedding me, Laurel's place in society will be secured. I'm a bloody duke. Once she's my duchess, no one will dare speak ill of her—else they have the both of us to answer to."

He sat straight again. "You'll need to break the news to your family. Now. They should be prepared for the announcement."

"I want to speak to Laurel first," Everton said.

"Follow me."

Anthony exited the supper room and strode toward the ladies' retiring room. Laurel was just emerging. Her eyes widened as she met him. He turned and saw not only Everton behind him but the man's duchess and two other couples, along with the dowager duchess, who had been seated at the table.

Her family surrounded them as Everton said, "Laurel, do you truly wish to wed Linfield?"

Anthony heard the gasps and felt her family's eyes bore into him. Anthony focused on her instead. Their gaze met and she nodded.

"Yes, Jeremy. Yes, I do."

A woman, most certainly a St. Clair, said, "I told you to kiss a few men, Laurel. Not compromise yourself and be forced to wed one, especially the second day of the Season." She turned and glared at him. "How dare you ruin my sister, you bloody fool!"

"Keep your voice down, Rachel," Everton warned. "We already will have a bit of a scandal with Laurel wedding so quickly." He looked at her again. "You're certain."

"I am," Laurel said firmly and came to him, slipping her arm through his. "Anthony and I know what we want."

In that moment, he felt pride at marrying a woman who stood strong in the face of adversity.

"Then let's return to the supper room. We may as well make the announcement now," Everton said. The duke watched his family turn and walk away but he hung back and said to Anthony, "I expect you tomorrow at three. You will produce the special license and we'll make the arrangements for the wedding."

With that, the Duke of Everton strode away.

"His anger will subside," Laurel said quietly as they followed. "Jeremy only wishes for me to be happy. He and Catherine are a love match. So are his two siblings. They'd wanted the same for me."

Anthony stopped. "I have offered you marriage, my lady. Love has nothing to do with it," he said stiffly.

"I quite agree. I come from a life where love between a husband and wife isn't important. I want children. I'll do what it takes to get them."

"I want them as well."

"Good. As long as you can treat me with respect and act as a good father to our children, it's all I'll ever ask. You are free to do as you wish the rest of the time. I understand that to be the way of the *ton*."

"Agreed," Anthony said, though as they entered the supper room, the bargain they'd struck left him less than satisfied.

CHAPTER TEN

ANTHONY RANG THE bell to the Everton household at precisely three o'clock. A butler with a look of disdain on his face admitted Anthony. He presented his card, which the servant refused.

"You are expected, Your Grace. No need for that. If you'll follow me," he said haughtily.

Tamping down the trepidation rumbling inside him, Anthony followed the butler to the Duke of Everton's study and was announced.

"Would you care for tea to be brought, Your Grace?" the butler asked.

"I would not," Everton said and the butler left.

He could see the duke's anger regarding the betrothal had yet to cool. Without bothering for an invitation, Anthony took a seat in front of the desk Everton sat behind and removed the special license he'd obtained this morning, setting it on the desk.

"I visited Doctors Common this morning. Are you ready to discuss the settlements?"

Everton steepled his fingers and studied Anthony. "Why did you do it, Linfield?"

"Do what, Your Grace?"

"Compromise my sister. You're a duke. You could have had any woman in the *ton* that you desired. Why Laurel?"

"I surprised myself, Everton," he admitted. "I wasn't planning to wed so quickly. Lady Laurel is unique, though. The life she led before she came to you St. Clairs and all she has experienced has made her immeasurably strong. Yet, I see a vulnerability in her. She is intelligent. Wise beyond her years and full of common sense. I find her quite extraordinary and believe she will make for a fine duchess."

"It sounds as though you admire her," the duke noted.

"I do. Neither of us has had an easy time in life. With my new title and power, though, I have the ability to protect her. Give her everything she has previously lacked. Laurel will bring an unmatched perspective to raising our children. They will be better, kinder individuals because they will be made aware that not everyone in society has the advantages they will hold."

"I see." The duke studied him. Anthony focused on even breaths, trying to remain calm under such scrutiny.

"It seems you will treat Laurel with respect."

"Of course. She will be my duchess."

"What of fidelity?" Everton asked.

"What of it?" he countered, remembering how Laurel mentioned that St. Clairs wed for love. "I am not a man to take any commitment lightly. Marriage is the greatest one of all. I will be faithful to my wife, Everton. Never doubt that."

"Do you love her?" the duke asked softly.

"No," he said, not wanting to tell Laurel's blood kin that would be impossible. "I haven't known her long enough. I do greatly respect and admire her. I'm interested and intrigued by her. We've found common ground between us. I believe we have the makings for a solid foundation for a marriage. That's more than most couples who wed can say."

His answer seemed to satisfy Everton. The duke picked up the special license and scanned it. "Are you ready to hammer out the marriage settlements?" he asked, a look of cunning in his eyes.

Anthony was eager to go toe to toe with him and responded, "Prepare to grovel, Everton. I plan to get everything I want—and then some."

"Duly noted," the duke replied, a slow smile spreading across his face. He cracked his knuckles. "I suggest removing your coat and rolling up your sleeves, Linfield. We've contracts to work out—and I plan to squeeze you until you scream for mercy."

Two hours later, an agreement between the pair had been reached. Everton offered his hand and Anthony took it.

"Welcome to the family, Linfield."

"Thank you, Your Grace. You are a worthy adversary. I only hope Laurel hasn't your skills in negotiation else I fear she will rule our roost."

Everton laughed. "She's a St. Clair, man. She'll run over you while smiling—and you'll never know what hit you."

Anthony had a feeling that's exactly what would occur.

And he was perfectly fine with it, knowing he could enjoy marriage to Laurel and keep his heart intact.

LAUREL ALLOWED HER female relatives to fuss over her as they prepared her for her wedding. Even she could tell their gaiety was forced. Left unsaid was how this marriage—though not forced—wasn't the typically happy St. Clair union the three women in the room had experienced.

It didn't matter to her. Linfield would give her his name, which included his protection, as well as children. That was what was most important. It would help shield her new St. Clair relatives from the vicious gossip that would erupt if she and the duke hadn't wed.

She did feel a bit sad, having expressed her wish that Luke and Caroline not attend. With Caroline's delicate condition, she didn't want her sister-in-law to have to endure another coach ride to London and back, especially since the wedding occurred so quickly. She had told Jeremy she would write to the Mayfields and share her good news. Hopefully, Linfield wouldn't mind her visiting them once their baby came in June. She was eager to meet her new niece or nephew.

"There," Catherine said. "I think you are ready." She stepped back and admired Laurel as she rose. "You make for a very beautiful bride. Linfield is an exceptionally fortunate man."

"Thank you all for helping me get ready." She hesitated and added, "I would like a few minutes alone to collect my thoughts."

Realizing they were being dismissed, Catherine and Leah nodded and left the room.

Only Rachel lingered at the door and said, "You didn't say what happened with Linfield. Did he do more than kiss you?"

"No," Laurel replied. "We were observed kissing. That was enough."

Her sister gazed steadily at her. "Did you at least enjoy the kiss?"

"It was pleasant," she began. "I was upset. He wished to console me. It somehow led to a kiss."

Rachel frowned. "Pleasant?"

"Well, I have never experienced a kiss before. This one . . . changed somehow." Laurel paused, unsure how to describe what had happened between them. She had thought about it constantly ever since it occurred. "It was as if Linfield became . . . hungry for me. The kiss started in comfort and turned into . . . something else. It was as if he needed me. And I needed him."

Her sister grinned. "Was that part more than pleasant?"

She sensed her cheeks heating. "Very much. I wish . . . I wish we hadn't been interrupted," she declared. "I would have liked to see where it went."

Relief swept across Rachel's face. She came toward Laurel and hugged her tightly. "Where there is hunger, there is desire. Desire leads to passion. And passion leads to love." She kissed Laurel's cheek. "You may marry Linfield now. I'm satisfied things will work out as they should."

What Laurel didn't tell her sister was that love would never be a part of this union. That moments before Jeremy announced their engagement to the *ton*, her future husband had told her love wouldn't play a role in their marriage. Laurel accepted it for what it was worth. If they could be friendly toward one another, that was all she would expect. People in the *ton* married and had children all the time. Lovemaking didn't necessarily include the two participants loving one another.

A knock brought her to her feet and she answered it. Standing at the door were Hudson and Jeremy.

"You don't have to do this," Hudson proclaimed. "He's a stranger."

"He's a *duke*," she reminded her brother. "The match is more than I could have hoped for."

"But you don't know him, Laurel," Hudson protested.

"We will have many years to get to know one another. I want this, Hudson. Truly. For you as much as me."

"Me?"

"Yes. There's already enough gossip about me as is. Marrying Linfield and becoming his duchess in a hasty marriage will lead to more—but it will soon die down and new scandals will arise. By the time you finish your education and enter society, I will be an old, married matron, hopefully with a few children. You will be able to wed the lady of your choice."

His face hardened. "I've told you I have no interest in marriage, must less wedding a member of Polite Society."

"You have. But at least this way if you change your mind, there will be no obstacles in your way." She took his hand. "Hudson, you know I want to wed and have children. It might as well be with the Duke of Linfield. We have reached an understanding and he will give me more freedom than I would have expected. Please, accept this and wish me well."

She saw stubbornness on his face but his features softened.

"I love you, Laurel."

"And I love you."

Jeremy finally spoke. "Are you certain, Laurel? You speak with conviction but only say the word and I will put a halt to the proceedings. We can withstand any amount of gossip. We are St. Clairs and will always stand together."

His words touched her but she refused to put her new family through the hailstorm of gossip that would occur if she didn't marry Linfield.

"Thank you, Jeremy, but I am perfectly willing to go through today's ceremony. It may not be the St. Clair way of wedding but it is the Wright one for me."

He studied her a long moment and then finally nodded. She saw he understood the pun she'd intentionally spoken. Offering his arm, he said, "Then Hudson and I would both claim the privilege of delivering you to your groom."

She took his arm and Hudson's and the two men led her downstairs to the drawing room. The only guests gathered included their families. She'd told everyone she wanted a simple affair. Since they were wedding only two days after her come-out ball, it was easier to prepare for such a small group.

At the far end of the room she saw the clergyman, whose name she couldn't recall. Standing in front of him was her groom. Linfield appeared both elegant and intimidating in his wedding finery, his shoulders impossibly broad, his thick, blond hair swept back from his face, making his cheekbones stand out. Jeremy released her and took her hand, placing it on Linfield's arm. Hudson held back a moment and then hugged her fiercely, leaning in to whisper in her ear.

"You'll always be a Wright to me. I love you." He withdrew and moved away.

"Are we ready to begin?" the clergyman asked.

Laurel glanced up at her groom and then back. She nodded.

The next few minutes passed in a haze, as if a thick fog had rolled in and she couldn't see a thing. She heard words being spoken. She repeated her vows, the words not really making much sense. It all seemed like a distant dream. Her groom slipped a slim wedding band onto her finger and she looked down at it, thinking it would be something always with her. She would never remove it.

Then the reverend stopped speaking and her new husband turned her toward him. He gave her a chaste kiss, nothing like what had passed between them before, and then lifted his lips from hers.

They were married. There was no going back.

Her family and his approached them, offering their good wishes. Hannah embraced her and said, "Now I have the sister I've always wanted."

"I feel the same," Laurel told her friend.

"You must call me Aunt Constance. You are family now."

"I will be happy to do so," she replied.

"Barton says the wedding breakfast is ready," Catherine announced.

The group followed Catherine from the room. Only the bride and groom remained behind.

Linfield gazed into her eyes. "Are you ready for this?"

She chuckled. "This will be easy. It's merely dining with our families. Everyone seems to get along nicely. The real test will be stepping out into society together."

"When do you wish to do so?" he asked.

"We can discuss it later. Let's join the others now."

As always, the food was delicious. Now that the vows had been spoken, the charged atmosphere had become happy and relaxed. Jeremy offered a champagne toast, the first time Laurel had ever drunk the frothy liquid. She remembered the first day that she'd met Jeremy.

He'd offered up champagne then, but the idea faded away when she had mentioned Hudson and Jeremy had run off to make sure her twin brother was found immediately. The bubbles tickled her nose and she giggled. Her new husband looked at her a moment and then smiled. She had the impression he did so rarely. He seemed very self-contained, as if he never wanted the world to know what he was thinking. She wondered how well they would get along.

Both in and out of bed.

The thought of him bedding her made her cheeks burn. She quickly downed the rest of the champagne and a footman refilled her flute. She drank that glass, too, and immediately felt lightheaded. She needed to keep her wits about her and set her glass down, determined to stay in control.

By now, everyone had finished eating and Laurel knew it was time for her and Linfield to depart. Her trunks had already been delivered this morning to his townhouse, with another one to go with them to the country. Anxiety filled her as she thought of leaving her new St. Clair home and everything familiar and going somewhere different to live.

She summoned Barton and said, "I would like to speak with Mrs. Talley and Cook before I leave."

"Yes, Your Grace," the butler said and slipped away.

It was the first time someone addressed her by her title. It felt a little surreal. She was Laurel Wright, a simple shop girl who'd barely had enough to eat two months ago. Now, she was a duchess, married to a wealthy man who probably owned countless properties scattered across England. Her life had done far more than turn upside down. It had gone sideways, spiraling out of control. She promised herself she would remain humble, always remembering her beginnings, and that her children would not become spoiled brats but rather behave in a thoughtful, kind manner to everyone.

Everyone surrounded her, embracing her, and she promised she would see them soon. Because Hannah was still involved in her come-out, Linfield had told Laurel they would go and spend a week at Linwood, the main ducal country residence located in Surrey, before returning to escort Hannah to events during the remainder of the Season. For now, her family had said they would see to properly chaperoning Hannah to social events.

As they moved to the entry hall, Barton approached.

"Your Grace? Mrs. Talley and Cook are waiting."

She told him to stay and motioned the two servants over.

"I wanted to thank all three of you. You made my short time here most welcomed. I know how hard you worked to make my wedding a memorable one. I appreciate it more than I can say."

She saw tears glimmering in Mrs. Talley's eyes, while Cook's tears flowed freely and she mopped them with her apron.

"It has been a pleasure to serve you, Your Grace," Barton said with dignity. "We hope to see you in the future."

"I will be here frequently, Barton," she promised. With that, she looked to Linfield.

He said to the group, "Thank you all for attending our wedding and for looking after Aunt Constance and Hannah while we are away."

He offered his arm and she took it. They went outside to the waiting carriage and her husband handed her up. He took the seat opposite her and, for a moment, Laurel felt disappointment. She squashed it and looked out the window, waving to everyone as the coach pulled away.

Once they'd left London, she asked, "How long will it take to reach Linwood?" she asked.

"Between three and four hours," he replied, his jaw tightening.

"What is it like?"

"I don't remember much about it," he said rigidly.

His answer confused her. "When was the last time you were there?"

"I was eight," he said succinctly and turned his gaze out the window.

Eight years old?

She supposed boys in society went away to school at about that age. Why had Linfield never returned?

"You went to other estates your father owned during your school holidays?" she asked, thinking it odd that he hadn't seen the main residence in a good number of years, probably two decades or more. It struck her she had no idea even how old her husband was, much less how long he'd been the Duke of Linfield.

He continued staring out the window and said dismissively, "I don't wish to discuss it."

Laurel's gut twisted. Something was wrong. Very wrong.

What had she done by agreeing to wed a stranger?

CHAPTER ELEVEN

ANTHONY COULD HAVE kicked himself for answering Laurel the way he had. A few hours had passed and not another word had passed between them. She had stared at him a good while but he'd never turned toward her. He couldn't. Humiliation at how his father had treated him filled him. The more miles that passed, the angrier Anthony grew at the memories. At how he'd been cast aside, while Theodore had all their father's attention.

He was also angry at himself for treating his bride so coldly. They had been married a little more than an hour when he'd snapped at her. Put her in her place. Spoke so firmly that it was obvious he'd brook no more conversation between them. Yet he knew this St. Clair. At least parts of her. She would not let it go. She would be after him, little by little, creating chinks in the invisible armor he wore to protect himself. That was something he couldn't allow. He didn't know if he should lie about all the years he missed being at Linwood or ignore any future questions she had regarding his childhood. Laurel was clever, though. She would easily sniff out a lie—and she certainly wouldn't be put off from asking him. He believed the only reason she remained silent now is that she contemplated why she had even married him. They'd had no choice, though. Despite the fact he felt she was entirely the wrong type of wife for him, he liked her. He wondered if they might even become friends.

He certainly couldn't wait to become lovers. The kiss they'd shared had morphed from sweet to explosive. It brought a whirlwind of emotions he had never felt, not to mention stirring his blood. He might not be able to give Laurel love—which she claimed she wasn't interested in receiving—but Anthony would make certain he satisfied her in bed.

And out?

He couldn't say. He had no idea what they would do during their week together at Linwood. He'd written the estate's manager and notified him he was bringing his duchess home for a brief visit. He assumed the man, if he hadn't expired from shock, had informed the housekeeper. Since it had been so long since he'd been to the estate, he needed to explore the grounds. The house, as well. He had a vague idea what it had once looked like. The only room he clearly recalled was his bedchamber and that wouldn't be where he and Laurel spent tonight.

The thought of lying in the same bed where his bastard of a father had caused nausea to rise within him. His fingers curled into fists and he had to force himself to relax them against his thighs. He couldn't think like this. Linwood wasn't his father's estate. Or Theodore's. It was his. He would do what he could to see his hand on it.

Turning to Laurel, he said, "Have you any talent in decorating?"

She startled at his words, turning from where she gazed out the window. "I haven't a clue what that might involve. We three Wrights lived in a space so small that I'm sure your dressing room would be larger. Why do you ask?"

They'd gotten off on the wrong foot. He wanted to correct that now, before he made a mess of their marriage.

"I'm sure it's been many years since anyone changed anything about the décor of any of the rooms. I want you to know you're free to do so. If you wish for new carpets or curtains. New furniture. I want you to put your mark on the house. Make it a home." Anthony smiled. "After all, it is where we will raise our children."

"Will we?" she challenged.

"Yes. It is the main residence of the Duke of Linfield. While eventually, I will have us visit the other numerous properties I hold, I'd hope the children would be raised more in the country."

"Yet you haven't been to this home in how long? How old are you, Linfield?"

Hearing that name on her lips rattled him. "Anthony," he prompted. "Remember?" When she didn't reply, he said, "I am twenty-eight years of age. I completed Eton and took the commission the duke purchased for me and entered His Majesty's army at eighteen. I remained in the army for almost a decade, fortunate enough to serve on Wellington's staff for several years. Once Bonaparte was finally defeated at Waterloo and exiled, I came home to England and found both my father and brother had died. That I was the Duke of Linfield."

She worried her lip, a look of pity in her eyes. He didn't want her pity—but he most certainly wanted to sink his teeth into that full lip.

"I'm sorry you came home and were greeted with such sad news."

"I wasn't sad at all," he said brusquely, watching her eyes widen in surprise. "I was never close to either of them. Their deaths meant nothing to me."

"I see."

He wondered if his words shocked her. She continued worrying her lip and he looked away. If he didn't, he might scoop her up in his lap and kiss her.

After a few minutes, she asked, "You've been in London this whole time? I mean, after selling out?"

"Yes. Enough about me. Tell me something about you."

A veil seemed to drop over her. Anthony wondered if Laurel had any secrets of her own.

"There's not much to tell. I went to school, at least part-time, until I was twelve. I held a variety of positions. The last two years I waited on customers at a chandlery. When the work day ended, I stayed after to balance the ledgers."

Anthony sat up. "You did?"

"I have an affinity for numbers. Mr. Cole was terrible at them. He was better at ordering goods for the store but even then, I would go back and check his numbers and the bills of sale." She paused. "There's not much else to know, other than I sewed for others at night. Mama's eyesight grew worse and she had trouble completing orders. You've meet Hudson. He's very smart and will do well at university. Mama did the best she could for us until her heart weakened. She was quite ill for some months before she passed." She looked down at her folded hands in her lap.

He gazed at her until she raised her head and their eyes locked.

"You told me you worried about putting food on the table and how to pay your rent. Was your brother not working while you held two positions?"

Anger sparked in her eyes. "Hudson also worked long hours, during the day as a coal porter and by night as a waterman."

"Then why did you have trouble making ends meet?" he asked, truly wondering.

Laurel snorted. "Spoken like a true member of the *ton*."

"I worked for my living, Laurel," Anthony said. "Being an officer, especially in a time of war, isn't fun and games. Every time I went on the battlefield, I wondered if I would return alive—or if I'd be missing an arm. An eye. A leg. War crushes a man's soul. His spirit. It crams his civility so far down that many find it hard to even return and live in society. I hate the man I had to become in order to survive. And I hate that I lost so many men under my command. I was lucky enough to come home, while they are lying in graves on the Continent."

He fell silent, wondering why he'd bared his soul to her in such a manner. He turned to the window again, watching the rolling landscape pass.

Then he sensed her beside him. She had moved from the bench

across from him to sit next to him. She took his hand in both of hers and lifted it to her lips, kissing it tenderly.

"I'm sorry war was so brutal, Anthony. That you had to fight to live every day. That guilt fills you because you survived and some of your command did not."

He turned to chide her. To tell her he never wanted to speak of the war and his role in it. Instead, Anthony found himself lost in those luminous St. Clair eyes. The rosewater scent he'd noticed from the night they'd danced seem to fill him.

He wanted her. Now.

He refused to take a virgin in a moving carriage, especially since they must be close to Linwood. He could, though, indulge in a kiss.

His free hand moved to her nape, holding her in place as he moved closer to her. He brushed his lips softly against hers. Her hand tightened around his. It wasn't enough, though. The need to taste her again tempted him and he eased her mouth open. His tongue slipped inside, colliding with hers. The faint taste of the strawberries and champagne they'd had at their wedding breakfast lingered. He swept his tongue around hers, teasing it, calling hers out to play with him.

And she responded. Lord, did she respond.

What she lacked in experience, Laurel made up for with enthusiasm. Her hands left his, sliding up his chest and latching on to his shoulders. Her tongue mated with his and then went to war, each of them wanting to dominate the other. His arms went about her, drawing her near, but it wasn't enough. He grabbed her waist and pulled her into his lap, turning her so she leaned against the corner of the carriage.

Anthony kissed her as if there would be no tomorrow. That the only time they would share was here. Now. He kissed her slow and long. Deep. Then hard and fast. He broke away and kissed her cheeks. Her eyelids. Her brow. He returned, feasting on her mouth, ripples of desire coursing through him. The need he had for this woman surpassed anything he'd ever experienced. His mouth moved to her throat and licked where her pulse pounded. He nipped at it and she gasped, then he soothed it with his tongue. Her hands pushed into his hair and then held on to it tightly as she began kissing him and the process started all over again.

He might have kissed her until the sun fell and then rose tomorrow morning, but he sensed the carriage turning. Instinct told him they now moved up the lane and that Linwood was in sight. Anthony broke the kiss and cradled her cheek.

"We are almost there."

"Oh!"

She started to scamper from his lap but he needed a final kiss. He made it soft and tender and then lifted her from his lap and seated her beside him. Her face was flushed with color and her lips swollen. Her green eyes sparkled with desire. He smoothed her skirts, hoping the servants would think they'd wrinkled during traveling. Fortunately, he'd refrained from pushing his fingers into her hair and freeing the raven locks. He would have hated to arrive at Linwood with pins scattered along the floor of the coach, her hair tumbling down her back.

The carriage made a wide sweep, coming to a stop. The door opened and Anthony climbed out. Surprise filled him. Two long lines of servants had formed, awaiting the arrival of the duke and duchess. He faced the carriage again and offered Laurel a hand. As her feet touched the ground she froze, seeing the mass of people that awaited them.

Turning to her, he bent and said low in her ear, "You are the Duchess of Linfield. These are your servants."

He sensed her straighten as she looked out and a smile appeared, melting his heart and probably every one of the servants that stood before them.

A man stepped forward and Anthony assumed this was his butler.

"Welcome home, Your Graces. I am Sanders." He indicated the women who had joined him. "Mrs. Wallingford, Linwood's housekeeper."

Neither servant appeared familiar to him. He would have to check the estate records and see when they had been hired on.

"Thank you, Sanders," he said crisply. "We'll need baths for us both. My valet, Monkton, and Her Grace's maid, Retta, are in a coach behind us. They can attend to us upon their arrival."

"Very good, Your Grace," Sanders said. Looking to Laurel, he asked, "Would you care to meet the Linwood staff, Your Grace?"

"Yes, Sanders," Laurel said eagerly.

Anthony accompanied her, thinking she would nod and smile as she worked her way down the line. Not Laurel. She asked the name of every man and woman in both lines and remembered when she heard a surname twice, learning there were two sets of sisters who worked as maids and a pair of brothers who were grooms. She had a kind word for each servant and he could tell she was making a very good impression. It was for the best. She would be the one dealing with them, not him.

At the end, he recognized a man in his mid-fifties. They paused before him.

"Ross Woodward, Your Graces," he said. "I don't know if you remember me or not, Your Grace. I was an assistant steward when I first came to Linwood."

"I do remember you," Anthony said brusquely, ready to go into the house and avoid any talk of the past.

"Oh, you knew His Grace when he was a boy?" Laurel asked eagerly.

"I did, indeed, Your Grace. He was a sturdy little fellow. Athletic. Always into mischief."

Anthony glared at Woodward and he immediately fell silent.

"You'll have to tell me more some time, Mr. Woodward. I'd also enjoy hearing all about the estate. I adore numbers. Could I examine the ledgers? I'd like to see what is grown at Linwood and learn something about our tenants."

"I'm sure you'll be much too busy with household affairs," Anthony said. "Shall we go inside?"

Laurel didn't budge. "I have always been very organized, Linfield," she said sweetly. "Although I know supervising the household will take up some of my time each day, I have Sanders and Mrs. Wallingford to help with that." She looked pointedly at Ross Woodward. "I will see the books, Mr. Woodward. His Grace and I will also be going about the estate and visiting with our tenants."

Turning back to him, she said, "Let's go inside, Linfield. I'm a bit parched after our journey from London."

Fuming, he led her inside.

Mrs. Wallingford followed close behind. "I'll bring some tea to you, Your Grace. Sandwiches, too. Let me show you to your rooms first. You, too, Your Grace," she said, looking to him.

Laurel clasped his arm as Mrs. Wallingford led them up the staircase and down a corridor. The housekeeper stopped.

"These are your rooms, Your Grace." She opened the door and indicated for them to enter. Following them, she said, "This is your sitting room. Right this way and through the door, you'll see your bedchamber."

Mrs. Wallingford pointed out the duchess' dressing room next and mentioned that it led into the duke's dressing room as they continued their tour. On the other side of it lay his bedchamber and a study.

A maid appeared and announced that the second coach had arrived and that the duke's and duchess' trunks were being brought up.

"Would you like your maid to unpack for you, Your Grace? I can send more help if you wish."

"Retta can handle things, Mrs. Wallingford. Thank you. Could you please see about the tea now?"

"Of course, Your Grace."

The housekeeper left and Laurel said, "This is a very dark room."

Anthony had noticed it immediately. It reminded him of the darkness of his father's soul.

"You said I might try my hand at decorating. Would you mind if I lightened it up a bit? I believe I would like a few new things in my rooms, as well."

He moved and closed the door that Mrs. Wallingford had used as she left. Since they were alone, he needed to address an issue with her.

"Never make me look like a fool again, Laurel. Especially in front of the servants."

Her eyes narrowed. "Do you mean when you made me look like a featherhead? Oh, the poor Duchess of Linfield. She hasn't a brain in her head. What would she want in seeing ledgers and examining records of the estate?" Her hands fisted and went to her waist. "You said I would have freedom, Anthony. This is to be my home. Our children's home. Why wouldn't I want to learn everything about it?"

"Because it's not the kind of thing a duchess does," he barked.

"Oh, I see. You swayed me with pretty words before our wedding, telling me I wouldn't have to follow the rules *because* I would be a duchess. Yet the moment the vows are spoken, you're already ordering me about. I won't have it."

She crossed her arms in front of her, defiance written on her face. "Besides, you've been gone a good twenty years. Even when you became Duke of Linfield, you didn't bother to come and see your home. I'll wager the first time you saw Aunt Constance and Hannah was when they came to London for the Season."

"So?" he asked, his voice laced with sarcasm.

"If you don't want to care about Linwood, I do. It will be our children's home. Hopefully, I'll produce a son who will inherit it. I want it to thrive for him." Her voice softened and she placed a hand on his forearm. "For us."

"I plan to take a firm hand in estate matters now."

"Will I be allowed to investigate the ledgers? Or were you merely paying me lip service?"

"You may look at whatever you wish. Linwood is your home," he said stiffly.

"Thank you." She looked about. "I don't know if I can sleep in here tonight. This room is so dreary. I suppose you'll have to come sleep in my bedchamber until I can make some changes."

Her words floored him. "Sleep with you? Why would you say that?"

Laurel let out an exasperated sigh. "We can't very well make a baby if you're in here and I'm in there."

He said firmly, "I will come to you. When we are done, I will return to my rooms."

She frowned. "We won't sleep together as man and wife?"

"That's not how it's done. We will . . . come together. Then I will take my leave."

"Jeremy and Catherine don't do that. She uses her bedchamber for storing her gowns and readying herself but she and Jeremy always sleep together. I know Rachel and Evan—"

"I don't care what the bloody St. Clairs do during the night," he shouted. "We will follow society's lead on this matter. You will sleep in your bedchamber. I will sleep in mine. I will come to you and—"

"Don't bother coming tonight, Your Grace," she said angrily. "I will be too tired to service you."

With that, Laurel Godwin, Duchess of Linfield, stomped away, slamming the door behind her.

CHAPTER TWELVE

L AUREL BRISTLED WITH anger at her new husband but knew better than to take their argument public. No servants had been present, for which she was thankful. She drew in several deep breaths, composing herself, and then continued through the dressing rooms. She reached her own bedchamber and saw Retta already there, bustling about as she unpacked.

"Your tea just came, Your Grace. I had it placed in your sitting room. Do you know what you wish to wear to dinner this evening?" her maid asked.

"Just finish unpacking, Retta. I don't think I'll be going downstairs for dinner tonight. I'm very tired after the wedding and the journey to Linwood. Tea will suffice."

Her maid gave her a sly smile and Laurel realized what the servant must be thinking. Instead of protesting, she kept silent and went into the other room. She poured herself a cup of tea but had lost her appetite. She sat contemplating what the rest of her life would be like.

Linfield had certainly proven himself to be a typical member of the *ton*. His behavior shouldn't have surprised her. A man would do or say whatever it took to get a woman to wed him. Once she had, she was powerless. At least when Laurel had worked for Mr. Cole, she earned her living. Now, though, she was dependent upon her husband for everything. The food she ate. The clothes on her back. She couldn't work. She couldn't own anything. Even the hefty dowry Jeremy had settled upon her would have gone to Linfield.

Frustration filled her. She hadn't asked for this life or marriage to a duke and now she felt trapped. What upset her even more was, despite her husband's high-handed manner, she had begun to develop feelings for him. She hurt for the little boy, one who had suffered a lasting trauma that had closed him off from the world. She ached for the young, idealistic man who had gone to war, only to have his soul shattered by the very actions that had allowed him to survive. Even worse, this duke stirred her blood in a way that might crush her. She didn't want to love him. She would refuse to do that. His kisses certainly made her desire him, though. She must separate the physical want from any emotional attachment. Surely, she could do so. Members of society did it every day. They wed. They came together to make a child. Then they led separate lives beyond those few minutes in the bedroom. She could do the same. She was made of strong stuff, else she never would have survived in her former life as a Wright.

Retta appeared. "Everything is unpacked, Your Grace. When do you wish me to return to ready you for bed?"

Laurel only wanted to be alone so she said, "You may do so now. I will not be leaving my rooms until tomorrow morning."

"So, the duke will come to you then," the maid observed. "Very well."

She held her tongue, not bothering to protest. The duke certainly wouldn't be coming to her tonight. Not after the scene between them.

Following Retta to the bedchamber, she allowed the maid to remove the wedding dress, which had been meant for a ball. She would wear it again later this Season and try not to think of this day and the disappointment it had brought.

Retta replaced it with a filmy night rail, which had been a gift from Catherine, as was the silk dressing gown the maid helped her slip into.

"You look lovely, Your Grace."

"Thank you," she replied, feeling hollow inside.

"Thank you again for allowing me to come with you. It's an honor to serve you. Good night."

Laurel paced restlessly once her maid left. She finally went to the desk and found parchment and ink. She wrote to Luke and Caroline of her marriage and how she was eager to see them and their baby come June. She set the letter aside to be posted in the morning and retreated to a chaise lounge, her thoughts so muddled that they made no sense. Finally, she went to her bedroom to retire. She was weary, both physically and emotionally, and hoped the mattress was comfortable and that she would fall asleep quickly.

Retta had already turned the covers back and Laurel stared at the large bed. She would spend time with Linfield in it at some point. It would be here they would make a child. Hopefully, more than one. Her eyes misted with tears, thinking she'd mucked up things between them with her flash of temper and wondered how she could apologize.

A soft knock sounded, so faint she almost didn't hear it.

It came from her dressing room door.

Gathering her courage, she crossed the room and opened the door.

The Duke of Linfield stood there, wearing a dark maroon dressing gown. No coat or waistcoat. No shirt or cravat. She could see a bit of his throat and bare chest. The sight caused her mouth to go dry. She stepped back and he entered the room, closing the door behind him.

"I said not to come," Laurel said stubbornly, not ready to yield control to him, though she knew it would be a losing battle. He had rights over her in every way.

Including her body.

"I know," he said softly. "I hoped you might have changed your mind."

His hands went to her waist. His thumbs began stroking her ribcage. Laurel shivered.

"I know you want a child as much as I do. Do you think we can set aside what happened before between us?"

"I suppose so," she said begrudgingly. "But I don't want to kiss you."

He frowned. "Why not?"

She swallowed. "It has nothing to do with making a baby."

The truth was his kiss set her afire—and she didn't want that. She wanted to hold this man at arm's length.

"All right," he agreed. You don't have to kiss me."

Linfield took her hand and led her to the bed. Those crystal blue eyes blazed. Holding her gaze, his fingers went to where Retta had tied Laurel's robe. Slowly, he undid it and pushed the dressing gown from her. It fell to the floor. His hands cradled her face. The air filled with electricity. She had told him not to kiss her but now she wanted nothing more than his mouth on hers.

Instead, he lifted her night rail from her and tossed it aside. Laurel now stood bare before him, her knees wavering. Her husband studied her at length. She felt herself turn red from her toes to her brow.

His hands returned to her face, cupping it. "You are very beautiful, Your Grace."

She couldn't reply. She wanted him so badly. Boldly, her hands moved to his sash and she repeated his actions. Undid the knot. Parted his dressing gown. Pushed it from his shoulders.

He wore nothing beneath it. Her eyes took in the broad, muscular chest, dusted lightly with golden hair which trailed down past his belly. His manhood jutted from him and she refrained from gasping. She didn't see how it would fit inside her.

Linfield scooped her up and placed her on the bed. Her heart pounded fiercely as nerves consumed her. She lay on her back, staring up at the ceiling, not daring to look at him. He settled on his side, his head propped up and resting in his hand. His free hand stroked her throat and slid down to cup her breast. As he kneaded it, his lips touched her throat.

"No kissing," she said, her words a whisper.

"You said you didn't want to kiss me—and I agreed. We said nothing about me kissing you."

Laurel wanted to protest but his warm lips were on her throat again as his hand continued fondling her breast. His mouth moved lower and suddenly it took in her breast. His tongue teased her nipple, causing her back to arch. Then his teeth grazed it and she almost came off the bed.

"Kissing . . . doesn't have . . . anything to do with . . . making a baby," she managed to get out.

He continued worshipping her breast and then moved to the other. By now, a throbbing between her legs had begun. The more he suckled her, the greater it pounded, demanding attention.

His attention . . .

"Please, Linfield."

He stopped. "Anthony," he said, his voice low and rough. "I insist, Laurel. Call me Anthony."

"Anthony," she repeated and then sucked in her breath as his hand touched her womanhood.

He began stroking her there, the throbbing consuming her.

"Do you have to do that?" she asked.

He stopped. "I need to ready you for what comes next, Laurel. The first time will hurt."

"How do you know when I'll be ready?"

He slipped a finger inside her and her hips rose. "I'll be able to tell. Trust me. I have experience."

Of course, he did. He was a man. He'd done this sort of thing all the time. The thought of him with other women angered her and she had no idea why.

Then rational thought became impossible as another finger joined the first. There was only need. Something building inside her. Something fierce and powerful demanding to be released. As his fingers worked some kind of dark magic, she began moaning. Whimpering. Sounds came from her that she'd never made before. But then again, she didn't understand what he was doing to her. Only that it was wicked and wonderful and she wanted more.

Whatever built within her now screamed to get out. Her body didn't seem her own anymore. It was his, to do with however he pleased. A sudden, blinding warmth filled her as a wave of pleasure so intense filled her. She cried out and her body shuddered. Ripples continued through her as she bucked and moaned, tears escaping from the corners of her eyes and streaming into her hair.

Then he was above her. "I'm sorry."

He thrust into her and the pain he'd promised became a reality. She clawed at his back and realized he wasn't moving.

"Get used to me," he said hoarsely.

He certainly filled her. She was stretched as never before. Then he began moving—and she felt the urge to move with him. They began a kind of dance. She caught on quickly and found him the perfect partner. He kissed her brow. Her cheeks. Buried his face against her throat.

But he didn't kiss her mouth.

It didn't matter. His movements brought a delicious feeling and she met every thrust. He increased the speed and began to plunge deeper and deeper into her. His hand came between their joined bodies and teased something that drove her to the edge of madness. Then Laurel was falling, falling, falling. He thrust one last time and then shouted his own cry, collapsing on her. Quickly, he rolled away and she came with him. For a moment, she forgot the harsh words that had been spoken between them, only relishing the feel of his arms about her and him still inside her.

It didn't last. He took her shoulders and moved her away. He slipped from the bed and found his dressing gown, shrugging into it and belting it. Without a word, her husband left, returning to his rooms as he'd said he would. All the happiness and wonderment she'd felt soured within her. Laurel beat her fist into the pillow, cursing him.

ANTHONY RETURNED TO his bedchamber. He could still smell Laurel on his skin and cursed.

She just wasn't on his skin—she'd wormed her way under it.

He paced aimlessly. He'd gone to her tonight and made love to her simply because she had forbid him to do so. He needed her to understand that this wasn't some partnership. They were not and would never be equals. She was nothing more to him than the woman who would bear his children.

Or so he told himself.

Instead, he wanted nothing more than to charge back into her bedchamber and make love to her again. He would never do that. She couldn't learn that he was fast becoming obsessed with her. A woman who knew her husband was besotted with her was a man who would lose any power he had over her. No, Laurel was not going to make him dance to her tune. He was the man. He would be leading in any dance they engaged in, be it in or out of bed.

Oh, but her body. Its satin skin and tempting curves. He swallowed at the memories just created between them. Laurel St. Clair was different from any woman he'd ever bedded. No, not just any female. Laurel was now his. His duchess. His wife. Yet it was the St. Clair in her which tempted him beyond reason.

He'd given in to her demand and not kissed her mouth. He wouldn't do that again. The only reason he had was so that she would let him to make love to her. Anthony had feared after their argument that she might press for an annulment and return to her family. He couldn't allow that. He'd needed to make her his—and he had. But the next time, they would kiss. For hours, if he wanted them to. Laurel was his wife. She was to be subservient to him in every way.

Yet he didn't want to break her spirit. It was one of the most attractive things about her.

He threw off his dressing gown and fell into bed, doubting that sleep would come. Surprisingly, he woke hours later, dawn still a while away. He must have been tired. He fought the urge to return to his new wife's bed. He needed to retain the power in this marriage. Going to her again so soon would show her how weak he was. In fact, he wouldn't touch her tonight. Let her see what she thought of that.

Anthony dressed without ringing for Monkton. He went to the stables, the sun just peering over the horizon, and saddled Bucephalus himself. He was eager to see Linwood and rode around the estate for two hours before returning to the house.

This time, Monkton awaited him, as did a hot bath.

"When I saw you were gone, Your Grace, I took the liberty of checking at the stables. I knew you would need a hot bath when you returned from your ride."

"You anticipate my every need, Monkton. That will be all."

He shucked off his clothes and eased himself into the steaming water. He closed his eyes for a few minutes, savoring the warmth surrounding him. Then he slid beneath the surface and came up, his fingers pushing his hair away from his face.

"I would like to see the estate today."

He opened his eyes to find his wife standing there.

CHAPTER THIRTEEN

L ORD, BUT THIS man was a feast for the eyes.

Laurel had cut through their adjoining dressing rooms, wanting to speak to her husband before breakfast. Having spent enough mornings in Jeremy's breakfast room, she knew there would be footmen stationed about to wait on them. If Linfield wanted to argue about her request, she wanted to do so in private. She owed him that much. It wouldn't do for her to undercut him. She certainly didn't want the servants discussing the tension between the newlyweds. He was as new to Linwood as she was and for some reason, she didn't want him making a bad impression. He hadn't seemed to know any of the servants when they'd arrived yesterday, so their early perceptions of him would be lasting ones.

The only man he'd recognized had been Ross Woodward, the estate's manager. Mr. Woodward's remarks about the duke when he was a boy had brought about tension and her husband had shut down the man's comments. She still knew there was some mystery that needed to be solved. If she could learn what had happened to eight-year-old Anthony Godwin, she might better understand the Duke of Linfield, the man he had become. Perhaps Mr. Woodward would be willing to share what he knew of the long-ago incident which had turned her husband into a stiff, unemotional man. She should have thought to ask him when she claimed the ledgers for the previous years this morning.

Looking at his bare chest, glistening with water, made her think of their coupling last night. Linfield wasn't unemotional when it came to her. Though he would never have admitted it, Laurel believed he had feelings for her. At least she hoped he did. She wanted to be on good terms with this man. He would be the father of her children and she wanted their household to be peaceful and loving. If they could be friendly and behave respectfully toward one another, it would be a good environment in which to raise their children.

She feared, though, that he would withdraw from her, only coming to her when he wanted her physically. Already, he was fast becoming something she needed, like the very air she breathed. She swore she would never let him see how taken she was with him. If she revealed how drugging his kiss was, he would use it to his advantage.

Laurel needed to remember she was a St. Clair. Though she hadn't held the name long, she understood it was a part of her blood. She'd learned St. Clairs could be headstrong and passionate. Stubborn and bold. She would need to stand firm against this man and never let her true feelings show. She already liked him a great deal. It wouldn't do to move beyond that. She would have to keep her wits about her whenever he was near.

Especially in her bed.

Suddenly, he plunged beneath the water and then emerged, pushing his hair back. Her mouth watered. She wanted to lick every drop from his chest. The thought enticed her—and appalled her.

Before he could open his eyes and find her drooling over him, she said, "I would like to see the estate today."

Suddenly, those crystal blue eyes pierced her. Laurel stood her ground, her nails digging into her palms as she kept a bland look on her face.

"Why?"

"Why do I want to see the estate?"

"Yes."

"Because it is my new home. I am curious about it."

"This house is also your new home. Surely, you'd like to tour it with Mrs. Wallingford."

"I plan to do that, as well. In fact, I was hoping you would do so with me. See both the house and then ride about the estate." When he didn't reply, she added, "I know it's been many years since you were here. You couldn't remember everything about the house. It's your home, too, Anthony. Shall we see it together?"

She watched as he pondered the question and then he nodded. "All right. We'll have Mrs. Wallingford take us about after breakfast."

"And what about seeing Linwood?"

"Maybe tomorrow. I would prefer to meet with Woodward and discuss various details regarding the estate. Once I'm more knowledgeable, I will know what to look for when I'm out and about."

Figuring he would turn down her request, she asked, "Might I sit in when you have this discussion with Mr. Woodward?"

"I'll think about it."

Laurel thought he merely mollified her but at least he hadn't totally rejected the idea.

Without warning, he rose from the tub. Water streamed down his toned body. He looked like a Greek statue brought to life, his proportions perfect. Yet he was a living, breathing man.

She heard him chuckling as she dashed from the room and returned to her bedchamber. Laurel paused before the mirror and saw the color in her cheeks. He'd stood deliberately, wanting to embarrass her. Seeing him in all his golden perfection hadn't embarrassed her. It had only made her want him even more—and that's why embarrassment reddened her face.

Leaving her rooms, she made her way downstairs and asked for a cup of tea. Sanders, the butler, asked what she wished for breakfast and she placed her order. By the time her plate arrived and she'd begun eating, her husband entered the room, immaculately dressed. It was sinful the way he filled out his buckskin breeches and bottle green coat. His hair, still damp, looked darker than usual. She fought the urge to run her fingers through it.

He told Sanders what he wished to eat and had a cup of coffee brought to him.

Glancing at her cup, he asked, "You prefer tea to coffee?"

"I do. While the smell of freshly-brewed coffee is heavenly, the taste leaves much to be desired."

"The women I know douse it heavily with cream and sugar."

Laurel sniffed. "*This* woman prefers not to imbibe it at all."

He smiled. It caught her by surprise. When he did, his eyes lit up. It made him even more handsome than usual. She had better steer clear from amusing him because a smile like that was intoxicating. She wanted to keep him at a distance, not entertain him.

They finished their meal without further discussion. He inhaled his food and finished at the same time she did.

"There was no need to rush, Your Grace. I would have waited for you."

He looked sheepish. "I tend to wolf down my food. In the army, you never knew when a meal might be interrupted by the enemy shelling your position. I went without food and sleep for three days once when we were under attack. I suppose some of that feeling of not being able to finish lingers. I apologize. I will be more aware of my manners in the future."

Again, she was surprised, this time by his words. She placed her hand over his.

"I'm sorry. I wasn't upset with you. I know it must be hard to be living in society after spending years on the warfront."

He gazed at their hands and she slipped hers back to her lap.

Rising, she said, "I will see if Mrs. Wallingford can show us the house now."

Linfield nodded. She felt her face flushing. Merely touching him seemed to fluster her. Laurel knew she better get her emotions under control.

She found Mrs. Wallingford and the housekeeper was more than willing to give them a thorough tour of the house. For the next two hours, they accompanied her as she took them from the wine cellars to the attics. Laurel was impressed by the magnificent library and couldn't wait to start reading the books within it. Though a good student in school and an avid reader of the newspaper, she'd only discovered novels when introduced to them by Leah and had enjoyed discussing them with the book club members. It still amazed her that she had idle time in which to sit and enjoy reading.

She also found the schoolroom to her liking. It smelled of old books and chalk. She thought of her children sitting at the table, learning to read and computing sums. She felt her husband's eyes on her and looked up. Somehow, she knew he'd read her thoughts.

Located directly across from the schoolroom was the nursery. It looked forlorn, not having been used in many years.

"We'll need fresh paint in here. New carpet, too," she pointed out. "I don't want the babies crawling about on a cold floor."

"You know you may do whatever you like," Linfield said. "The same with any room in the house here or in London."

"Thank you, Your Grace. I will make a list of the things I'd like done. I'd also like to talk with Rachel and have her visit Linwood. She has a fine eye for detail and I'm sure she'd make some excellent suggestions. Perhaps after the Season ends, she and Evan can come for a visit."

He merely nodded and stepped back into the corridor. Laurel wondered if he minded her sister and brother-in-law coming to visit. It didn't matter. She wanted them to come. In fact, she wanted all her relatives to see Linwood. It surprised her how it had only been one day since she'd seen most of them and yet she missed them terribly.

She thanked Mrs. Wallingford for showing them around and the housekeeper left. Linfield lingered in the hall, waiting for her.

"Do you remember having lessons in the schoolroom?" she asked, knowing he probably had no memories from his time in the nursery.

"Vaguely. Theodore and I had a tutor. When Theodore left for school, the tutor only stayed a short time and then he was gone."

"What about your bedchamber? Did you recall which one was yours?"

"Not really. It's been too long since I was here."

With that, he turned and walked away.

ANTHONY HAD TO escape. He'd listened to Mrs. Wallingford go on and on about the house. She had a story for each room they visited—and they all included his father or Theodore. He'd gleaned that she'd arrived at Linwood about a year after his departure. Sanders, the butler, had come aboard a dozen years ago. As the woman prattled on, he wondered if she or any of the other servants had even known about him. If they wondered who this new Duke of Linfield was and why he'd been sent away as a child.

He had recognized his bedchamber, lying to Laurel about that. He'd spent many hours locked within it, receiving only bread and water as punishment for one of his many transgressions. His father had removed all books and toys from the room, wanting him to suffer from boredom. He knew every inch of the room, from the one loose plank near the corner to the wallpaper he'd peeled from behind the bed. Just standing in the room made him break out in a cold sweat.

The schoolroom was different. He'd been smarter than Theodore and could remember their tutor praising him. He'd never understood where the man went. Anthony had thought the tutor would remain until it was time for him to join Theodore at school—yet one day he'd simply vanished. After that, Anthony had roamed the estate as he pleased. Read the books he wanted to. Played with his toy soldiers, lining them up and fighting imaginary battles. He'd slipped open a drawer while Laurel was distracted and found the set of soldiers still sitting where he'd last left them. His throat had thickened with unshed tears for the little boy no one had seemed to want.

He ventured to the office which had housed the estate manager years ago and found Ross Woodward at work. He shot to his feet at once.

"Your Grace! I wasn't expecting you."

"Have a seat."

"Please, take mine," Woodward said and came from behind the desk, seating himself in the chair in front of the desk.

Anthony went and took Woodward's place. It felt like home. Many years ago, before he'd been exiled to Aunt Constance's country house, he'd come and visited the estate's manager regularly. The man, whose name escaped him, had explained things to Anthony and let him sit in this very chair. He'd felt important and special, knowing it was his brother who was have Linwood—but that he would know things about the place that Theodore never would.

Who knew over two decades later he would be the duke?

"I'd like you to give me a general accounting of the estate," he began. "I know you sent letters to me but start from the beginning. Take as long as you wish. We can examine the ledgers later."

Woodward started to speak and then nodded. Anthony decided the man didn't know where to begin, being overwhelmed in the presence of the new duke.

"Tell me about the number of tenants at Linwood," he suggested. "Those who have been here the longest. What crops are grown and the approximate yields of the past ten years. I'm sure that will lead to other questions I may have."

For the next two hours, Woodward spoke. The man was knowledgeable and obviously very good at his job. He referred to no notes, simply speaking from the heart. Anthony let him talk and when he seemed exhausted, the duke let him pause. At that point, Anthony began discussing what he would like to do to improve the estate, based upon what he had seen during his early morning ride. The additions he had in mind. An unused section that he believed would be useful for storage and even additional farms. As he laid out future plans, Woodward joined in eagerly. The two men talked for several hours. By the end of their discussions, Anthony was eager to get out on the estate once more to see some spots and examine them in more detail, as well as talk with his tenants.

"I'll leave you to get started," he said. "I'll ride the estate again in the morning and we'll speak after that."

"Very good, Your Grace."

"And Woodward. One more thing. My wife . . . is a very curious woman. If she asks about the past—my time here at Linwood—be so good as to tell her you don't really remember much. That you were merely being kind when you met her. That I hadn't truly made an impression on you when I was a child."

The manager nodded slowly. "Yes, Your Grace. I truly don't recall much. Only that you were a bit rambunctious and then you went off to school. No one was very clear why you never returned." He looked away and added, "Your father . . . never mentioned you again."

"I see."

"Your Grace, Her Grace has already come for a few ledgers early this morning. I gave them to her. I hope that was all right."

Anthony didn't show his surprise. "It's not a problem, Woodward."

It was, though. He'd specifically told her not to engage with them. Every servant in line had heard him suggest to her yesterday that her role was in running the household, not investigating the estate. Naturally, Laurel had ignored his directions. He remembered at school how stubborn both Jeremy and Luke St. Clair had been. Though she hadn't been raised in their household, Laurel was proving to be the most determined St. Clair of all. One kiss and his plans to marry an unassuming wallflower had flown out the window.

He left the office, his stomach rumbling. As he passed the grandfather clock in the entryway, he heard it chime four o'clock. He hadn't realized it was so late.

Guilt filled him having left her alone all day. Once again, he'd left things poorly with this new wife when he'd walked away from her this morning. She'd desperately wanted to sit in on his meeting with Woodward. He hadn't wanted her present merely because she wanted to be there so badly. Anthony told himself she would have to learn that she couldn't get her way every time. She'd already obtained the ledgers behind his back. He would let that pass. Right now, though, he owed his bride a little attention, having abandoned her for most of her first day of being married and coming to a strange place. They could take tea together and he would share some of the improvements he wished to make at Linwood. He'd even be willing to listen to any opinions she might have regarding this. With Laurel, he was certain there would be opinions aplenty.

He went to the drawing room and rang the bell. A maid appeared. He asked for tea to be brought and for his wife to be found so that she could join him.

The tea arrived ten minutes later, a maid pushing the cart. Mrs. Wallingford accompanied her.

"Her Grace isn't here, Your Grace," the housekeeper told him. "While you were meeting with Mr. Woodward, she decided to ride out and meet some of the tenants."

CHAPTER FOURTEEN

L AUREL HADN'T WASTED a moment. The second she learned
Linfield was behind closed doors with Ross Woodward, she told
Mrs. Wallingford where she was off to and headed directly to the
stables. She'd only been riding for two months now but she had taken
to it as she had dancing. Being atop a horse was the most liberating
thing in the world.

The head groom had helped select a mount for her after asking a
few questions about her experience. He'd even had two different
horses brought out and let her try each one, riding around in a wide
loop before returning. They settled on one and he assigned Tam, one
of the grooms, to escort her about the estate. Tam led her several
places that had the advantage of height so that she could see wide
portions of the estate without having to ride so far. Laurel told herself
she would travel the entire perimeter tomorrow, seeing more of the
land up close.

Now that she had a good idea of what the property consisted of,
she told Tam she wished to meet as many tenants as she could during
the rest of the afternoon. She assumed Linfield would be tied up the
rest of the day with Mr. Woodward and wanted to make the most of
her time.

Tam's parents had resided at Linwood since they were both children and had taken over Tam's father's cottage and plot of land.

"Didn't you have any interest in farming?" she'd asked.

"No, Your Grace. It's always been animals for me. Horses, in particular. I was lucky to gain a position in the stables. I get to do what I
love and still see my parents every week. My sister, too, since she
married last year, one of the tenants on the far east side of the
property."

"Where are your parents located?"

"Here to the west."

"Then I shall call upon them first."

She regretted not having taken time to go to the kitchen to collect
some kind of treat for those she visited but she soon learned her
company was as cherished as any gift that she might have brought
with her. Laurel met Tam's parents and a dozen other families. Tam
also took her to an area between the tenants' land and the main house,
where he introduced her to the blacksmith and his farrier. She learned
the blacksmith shoed horses and made various wrought iron products
for the farmers and people at Linwood, while the farrier also shoed
horses and acted as a type of horse doctor.

Laurel met the estate's wheelwright, who built carts and wheels
and one of its two gamekeepers. Everyone was interested in her and
her marriage to the new, mysterious duke. A few mentioned knowing
the former duke and his eldest son. When their names came up, a
quietness seem to settle as a blanket. She was smart enough to read
between the lines and understand neither man had been fondly looked
upon by these farmers and laborers.

"I promise I will bring my husband back with me tomorrow. He is
eager to meet everyone. He would have come with me today but he
and Mr. Woodward had a great deal to discuss regarding the estate."

Tam finally told her it grew late and they needed to return to the
stables. As they rode in the direction of the house, she saw a horse
approaching at a fast clip and recognized the rider as Linfield. Her gut
told her he was furious with her and she signaled to Tam to come to a
halt.

"His Grace approaches, Tam. Why don't you return to the stables? My husband will see me home safely." She smiled sweetly, though her insides quaked.

"Yes, Your Grace. It was a pleasure escorting you today. If you ever need anyone to accompany you again, just ask for me."

"I certainly will, Tam."

He kicked his horse and rode off, passing Linfield, who turned and looked at the groom. Laurel feared he would stop Tam and berate him but the duke must have thought better of it, riding toward her instead. She remained in place, waiting for him to arrive.

His horse was reddish-brown, what Luke would have called a bay. Her brother had been the one to teach her to ride and had imparted all kinds of miscellaneous information to her regarding horses. She'd seen this horse attached to the carriage that followed them to Linwood and assumed it was Linfield's personal favorite. With its great size, she guessed that the animal had been at war with him.

He pulled up alongside her, his eyes flashing with anger.

"You went out on the estate."

She answered him calmly. "Yes. I wanted to see where my future children would play."

"Our children."

"Yes. Our children," she agreed. "I also wanted to meet some of the tenants. They are most eager to make your acquaintance."

"I told you the household required your attention."

"And I told you that I—we—have an excellent staff," she snapped. "I've already spoken to Cook about menus for the remainder of the week we will be here. That's a very duchess-y thing to do." She paused. "I had the time and thought I would use it to see Linwood."

"I would have preferred to show it to you myself."

She softened. His voice had a catch in it and she realized it might have meant something to him to be the one to show her around. She pictured the little boy he'd been and wished whatever had happened had not affected him the way it had.

"I only saw a few parts of it. Tam, the groom who accompanied me, led me to a couple of high points so I could see for miles. It's beautiful, Anthony. You are very fortunate to have such an impressive place."

"It's ours," he said, his anger subsiding. "One of many properties but the one I believe we'll spend the most time at. At least until we have children."

Laurel frowned. "But I thought you told me that we would raise our children here. I don't understand."

"You know I need an heir. A spare would be even better. Once I have them, I told you that you would be free to—"

"To what? Take a lover?" she asked, her heart sinking but her anger rising. "Like women of the *ton* do? Like you will?" Bitter disappointment filled her. "I thought when you said I would have my freedom it meant I would be able to participate in things I am interested in. I would love to do charity work, especially in my former neighborhood. Work with furthering the education of the less fortunate. Help feed the hungry."

She shook her head. "I had no idea you merely wanted me for your brood mare. While I didn't expect you to be entirely faithful because most men aren't, I would never bring another man to my bed. I want to be a good example to my children. To show them the difference between right and wrong. To have them be kind to others. To teach them to honor their word."

Laurel gripped her reins. "You'll get your heir and spare and then you're welcome to spend all of your time in London. The children and I will be perfectly happy here at Linwood without you. Go to your other estates. Chase all the lightskirts you wish. Take on as many mistresses as you choose. We won't need you."

With that, she urged her horse on and raced toward the stables. She arrived and dismounted, tossing her reins to Tam, who looked puzzled. Moments later, Linfield rode up and Laurel hurried away, as fast as her skirts would let her. She rounded the stables to head toward the house, knowing she wouldn't reach it.

As she expected, a hand seized her elbow, halting her forward motion. Her husband jerked her and she stumbled, her back pressing against the stable wall.

His other hand gripped her elbow, his body close, blocking her escape. Fury blazed in his blue eyes.

"I do want an heir," he ground out. "I want several children. And I want to be a good father to them. The kind of father I never had."

His eyes fell to her mouth. "I also want my wife. Only my wife. I plan to honor my marriage vows, Laurel. You are the only woman I want."

With that, his mouth took hers roughly. The kiss was one meant to punish her. Hard. Brutal. Angry. Yet it had the opposite effect. Instead of putting her in her place, it only stirred the fire of passion inside her. Within him, as well. Her hands clutched at him, her fingers finding cloth and tightening. He jerked her to him, his mouth devouring her, his kiss deep. Through his clothes she could feel the furnace of his body as hers melted into him. They may not like each other much but the passion they felt for one another was undeniable.

He broke the kiss, his forehead resting against hers.

"I don't know why I respond to you like this," he muttered. "Why I get so angry."

"I feel the same," she replied. "No one has ever infuriated me more—and yet I want you inside me now."

He released her elbows and cupped her face. His eyes drank her in. "It's still daylight, Your Grace. Should we scandalize the servants and retreat to your bedchamber?"

Her mind shouted no but her body betrayed her when her lips whispered, "Yes."

Disregarding every rule of propriety, he scooped her into his arms and strode toward the house. Flabbergasted, she remained mute as he entered the house and trotted up the stairs. They passed a maid whose jaw dropped. Laurel buried her face against her husband's chest, muffling her laughter. She didn't know if any other servants observed their outrageous behavior because she didn't look up until he set her down safely within her rooms.

Linfield struggled with unfastening her fitted riding jacket and finally jerked it open, buttons flying everywhere. He peeled away her layers of clothing and when she stood naked in front of him he began kissing her hungrily. His hands were everywhere, touching her, sliding up and down her bare back, pulling the pins from her hair. It came tumbling down and he ran his fingers through it, kissing her again and again.

She began undressing him, undoing buttons and unwinding his cravat. As she pulled it away, she kissed his throat, feeling his pulse jump. He growled and lifted her off her feet, carrying her to her bed and tossing her upon it. She watched as he quickly rid himself of the rest of his clothing before his body covered hers. He made love to her frantically, as if he couldn't get enough of her. When he entered her, she tensed but felt none of the pain of the night before. Apparently, he had been telling the truth that it only hurt the first time.

He had her wrap her legs about his waist as he continued thrusting into her. It allowed him to penetrate deeper. His tongue imitated his manhood, plunging into her mouth, plundering and tasting. When her release came, his mouth covered her cry. Soon after, he shuddered violently and collapsed atop her, pushing her into the mattress. She welcomed the weight of him, her arms and legs still wrapped around him.

He pushed away and left the bed, heading toward their dressing rooms.

"I will see you at dinner. Eight o'clock. Come to the winter parlor."

With that, he was gone.

ANTHONY ENTERED THE breakfast room, surprised to find Laurel already there. They had dined together last night in a small room that he remembered eating in once on his last birthday at Linwood. His aunt, Constance, had been present and it had been a happy occasion. Even Theodore, who usually wanted all the focus on him, allowed Anthony to bask in the attention he received that night. He had escorted Laurel to her room after they finished eating and left her alone. Though he would have liked nothing more than to stay, he still held back from her. He couldn't let her see how much she affected him. How he looked forward to her company. She threatened to worm her way into his heart and he would shield it at all costs. While she would make a good duchess and a very good mother, based upon what he had seen, he didn't want to let down his guard. He needed to keep a part of him separate from her.

The truth was, Laurel seemed a very good person, despite her humble beginnings. He, on the other hand, still felt like an imposter, allowing everyone to address him as Your Grace as they fawned over him, treating him as if he were someone special. He didn't feel like a duke. He knew he needed to concentrate on learning more about his vast responsibilities—and focus less on what he wanted to do in bed with his new wife. He hadn't been a nice man before or after the war. He was afraid if he let Laurel become too close to him, she would see he was a fraud.

And not want him anymore.

Anthony seated himself at the head of the table, his wife sitting to his right. Laurel wore a rose-colored gown, which turned her hair raven black and made her emerald eyes stand out. Over dinner, he had shared with her some of the things he'd learned from Woodward and they decided the route to take across the estate today. She wanted him to meet the tenants she'd visited with yesterday. He wasn't thrilled with the idea. Despite his façade, he was nervous around people. Even at his club, he didn't say much. The only time he truly felt himself was when he boxed at Gentleman Jack's, pounding his fists into some poor sparring partner. He supposed violence permeated his soul, burned into him by war. No one could save him since he had no soul left to save.

He finished his meal and swallowed the last of his coffee.

"Can you ride out in a quarter hour?" he asked.

"Yes. Let me change into my riding habit. I'll meet you at the stables."

She left and Anthony, already in his riding clothes, went directly to the stables. His head groom raved about Bucephalus' splendid lines. He asked for the horse to be saddled and one for his wife, as well.

"What mount was Her Grace given yesterday?"

The groom told him and had it brought out with Bucephalus. The horse seemed adequate but he wanted something far better for her. After all, Laurel was a duchess and deserved the best. He wouldn't have her ride anything but the best horseflesh available, especially when they returned to London. He knew the *ton* would sink their teeth into her and her reputation as it was. He wanted her dressed in the finest clothes. Wearing the best gems. Riding the best mount.

He turned and watched her approach. Yesterday, she had worn blue. Today's riding habit was a rich forest green, the tight riding jacket snug against her breasts. The sweeping skirt hid her beautiful, long legs. Anthony had a vision of them wrapped about his waist and almost grabbed her hand to drag her back to bed. Instead, he greeted her.

She smiled but went straight to the horse and offered it an apple. A simple gesture but a thoughtful one. His duchess excelled at thoughtfulness. He remembered her seeking out staff at the St. Clair townhouse before they left to come to Linwood, complimenting them on the wedding preparations and thanking them for all they had done for her while she had lived under their roof. She'd been just as gracious when she'd meet her own staff at Linwood and already used the names of various servants. He could barely remember Monkton's name most days.

Laurel stroked the horse's mane and kissed its nose. "That's my good beauty," she purred.

Anthony wished she stroked him. That instead of climbing atop this horse she would mount and ride him.

"Are you ready?" he asked and handed her up before climbing atop his own horse.

"What is his name?" she asked.

"Bucephalus. He's named after Alexander the Great's horse."

She leaned over and brushed her hand against the horse's neck. "I will bring you an apple next time, Bucephalus," she promised. "You look the greedy type so I might slice it into pieces and feed them to you to keep you from gobbling it down."

Anthony pictured her feeding him. Naked. He shook his head, trying to rid himself of the image.

They spent close to two hours riding various portions of the property and then rode to the highest part of the estate. The April day was sunny and clear and they could see a great distance. Laurel slid from the saddle and went to stand at the edge.

"It's hard to believe all this is owned by one man," she said, awe in her voice. "That one day our son will inherit it."

He had also dismounted and came to stand beside her. He refrained from standing behind her and slipping his arms about her. He had heard of wounded soldiers becoming addicted to laudanum, the drug becoming their entire reason to exist. This woman was like an opiate that he was having trouble staying away from. He must learn to temper his lust and only come to her every now and then. He prided himself on his control, even managing to harness his constant rage, only unleashing it to serve him. His growing attraction to Laurel threatened to upset the balance of his neatly ordered life.

"Shall we?" he asked.

He assisted her into the saddle and mounted Bucephalus. They rode to the first of the tenant farms, where they were warmly greeted. More people showed up, wanting to meet him and visit with the duchess again. Over and over, farmers pulled him aside, praising Laurel. In one afternoon, she had gained the love of their people without even trying. He tamped down the jealousy he felt and tried to smile and thank everyone.

It just showed Anthony, though, how dangerous his duchess was. He would get children off her—but it was best that they lead separate lives. He would remain faithful to her but he couldn't be around her every day.

If he were, she would eventually break down all his walls and find out who he really was.

CHAPTER FIFTEEN

LAUREL AWOKE, HER eyes grainy from lack of sleep.

Anthony hadn't come to her last night.

She'd stayed awake as long as she could, thinking of the day they'd spent together. While he hadn't been as warm toward the tenants as she would have liked, she understood as a duke, he needed to keep a certain distance from everyone. They'd returned after being out all day and once again, after bathing, eaten in the winter parlor. She enjoyed the small room. Sanders had rolled in a cart both times and placed their plates and wine in front of them before leaving. After having footmen always present, Laurel liked the intimacy of dining alone with her husband—almost too much.

She reminded herself that he was just her husband. That while they got along for the most part, they were two very different people. It wasn't her plan to ever fall in love.

But if she had, it would have been with Anthony.

Her warring feelings gave her pause. At times, she thought of him as Linfield, the haughty duke who contained his emotions. When he touched her, though, he was Anthony, the man whose need for her raged out of control. Laurel wondered if he thought the same of her. Was she truly two people when around him? Sometimes, she still felt as if she were that inadequate shop girl, too thin from not having enough to eat, trying to avoid the likes of Julius Farmon so she could stay safe another day. She might be the Duchess of Linfield but a part of her would always feel like Laurel Wright.

She stretched, telling herself she would hide her disappointment when she saw her husband. If he knew how long she had waited up for him, it would give him satisfaction. Sometimes, she felt they were at constant war with one another, jockeying for the superior position in their marriage. She knew society—and even the Bible—determined that a man was to be the head of a household and marriage. Why she couldn't accept that, she didn't know. She merely wanted to be herself, even if that self seemed to antagonize her husband to no end.

After ringing for Retta and dressing for the day, Laurel went to the breakfast room. A note rested at her place. She opened it and learned that Anthony had already eaten and had ridden out with Mr. Woodward. He promised to be back by teatime.

She folded the note again, the first from him. It was terse, with no mention of affection, much like the man who wrote it. Yet she knew he felt deeply. Laurel determined to solve the mystery of his childhood. She'd already tried, speaking with some of the longtime tenants. They remembered him as a boy, one who roamed the estate freely. He'd been curious and had a streak of mischief within him. Other than that, none of them knew much about him. It saddened her when one farmer said the boy had gone to school and never returned. The Duke of Linfield and his heir, Theodore, never mentioned Anthony the few times they were out and about on the estate. The farmer said no one asked what had become of the child because none of them wanted to anger His Grace.

The servants were no help, either. She'd spoken to many of them. None had been here during Anthony's time in the household, more than twenty years ago. Laurel understood servants came and went but she had hoped she might find at least one who could clear the muddy waters for her.

Once she'd finished breakfast, she walked through the entire house again, making detailed notes on what she would like done once they returned after the Season, when they would make Linwood their more permanent home. It made her wonder about Hannah and Aunt Constance. She knew the older woman had a country residence and supposed Hannah had been living with her. Would they return there—or come to Linwood? Of course, it was possible Hannah might very well find a husband by Season's end and marry and move in with him. It made Laurel eager to return to London and see these new family members, as well as visit with her own. Hudson would leave in a few months for university. She hoped he might spend at least part of his holidays with her at Linwood or their other estates. Anthony had promised to take her to see the properties he owned. She was curious as to their locations and just how many there might be. At least Linwood was located close to her St. Clair relatives and would make visiting them easy.

After she'd compiled her list, Laurel returned to her room and spent a few hours examining the ledgers she'd borrowed from Mr. Woodward. She was pleased to find that Linwood was quite profitable. She decided to return the ledgers to the estate manager's office since it was almost teatime and she expected Anthony to join her, based upon what his note indicated. When she entered, it surprised her to find Woodward sitting behind his desk.

"I didn't mean to interrupt," she apologized. "I've come to return the ledgers I borrowed."

"You haven't, Your Grace," he said pleasantly. "His Grace and I returned an hour ago."

"I hope you had a pleasant day together."

"His Grace is full of good ideas. I look forward to implementing his vision for Linwood. I believe he's eager to visit his other estates and see what work needs to be done at them, as well."

"His Grace and I are about to take tea. Would you like to join us? I'd love to hear about what you did today and also discover what other properties are in the family."

Mr. Woodward looked taken aback. "Are you certain you'd like me to join you? I . . . that is, I never took tea with the previous duke."

Laurel smiled. "You are more than welcomed. Come along."

She led him upstairs and rang the bell. The maid who answered told her that tea would arrive shortly and Laurel thanked her.

Since they were alone, she decided to approach Mr. Woodward regarding Anthony's past.

"You have been here a good number of years, I'd imagine," she began.

"Yes, Your Grace. I came as an assistant steward. My father was a steward at an estate a day's ride from Linwood and he trained me himself."

"Then you rose in position and took over all management of Linwood?"

"I did. I've been most fortunate to serve at Linwood for so long."

"You mentioned when we arrived that you recalled my husband as a child."

Woodward frowned, clearly uncomfortable with her comment. "I barely remember him as a boy," he said. "I'm afraid after so long a time, I was trying to curry favor with our new duke. He was only here a short while and then off to school. I really don't remember much about him at all."

He looked away, his fingers slipping under his cravat, pulling nervously at it.

"Didn't it concern you when he didn't return from school during the holidays?" Laurel pressed. "I know boys are sent away to further their education but they do come home to spend time with their families."

Woodward looked at her helplessly. "It's not for me to say, Your Grace."

"Woodward," a deep voice said.

The manager turned, as did Laurel, and saw the Duke of Linfield standing there.

"Do you have something to do, Woodward?" he demanded.

Woodward shot to his feet. "In fact, I do, Your Grace." He glanced back to Laurel. "Please forgive me, Your Grace. Thank you for your kind invitation to tea but I have a vast amount of work to complete."

With that, the older man hurried from the room.

Her husband didn't seat himself. Laurel nervously moistened her lips, waiting for his anger to erupt. It didn't. Instead, it was as if the room turned ice cold.

"My childhood is of no concern. I am an adult now. The Duke of Linfield. I haven't been a child in a long time, Laurel. Nor an idealistic man going off to war, thinking he might change the world. I'm afraid you're stuck with me as I am. I wish the door to the past to remain closed." He paused. "Do you understand?"

"Yes, Your Grace," she said, her heart pounding, more afraid of this cold, aloof Anthony than the distant or sometimes angry one.

"I'm glad we could come to an understanding. I think it's time we returned to London. Don't you agree?"

She felt as if he'd slapped her. They were supposed to spend the week here, getting to know one another. Except he didn't want her to know him at all. Or what had happened here between him and his father.

"Yes, Your Grace."

"See that your maid packs for you. We will leave first thing in the morning."

Anthony turned and walked away but Laurel wasn't going to let him do so again. She was tired of him leaving her.

"Aren't you going to stay for tea?" she asked.

He faced her. "No. And I will be out for dinner. I will see you in the carriage tomorrow."

With that, her husband abandoned her.

Again.

NOT A WORD passed between Laurel and Linfield during the coach ride back to London. She kept her gaze turned out the window, watching the lush, green countryside pass by, determined not to be the first to speak. She wanted to hide all her varying emotions. Her hurt. Disappointment. Anger. Frustration.

Would the rest of her married life be so up and down?

She found it exhausting and unsatisfying. Worse, she would have to keep all of this to herself. Her relatives would be curious as to how she and her new husband were getting along. Sharing the truth with them was the last thing she planned to do. The same went for Aunt Constance and Hannah, though it might prove harder to hide the rift with the two women living in the same house with the warring couple.

The carriage pulled up in front of the Linfield London townhouse. The door opened and her husband climbed out. He handed her down and immediately returned to his seat.

"I have business to attend to. I will see you tonight."

Laurel clamped down on her jaw, not wanting to show how startled she was. With a flick of the reins, their driver took off. Moments later, the second coach pulled into place. Retta and Monkton climbed out. By now, the front door had opened and a footman appeared. She assumed the trunks would be taken care of as she marched into the entry way, cursing silently.

The housekeeper appeared. "Your Grace." She sounded startled. "It is good to see you. Allow me to show you to your rooms."

Laurel followed the woman upstairs. The bedchamber was large and airy though the furniture looked quite dated and both the wallpaper and carpet were faded.

"Your dressing room is through that door. All of your clothes that came after the wedding have been placed in your wardrobe."

A footman entered, bearing her trunk, Retta on his heels.

"I see your maid has also arrived."

"Yes. Monkton, too," Laurel said. "His Grace had business to attend to but he will be home for dinner this evening." She paused and added, "We were eager to continue with the Season, which is why we decided to return early." She added that to hopefully throw off the woman, not wanting news of her and Linfield's estrangement to reach the servant's hall.

"Very good, Your Grace. Shall I tell Lady Constance and Lady Hannah of your arrival? They are in the drawing room." The woman smiled. "Entertaining a few of Lady Hannah's suitors."

"I will join them." She looked to Retta. "Familiarize yourself with everything and then get yourself settled."

"Will you be going out tonight, Your Grace?" Retta asked.

Laurel looked to the housekeeper. "What event takes place tonight?"

"A musicale at Lord Downley's."

"Yes," Laurel told Retta. "Choose whatever you wish for me to wear."

She left the bedchamber and went down a flight of stairs to the drawing room. Two men in their mid-twenties were present and stood as she entered the room.

"Laurel!" cried Hannah, rushing to her.

She embraced her sister-in-law. "It's good to see you."

"We weren't expecting you so soon," Aunt Constance said as they joined her and the two guests.

"I think Linfield worried about his sister while we were in the country." She turned to the men and Aunt Constance introduced Laurel to them.

They chatted for a few minutes and then both visitors rose and took their leave. Hannah promised she would see them tonight.

Once they'd left the room, she asked Laurel, "What did you think? Did either of them appeal to you?"

Laurel laughed. "I already have a husband, Hannah. The point is, does one appeal to you—or both?"

All three women laughed and Hannah said, "I do like them both. I've met several young men in the short time you and Anthony have been gone."

"Then you will have to introduce them to us this evening."

"Oh, will you attend Lord and Lady Downley's event?" Aunt Constance asked. "With Anthony?"

"Yes. We both plan to be there. I suppose I should write to Lady Downley to see if we can come."

"You're a duchess bringing her duke. Of course, you can attend," Aunt Constance said. "It would be nice if you let Lady Downley know, however, that you have arrived in town again and would enjoy their musicale."

"I will do so and also send word to my family that we are back," Laurel said.

"I'm going to decide what to wear this evening," Hannah said. "I never knew how difficult it was to make a decision about my appearance. Which gown to wear with what gloves. How to style my hair. Whether my slippers should match the gown or provide a contrast to it."

Both the young women rose to leave. Laurel allowed Hannah to go through the doorway first and then she heard her name called.

"Would you stay a moment longer, my dear?" Aunt Constance asked pleasantly.

"Of course," she replied and returned to the seat she had occupied, though she didn't want to. She knew now they were alone that the older woman would have questions. Ones she didn't have the answers to.

"How did you find Linwood?" Anthony's aunt asked casually.

"I see you are starting with easy questions."

"Should I dispense with them? Then I shall." Aunt Constance took Laurel's hand. "Why are you back in London so soon?"

"Honestly? I don't know. Or at least I don't know all of it." Tears welled in her eyes. "I'm not sure Anthony is happy with me."

Aunt Constance squeezed Laurel's hand and then released it. "I beg to differ. Tell me what happened."

"I adore the estate. The tenants are good people. The household staff is superb. I felt we were making progress, getting to know one another. There were a few flies in the ointment," she admitted. "Nothing too serious. Then I mucked it all up by asking about Anthony's past."

"Oh, dear," Constance murmured.

"Yes. That is what has driven a wedge between us. Mr. Woodward, Linwood's estate manager, was one of the few employees who knew Anthony as a child. I know something dreadful occurred between Anthony and his father many years ago. I thought if I knew, it would help me understand him better. Anthony came across us while I quizzed Mr. Woodward."

Laurel shuddered. "He was so angry, Aunt Constance. Not a raging anger but a cold, controlled one. So cold that it frightened me. The husband I was getting to know changed before my eyes. I'll be frank and tell you that the physical side of marriage has shown we are very well suited. Now, though, I'm not sure if he will ever touch me again. He made it clear that his past was to remain closed behind a locked door which only he has the key to unlock."

She wiped away the tears that began to fall. "I fear he's tossed away that key and whatever festers within him will never heal. That was when he said we were returning to London. Anthony has yet to speak to me."

"Even on the carriage ride back to town?"

"Not a word. I'm not sure what to do. I know the kind, caring man I married is buried somewhere inside him. I don't know how to apologize, though. I'm afraid to bring up the quarrel between us for fear of making things worse."

"Then you don't use words," the older woman proclaimed. "A kiss is where you start. Show Anthony the passion and tenderness you feel toward him. The wounds you seek to heal are very old ones, Laurel. My boy was horribly scarred by events in his past. Care for him. Love him. In time, he will see he can trust you. Only then will he be able to share what happened to him and allow you to be the balm for his wounds. It's not my place—or anyone else's—to share his past with you. It's for Anthony to do so. When he does, be prepared, for he will be in a world of hurt reliving it as he speaks of it. Until then, do all in your power to care for him and wear him down with love."

Laurel wiped her eyes. "Thank you. And please, not a word to anyone."

"Of course not." Aunt Constance smiled. "Go and write your notes, my dear. I will see you later."

She returned to her room and quickly penned a brief note to Lady Downley and rang for a maid, asking it to be delivered at once. She took her time composing short letters to Catherine, Rachel, and Leah, letting the three women know she was back in the city and would be at the musicale tonight. At first, she asked for them to attend tea here tomorrow afternoon and then set aside the notes and tried again, recalling that tomorrow afternoon was a garden party hosted by a viscountess who'd had Rachel design a new fountain and gardens for her. Laurel had been disappointed that they would miss the affair but now that she was back in town, she was eager to see Rachel's work firsthand.

Once more, she summoned a servant and passed the three notes along, which notified her family that she was back in town and asked them to tea the day after tomorrow. Though she had told Retta to pick out a gown for her, Laurel decided to take matters into her own hands. She chose one that Rachel had insisted become part of Laurel's wardrobe. It showed a little more of her bosom than she felt comfortable revealing—but that was the very reason she wanted to wear it. Hopefully, the dress would capture Anthony's attention.

Until he removed it from her later tonight.

CHAPTER SIXTEEN

ANTHONY HAD ALREADY instructed his driver to head to Gentleman Jack's once Laurel had been dropped off at the townhouse. His anger at her prying into his past had yet to subside. She was very persistent. And persuasive. Though he'd warned Woodward not to speak to her regarding the past, he doubted the man could have stood up under Laurel's interrogation. Thank goodness he'd arrived in the drawing room when he did, else who knows what the man might have spilled. Anthony knew it was wounded pride speaking, wanting to conceal how shabbily he'd been treated by his family. How he was the little boy not good enough to remain with his family.

He never wanted Laurel to learn of the treatment he'd suffered at the duke's hands. Though she infuriated him at times, he still wanted her to have a good opinion of him.

The most difficult thing had been to hang on to his anger last night and keep from going to her. He lay awake in bed for hours, fantasizing about his hands on her smooth, alabaster skin. His mouth on hers, taking and tasting. Thrusting into her, again and again. It had nearly driven him mad but he'd maintained control and stayed in his bedchamber.

They hadn't spoken during their journey back to London. As the miles passed and the silence thickened, he didn't know how to start a conversation. Instead, he'd let the swaying carriage stoke his anger until, by the time they'd arrived, it filled him. He knew how to control it, though. He'd seen her home and now came to vanquish his demons by using his fists.

He alighted from the coach and went inside. Gentleman Jack himself was the first to greet him.

"Back from the country already, Your Grace?" the former boxer asked. "I heard you've married a very pretty young thing."

"She's not pretty," he snapped. "My duchess is quite beautiful."

"I see. Are you merely working out with the bags or do you seek a sparring partner?"

"Both," he said succinctly. "I'll be at the bags shortly. Find me someone to fight."

The owner took his leave and Anthony headed into the rooms designated for changing. He unknotted his cravat, thinking of how Laurel had done so. He cursed under his breath, determined to push all thoughts of her from his mind. Stripping to the waist, he returned to the outer rooms.

"Boxing gloves, Your Grace?" a worker asked.

"No."

Anthony went to a vacant punching bag and attacked it viciously, pounding his fists into it. With each punch, frustration only built instead of subsiding. He continued pummeling the swinging bag until sweat dripped from him. Someone brought him a large tankard of ale and he drank the entire thing in one long gulp.

"I've found a partner for you, Your Grace," Gentleman Jack told him. "Follow me."

They passed several marked-off rings, all filled with gentlemen of the *ton*, sparring with men. Anthony suspected many of the employees allowed themselves to be beaten although he'd boxed with a few who would never give in. The man that watched him approach the ring was one of those. He was two inches shorter than Anthony but made up of pure muscle. From experience, Anthony knew his opponent's reach was longer than most men of his height.

Unfortunately, his competitor never stood a chance. From the moment Gentleman Jack gave the signal, Anthony seized the moment, advancing and immediately throwing hard punches to his opponent's midsection. Before long, the action between other boxers had come to a halt as everyone watched the Duke of Linfield beat a man to a bloody pulp.

Gentleman Jack called a halt to the match and two workers lifted his unconscious opponent, dragging him from the space.

"You've already cost me two employees, Your Grace. That might be a third. Perhaps you need to find another sport to help exorcise your demons."

Anthony glared at the former boxer. "You're saying I'm no longer welcome?"

The owner thought a moment and Anthony could see he didn't want to risk alienating one of his best customers.

"Let's strike a bargain, Your Grace. The next time you come, you fight with gloves. Until I tell you to go back to your bare knuckles. Fair enough?"

"All right," he said begrudgingly. He didn't like wearing them but he needed to box. If that was what Jack wanted, he would agree.

He returned to the townhouse and soaked in a hot tub for a long while as Monkton applied liniment to his bruised knuckles. After ten minutes, Anthony washed it away. He couldn't show up with the smell of liniment clinging to him. Besides, a duke would always wear gloves to evening social events so his damaged knuckles would never be seen. Monkton had already informed him of tonight's musicale.

Since he returned so late, he'd missed dinner. Monkton dressed him in dark evening clothes and Anthony hurried downstairs. Aunt Constance and Hannah were already waiting in the foyer and he apologized to them for his tardiness. They didn't seem to see anything remiss in him and Hannah chatted away, telling him about the two young bachelors who had visited this afternoon. Anthony nodded and kept glancing up the stairs, anxious for Laurel to appear. When she did, she stole his breath.

He watched her descend the stairs, the emerald green gown hugging her curves. He couldn't take his eyes from her. The neckline revealed her rounded breasts to perfection. His fingers longed to skim them. His mouth yearned to suckle them. She reached the bottom of the staircase and he noticed she wore the same pearls he'd seen before and they seemed wrong for this gown. He'd meant to give her jewelry. He had access to the numerous Linfield jewels now. Knowing every eye would be on his bride tonight, he needed her wearing something splendid.

"You look beautiful," Hannah exclaimed.

"Yes, she does," he agreed. "Will you excuse me a few minutes?"

Anthony returned to his bedchamber and the safe that held several sets of gems. More were at his bank and he decided he would go first thing tomorrow and claim them. He wanted everyone to see how splendidly his duchess wore them. He took a moment to locate what he wanted, hoping she would appreciate the gesture.

When he joined the others, he said, "I have something for you, Laurel. Would you remove your pearls?"

She cocked her head, frowning at him, but reached behind her neck and undid the clasp, lowering the necklace and handing it to his aunt.

"Could you help me unfasten my bracelet?" she asked Hannah.

Once the bracelet was gone, he came toward her and opened the box he carried.

She gasped. "They're stunning."

Anthony met her gaze. "Not as stunning as when you wear them."

Handing her the box, he lifted the diamond necklace from the case and moved behind her. He brought it over her head and fastened the clasp at her nape, brushing a brief kiss along it. She shivered. He removed the bracelet and encircled her wrist, closing it.

She shook her head in wonder. "It's lovely. Thank you, Anthony," she said softly.

"Shall we?" He offered her his arm and she took it.

Hannah couldn't say enough about the diamonds, claiming everyone would be jealous of Laurel tonight. His aunt caught his eye and nodded her approval.

They arrived at the Downleys' and entered. A musicale was more exclusive than a ball and so the guest list was much smaller. From the moment they entered, Laurel had the attention of every man and woman present. They greeted their hosts and then she was swarmed by others, including the female St. Clairs. His eyes swept the room and he saw the hungry, lusty looks as other men watched her greedily.

Anthony wanted to work his way about the room and smash every one of them in the mouth.

The Duke of Everton joined him. "Good evening, Linfield. Did you and Laurel enjoy your brief sojourn in the country? I thought you were staying a bit longer."

His eyes remained on his wife as he answered. "We did. Laurel seemed taken with Linwood. It is the main residence of the Godwin family. We will raise our children there."

"Laurel is a woman to be treasured," Everton said of his half-sister. "It's important to always treasure what we have—for we never know when we might lose it."

With that, Everton sauntered away.

Anthony moved toward his duchess, nudging others aside as he took her hand and slipped it into the crook of his arm.

"You look parched, my dear. Let's get you some ratafia before the music begins."

He led her away from the horde of admirers, claiming a drink for her and seating her on the end of a row so no one would be on her left. He took the seat next to her, his gaze falling to her lovely breasts.

Ones that he planned to feast upon tonight.

LAUREL AWOKE AND immediately knew she was alone. Disappointment filled her.

Last night had been divine. Her choice of gown, along with being newly married and making her first foray into society after her wedding, had guaranteed she received attention at the Downleys' musicale. If she'd learned one thing about the *ton*, it was that titles impressed them. The loftier, the better. As a duchess, she'd had a group surround her from the moment she'd entered the room. What she'd enjoyed was knowing her husband's eyes never left her. He'd come and swept her away, keeping her to himself. Then during the intermission, he'd insisted they leave. She'd pointed out that it wouldn't be fair to Hannah to depart so early but Anthony had told her he would arrange for the Evertons to take Hannah and his aunt home.

Once they'd gotten inside their carriage, Anthony had kissed her the entire way home. He'd come to her bedchamber with her, dismissing Retta by saying he would attend to his wife. Her maid had been unsuccessful in hiding her smile as she curtseyed and left the room.

Anthony had undressed her and made love to her twice, the first time swift and frantic, the second leisurely and just as fulfilling. He'd even held her in his arms as she drifted off to sleep. She'd hoped he would stay the night with her. Obviously, he hadn't. She didn't know why it seemed important to her—but it did. Just when she thought they were making progress and taking a step forward in their relationship, her husband retreated two steps.

She rose and rang for Retta, deciding to dress in her riding habit. She hoped she could convince Anthony to take her riding this morning. She selected her green habit over the repaired blue one, knowing instinctively that he seemed to prefer the first. As she left her bedchamber, she ran into him in the corridor. He was already dressed for riding, as well.

"Are you going to breakfast or will you ride first?" she asked.

He took in her outfit. "You planned on riding?"

"Yes. I thought I would eat something and then have a groom escort me to the park."

"I'll take you," he said firmly, giving her an inner glow.

They ate quickly and then went to the stables. He suggested to the groom which horse to bring her and soon it and Bucephalus were saddled. Anthony helped her into the saddle and they set off for the park. They rode for an hour and, once again, Laurel felt a sense of freedom on horseback that she knew would never grow old.

As they walked their horses back to the townhouse, she said, "I've invited my family to tea tomorrow. Will you be able to join us?"

"If I am available," he replied.

"I do want you to get to know my family. They are very important to me."

He didn't respond.

"I hope to do something, as all of my female relatives seem to do."

He frowned. "What do you mean?"

"Rachel designs gardens. In fact, the garden party today will show-case her work. Catherine writes children's books and donates the proceeds to various charities. Caroline owns a bookstore and tearoom. Even Leah has helped organize the bookstore's circulating library and a book club for women."

He looked thoughtful. "You want to do something similar?"

"I told you I am interested in helping others. With my new position, not only can I help the less fortunate, but I might inspire other women in Polite Society to do the same. I plan to speak to Catherine about it since she has experience regarding charity work."

By now, they had reached home. He brought his horse to a stop.

"I've business to attend to. I will see you later. What time is this garden party?"

"Four."

Anthony nodded and then turned his horse. Laurel wondered what business he had. He'd been so mysterious about it when they'd arrived in London yesterday. Curiosity ate at her, so much that she decided to follow him.

At first she hung back, not wanting him to notice her, but he never glanced over his shoulder. She closed the distance as traffic on the streets picked up. She didn't want to lose him. Finally, he stopped on Bond Street and dismounted, tossing his reins to a boy and striding into a building. She saw no markings other than the number thirteen and hadn't a clue what lay inside. Pulling her horse around, she watched from across the street as other well-dressed gentlemen entered at intervals. After three quarters of an hour, Anthony still hadn't emerged.

Laurel decided to go in.

She crossed the busy street and slid from her saddle, handing her reins to the boy who had taken Anthony's horse.

"I won't be long," she said breezily. "Keep my mount close."

His mouth gaped as she marched toward the door and entered. Once inside, the strong smell of liniment and sweat assaulted her. Looking around, she saw men stripped to the waist. Some fought one another in pairs, while others struck long, oblong bags hanging from the ceiling. She spotted Anthony immediately. He stood in front of one of these bags, a man holding it as her husband punched it repeatedly. He wore something over his hands as he struck the bag. Sweat glistened on his torso. With each hit, the muscles in his back danced.

The man released the bag and came around, demonstrating something. Anthony nodded and ferociously assaulted the bag again. The force he used made her cringe. She'd seen his knuckles bruised and had been too afraid to ask what had happened to them. Now, she knew.

The man who'd tutored Anthony began striding around the large room. He had an air of confidence about him. She didn't know if he owned this establishment or was one of its instructors.

Suddenly, he spotted her and strode toward her. Firmly taking her elbow, he led her outside.

"No women allowed, my lady," he said briskly though he didn't seem angry.

Raising her chin a notch, Laurel said, "I am the Duchess of Linfield."

He studied her a moment. "Hmm. So, you are, Your Grace. Your husband is quite the boxer. If he weren't a member of the *ton*, he would make me more money than Croesus ever had."

"He would be a boxer?"

"That he would, Your Grace."

"And your name, Sir?"

He grinned. "I'm Gentleman Jack, Your Grace. John Jackson, actually, but the gents who come for my lessons like that I dress well and speak even better. Hence, my nickname."

"You teach gentlemen to box?"

"I do. Your husband has taken lessons at my boxing club ever since he returned from the war." Mr. Jackson shook his head. "He's got anger in him, that one. The war did that to some men. I'd heard he gotten married, though. Maybe you can help tame the savage beast."

Laurel thought a moment. "What I would like, Mr. Jackson, is to learn more about boxing since it is important to my husband." She paused. "Would you consider giving me private boxing lessons?"

CHAPTER SEVENTEEN

ANTHONY LEFT GENTLEMEN Jack's and headed straight for Tattersall's. He knew any horseflesh worth buying would need to be purchased there. He was eager to find the right mount for Laurel. It was obvious she took joy in riding and he wanted a horse perfectly suited for her. Though she hadn't been riding long, she showed remarkably good skills. He wanted a horse as spirited—and beautiful—as his wife.

Their lovemaking last night had been the best of their brief marriage. When they'd finished, he'd been reluctant to leave her, gathering her in his arms and whispering for her to go to sleep. He lay there, utterly content. It wouldn't do, though, for him to stay the night. Much as he enjoyed her body next to his, he wanted definite boundaries drawn between them. Already, she was becoming far too important to him. He wasn't going to be some puppet for a St. Clair to tug about. That thought had made him slip from her bed. He'd returned to his own bedchamber and lain awake far too long, the scent of her lingering on his skin.

He arrived at Hyde Park Corner and saw the place was busy. Immediately, he was met and called by name, though he had never set foot in the establishment. It continually amazed him what being the Duke of Linfield meant.

"Are you looking for a team for your carriage or phaeton, Your Grace? We have a beautiful pair of matched bays that have just arrived."

"My wife needs a lady's mount. One with a smooth gait and a light mouth."

"Ah, yes, I heard that congratulations are in order for you and Her Grace. I believe her brother, the Earl of Mayfield, taught her to ride. Is the duchess a skilled rider or one lacking in confidence?"

Anthony had assumed she would have been given riding lessons but it made perfect sense for Luke St. Clair to be the one to have taught her. He'd had a way with horses when they were boys at school.

"She is a natural rider and has taken to it quickly. We have ridden in the country together and I've seen no hesitation on her part."

"Well, my name is Jesper, Your Grace. I believe I have just the horse you require if you'll follow me."

He led Anthony to the stables and inside. The scent of hay and horse filled the large barn. They passed several horses of interest to him and he considered the possibility of breeding them at Linwood. Finally, Jesper stopped in front of a stall.

"This is Clio, Your Grace. She has an even temper and yet is still spirited. What do you think? Shall I bring her outside and let you have a look at her in the sunlight?"

"Yes."

Anthony waited, watching as Jesper entered the stall. He spoke to the horse and gave her a few quick pats before putting on a bridle and leading the horse out. He allowed them to walk in front of him so he could observe Clio. Once outside, he studied the animal carefully, running his hands along the coat, checking her knees and teeth.

"Tell me about her sire."

Jesper filled him in on Clio's background and then swung up, trotting around a large ring. The horse had fine lines and its soft gray coat was an unusual color. By the time Jesper returned and came to the ground, Anthony had made up his mind.

"I'll take her."

He was led into an office and provided with documents regarding the horse's lines.

"Send the bill to my solicitor," he instructed, providing the man's name and address. "I'll also need a sidesaddle. The best you have."

"I'll fetch that," Jesper said.

Minutes later, Clio had been saddled and Jesper said, "I can take the horse to you now. I have another to deliver to Mayfair."

"Very good. I will let my groom know to expect you."

Anthony left, hopeful that Laurel would approve of the gift. Their wedding had been so rushed that he hadn't even thought of presenting her with something for the occasion. She'd received diamonds last night, which she had looked upon with awe. He wanted her to like Clio even more. He wanted to keep giving her whatever she wanted, just to see the smile that lit her face. He'd noticed a dimple in her right cheek for the first time at last night's musicale. He wanted to see it more often.

He called upon his solicitor on his way home to let him know to expect the bill of sale for Clio. They spent a good hour discussing other pressing business. He found he was becoming interested in it. The responsibilities at the doorstep of the Duke of Linfield had seemed daunting when he'd first arrived in England. With a wife now and the thought of an heir someday, suddenly Anthony found renewed interest and eagerly looked forward to learning all he could, not only about Linfield but his other properties and investments. His solicitor caught his enthusiasm and they made an appointment to continue their discussion since another client with an appointment had arrived.

When he reached home, his groom told him Clio had been delivered.

"She's a fine horse, Your Grace. As fine as Bucephalus in her own way. Her Grace will be most pleased."

Anthony couldn't wait to find Laurel and bring her to the stables.

It was half-past two and though they didn't have time for a ride, he knew he could introduce the two before Laurel had to dress for the upcoming garden party. He didn't look forward to attending it. Society events were not high on his list of things to do but he knew it was important for her to be there because her half-sister had created something they were supposed to go look at. Though Laurel hadn't known her St. Clair family long, she seemed quite close to them. He wondered if he would ever be comfortable around the St. Clairs and their spouses and children.

He passed the butler and asked where the duchess was, thinking she might already be in her rooms dressing.

"In the drawing room, Your Grace."

That was probably better. If he'd gone to her chamber while she dressed, they might have missed the garden party. He wondered what she would wear today that would entice him.

Anthony opened the door to the drawing room and came to a halt. The scene before him didn't make sense.

Gentleman Jack stood at the far end, demonstrating how to throw a punch. He was bent slightly at the waist, as he taught all the men who came to his boxing club to do. Laurel imitated him. The former boxing champ drew back his arm and thrust it forward. Laurel did so, as well.

"Do the sequence," Jack commanded.

Laurel commenced moving her feet. Her slippers moved forward and back and then from side to side, her face flush from the activity.

"That's good, Your Grace. Add the rest."

She struck her imaginary opponent with a straight on punch, followed by an uppercut with her left, her feet dancing all the while.

"Oh, this feels marvelous, Mr. Jackson!" she proclaimed.

Anthony strode across the room. "What in bloody hell is going on? Have you gone mad?"

She ceased moving though her bosom heaved as she panted. Wisps of hair had come loose from her chignon, framing her face.

"I'm learning how to box, Anthony," she declared, a radiant smile on her lips.

"No, you are not," he said firmly. Turning to Gentleman Jack, he said, "What were you thinking? Get out!" he shouted and glared at his wife.

Her smile fell. For a moment, she looked as if she might cry. Then he watched as a steely resolve entered her eyes.

"Thank you for the lesson, Mr. Jackson. We can continue this—"

"There's no continuing this," he roared.

The former boxer ignored him. Looking at Laurel, he said, "I regret that we won't be able to pursue further lessons, Your Grace."

"You're afraid of him?" she asked, astounded. Then her eyes narrowed. "No, I know you're not. You're only afraid of losing his business. Or that word might get out that you had the audacity to instruct a female. I am sorry, Mr. Jackson. Terribly so. You are an excellent teacher. I wish you well in all future endeavors."

"Thank you, Your Grace." Gentleman Jack bowed to her and left the room.

The moment the door closed, Laurel shouted, "How dare you treat him so poorly!"

"How dare he come to my home," Anthony snapped. "What were you thinking, Laurel? Are you mad? Boxing lessons? What a disgrace."

She marched to him, standing so close her breasts brushed against his chest. "Yes, I am mad. Not insane. Just extremely angry. At you."

"Boxing lessons are not appropriate—"

"Don't, Linfield," she said. "I don't need this lecture from you again on how a duchess—your duchess—is to act. You already lied to get me to marry you."

"I lied?" he asked, astounded. "About what? And we had to wed. Else your name would have been dragged through the mud by the *ton*."

"Oh, that's right. Place all the blame on me. All because I kissed a man even though it was a private moment. I never should have married you. You told me I could be my own woman and make my own rules but all you do is want me to behave like every other silly female in Polite Society. I would rather have had tongues wag. Another scandal would have come along soon enough and I wouldn't be saddled with you. Or you with me."

Angry tears splashed down her cheeks. "I only wanted to learn about boxing because you're interested in it."

"I don't want you interested in my life!" he shouted.

His words hung in the air. Anthony regretted them the moment they left his lips. He saw Laurel's face twist and knew he'd hurt her deeply.

Without a word, she fled the drawing room.

"Blast it all."

He went and poured himself a drink, downing it quickly and then sinking into the nearest chair.

He had told her she didn't have to follow society's rules, only to berate her when she was herself. He liked that she was her own person. It touched him that she'd somehow learned of his interest in boxing and arranged to have lessons, all to understand him better and please him. Yet what had he done? Yelled at her like some furious fishwife.

"You are an idiot," he told himself.

He poured another drink and sat moping. Why did he constantly pick a fight with her? He knew the problem lay within him. As far as he knew, Laurel was just this side of perfect. He owed her an apology. Setting aside the empty glass, he ventured upstairs and knocked on her door. Moments later, her maid opened it.

"Oh, Your Grace! Um, Her Grace isn't here. I'm . . . she . . . she went out. To a garden party."

She'd left without him.

"Thank you."

He hurried to his own room and stripped off his clothes. Monkton suddenly appeared and helped him sponge off quickly and dress again.

"Where is this garden party?" he asked the valet.

Soon, he was on his way. Walking because Laurel had taken the carriage, accompanied by Aunt Constance and Hannah. At least it was only a few blocks to his destination. Anthony had no idea what he would say when he saw Laurel. He prayed she would talk to him. Her family would be present and he knew she would not cause a scene and embarrass them. He dreaded the look in Everton's eyes. Anthony had wanted to make Laurel happy and yet, somehow, he continually caused both of them misery.

He arrived and found her the center of attention, men fawning over her. She had blossomed since they'd first met. The former shop girl was now the belle of the *ton*. She held herself with a natural grace and confidence. His duchess would be much imitated, from her sense of fashion to the good deeds that she was so eager to become involved in.

The earl on her left said something and she laughed merrily, that dimple making her even more attractive. A sense of despair washed over him.

He was holding her back. He might be a duke but he wasn't good enough for her.

His heart heavy, Anthony knew he'd caged this beautiful swan— and it was time to truly set her free. He turned and left.

CHAPTER EIGHTEEN

LAUREL AWOKE AFTER a restless night, surprised she'd finally dozed off. She'd stayed at the garden party until it ended and then accompanied Aunt Constance and Hannah back to the townhouse. Pleading a headache, she'd retreated to her room and remained in it the rest of the evening. She'd sat in a chair for a long time, watching the door that led to her dressing room, wondering if Anthony might come through it.

He hadn't.

She'd finally heard noise in the hall and slipped from the chair. Opening the door a few inches, she could hear him stumbling along, bumping into the walls. She waited half an hour and then tread softly through her dressing room and his, opening the door to his bedchamber. She found him sprawled across his bed, his clothes askew, reeking of alcohol. Disgusted, she returned to her room and went to bed, though sleep evaded her.

She'd never been more miserable. Not even when threatened by Julius Farmon. She'd found a way to escape Farmon.

She was linked to Anthony for life.

Divorce was unheard of among the *ton*. It was too late for an annulment. She might already be carrying their child. A child made in passion but one whose parents thoroughly hated each other. No, that wasn't true. He might loathe her but she didn't feel the same way, despite the fact they seemed to argue more than anything else.

Had she really done something wrong by wanting to learn about boxing? She supposed in his eyes, she had. He had been raised under an entirely different set of rules from her. Attended an all-male school. Then he'd gone into the military and had been thrust into the midst of war, where each day might have been his last. He was used to the company of men. She must seem like some foreign creature to him, especially since she wasn't of his social class. For God's sake, he was a bloody duke! She was an illegitimate working-class girl, a pretender in her fine gowns and jewels. She might be the darling of the *ton* now but society was fickle.

Laurel dressed on her own, not wishing to rouse Retta. She decided to apologize to her husband. Cutting through their joined rooms, she reached his bedchamber door and knocked. No response. She knocked again. Still nothing. Pushing open the door, she found his bed empty and wondered if he'd arisen to go for an early morning ride. She went to the window and saw him entering the stables.

Hurrying from his room, she went down the flights of stairs and out of the house. When she reached the stables, she was met by Tam.

"If you're looking for His Grace, you just missed him."

"Oh." She deflated, gloom settling over her. As she turned back toward the house, the groom asked, "Did you come to see your gift, Your Grace?"

Laurel wheeled. "What gift?"

"The horse His Grace bought for you," the man replied. "His Grace said he'd gotten it for you as a wedding gift. Her name's Clio. She's a right beauty."

Stunned, she asked, "May I see her?"

Tam led her to a stall and Laurel saw a light gray horse standing there. She was about fifteen hands high and had beautiful lines and intelligent eyes.

"She's gorgeous."

"She is indeed. His Grace bought her at Tattersall's yesterday. Said you wouldn't have time to ride her because the two of you had a garden party to attend but he was excited for you to see her."

The groom's words brought a world of hurt to Laurel. Anthony had bought her this mount as a wedding gift. He'd come in yesterday ready to share Clio with her, only to be disappointed by her un-duchess-like behavior. They'd argued and she'd left the house, attending the party without him. No wonder he'd gone out drinking. He had an unmanageable, unladylike, ungrateful wife. She determined that somehow she would make it up to him.

"Did His Grace go riding in the park?"

"I assume so. He favors Rotten Row this time of day."

"Please saddle Clio. I wish to go find him."

"Yes, Your Grace."

Tam worked quickly and led the horse from the stables. "Wait here. I'll saddle a horse and come with you."

He went back into the stable but Laurel didn't have the patience to wait. She needed to see Anthony now. Leading Clio to the mounting block, she stroked the horse's neck.

"We're going to go find my husband, Clio. I'm so glad to have you, my sweet girl. Let's go see Anthony."

With that, she climbed onto the block and mounted the horse, taking off quickly. Clio had a smooth gait and she reached the park in no time. At this early hour, it was deserted.

She went to Rotten Row and saw her husband riding in the distance. Her heart pounded as she watched him, man and beast seemingly one. Bucephalus galloped toward her and as they approached, she could see Anthony's coattails flying. He spied her and came to an abrupt halt. He was still too far away for her to see his face clearly so Laurel nudged Clio and cantered toward them.

When she reached them, she pulled up on the reins and moved to the ground. He did likewise, coming to stand before her. His eyes were bloodshot. Stubble covered his face. His hair needed combing.

He was still the most handsome man she knew.

Suddenly, it struck Laurel that she had gone and done the unthinkable.

She had fallen in love with her husband.

Her throat thickened. It was the last thing she'd expected. She'd never even thought it a possibility. But standing here in front of him, she knew beyond a doubt that she loved this man, warts and all.

"I've totally mucked up things," she said, her words tumbling out in a rush. "I don't want it to be like this between us. I didn't mean to be nosy. I can be what you want. I will learn to act like a duchess should." Tears welled in her eyes. "Just . . . please . . . promise you'll give me another chance. I won't invade your personal life again. I'll respect your privacy. I want things to be better between us."

His hands cupped her face, his thumbs wiping away her tears. "I didn't mean to box you in. I don't want to force you to be someone you aren't."

"I know you never wanted to marry me, Anthony. That you only did so because society expected it. I'm sorry you're stuck with me. I promise I'll be whoever you want me to be. Just let me in a little bit every now and then."

He pressed a soft kiss on her brow. "I did want to marry you, Laurel. It may not have seemed so. You are unlike any woman I have ever known. I don't want you to be someone you're not. I want you to be Laurel. My duchess. I'm sorry my temper got the best of me."

"I have a temper, as well," she said ruefully. "I say things I don't mean. I strike out and try to hurt others—hurt you—when I'm angry."

"It seems I do the same," he said softly. "I am sorry I hurt you."

"I'm sorry, too."

He kissed her. Not in passion but sweetly. As an apology. Laurel hoped it would signal a new beginning between them.

"I love Clio," she told him when he broke the kiss. "I've never had anything so grand. I never will."

Anthony gave her an odd look. "What about the diamonds you received last night?"

She shrugged. "They're very lovely. But I prefer my horse."

He kissed her again with enthusiasm. "We should go home, Duchess."

It gave her a thrill to hear him call her that. Jeremy addressed Catherine the same way sometimes, especially when he seemed tender toward her.

"I would like that, Duke," she replied.

He lifted her into the saddle and mounted Bucephalus. They cantered home and left their horses with Tam. Anthony threaded his fingers through hers and she felt closer to him than she had for several days.

Without a word, he led her to his bedchamber—and locked the door.

Slowly, he undressed her, kissing her with each piece he removed. Then he made love to her thoroughly, leaving no part of her untouched.

Lying in his arms afterward, she said, "I feel like a goddess who has been worshipped by a god."

He brought their joined hands to his lips and pressed a kiss against her fingers.

"I promise to be a better husband to you, Laurel. I may not always succeed but I will give it my best effort."

"I'll do the same." She kissed his hand. "It's good to see you smile, Anthony. You don't do it very often."

His eyes darkened. "Then why don't you give me something to smile about?"

ANTHONY THOUGHT IF they could only spend the rest of the marriage in bed that they would have no problems. Unfortunately, there was more to life than exploring the sweet curves of his beautiful duchess.

He'd gone to his room and summoned Monkton. Though the valet never said a word, he had a knowing look in his eye. It didn't matter. Anthony didn't care if the entire household knew what he and Laurel had been up to.

After bathing and dressing, he went downstairs. His solicitor would be arriving soon and he wanted to be prepared for their meeting. As he sifted through papers on his desk, he felt the air of the room change and looked up to find Laurel at the door.

"Come in," he told her. "I'm preparing for a visit from my London solicitor."

"Will you be long?" she asked.

"A few hours. Possibly more."

"Do you remember that my family is coming for tea this after-noon?"

He hadn't and was reluctant to be around so many boisterous St. Clairs.

"I have a good bit to do, Laurel. I sadly neglected my duties as Duke of Linfield when I first returned from the war. Now that I have a wife and a family to consider, I am much more aware of my responsi-bilities and need to pay attention to them."

She approached him, her emerald eyes reflective. "Family is very important to me, Anthony."

"It's never been to me," he said, regretting how harsh the words came out. "I'm sorry. I do like Aunt Constance. I tolerate my half-sister. She's a bit of a featherhead, though."

Laurel's eyes flashed and he wondered if her acknowledged temper would rear its ugly head. "Hannah is your sister. You're to quit all this blasted nonsense about her being a half-sister."

Her cursing shouldn't have surprised him. "Well, she is. I can't change the fact that the duke married again and had another child by a woman I never met. I only laid eyes on Hannah for the first time a couple of weeks ago."

"And whose fault was that?" she asked testily.

"Mine," he admitted.

"I am a bastard half-sister to Jeremy, Rachel, and Luke—yet they have openly embraced both Hudson and me. Did you know the three of them all have different mothers and they are all half-siblings? That the man who raped my mother wed three women?"

Anthony rose and took her hands in his. "I didn't know your mother was attacked."

"Oh, you thought Everton had taken her as a mistress? No. He brutalized her in the dress shop she worked in while his mistress was being fitted for a new gown at his expense. Mama was sixteen, Anthony. Younger than Hannah."

He squeezed her hands. Words were beyond him.

"The St. Clairs accept me as one of them. The least you could do is accept Hannah. She is a very sweet girl. A little talkative but she has a heart of gold and worships the ground you walk on."

"I resolve I will refer to her in the future as my sister. You have my solemn promise." It was the least he could do and would make both Laurel and Hannah happy.

"Good. I'll ask again—will you come to tea? I want everyone to get to know you and you to know them," she pleaded. "Just because family hasn't been important to you in the past does not mean it has to remain that way. You can change. Our children will be our family and I know you will love them. They will want to spend time with their aunts and uncles and cousins. Why, there already are so many little cousins for them to play with as it is." She paused. "Please. You need to be present when we have children. Focus on them. Listen to them. Play with them."

Anthony thought of how his father had done none of those things for him and wondered if he could actually be the kind of father Laurel desired him to be.

"I'll be at tea," he promised.

Laurel kissed him. "Oh, thank you. I'll leave now so you can work."

He watched her go and thought how simply by agreeing to attend an hour-long tea how much he had pleased her. He needed to do little things such as this more often.

His solicitor arrived and they had their heads together for several hours, making plans and discussing the business scene in London and beyond. The man recommended hiring a business manager who would help Anthony select the best investments and he decided he would speak to Everton about it at tea today.

At the appropriate time, he made his way to the drawing room and found it filled with people, including his aunt and sister. He watched Hannah for a moment. She was talking animatedly with the Duchess of Everton and he thought perhaps he'd been too harsh in his assessment of her. She favored her father a great deal, which had probably prejudiced him against her. He vowed to clear the slate and behave in a more brotherly fashion.

Laurel called a greeting to him and the others responded as he joined them. The maids rolled in three teacarts to feed such a large group. The women began talking about fashions they'd seen this Season, which led the men to a conversation of their own. He didn't know Alford or Merrick, other than being introduced to them at the wedding breakfast. He discovered both men were intelligent and clever. Merrick, in particular, had a wicked sense of humor. Anthony asked Everton who served as his business manager and the four men engaged in a long discussion on investment opportunities available. Everton invited Anthony to White's to meet a few other peers who might have some insight regarding good investments and Anthony agreed to do so tomorrow afternoon.

By then, the women claimed their attention again. Anthony

learned a great deal in a short time about Laurel's family. The group spent several minutes discussing the Duchess of Everton's latest book and her upcoming appearance and book signing at Lady Mayfield's bookstore. He began asking questions and discovered how long she'd been writing and how the proceeds were given to various charitable organizations, orphanages receiving the bulk. Laurel asked the names of the orphanages and learned that one recently added to Catherine's list was in her former neighborhood.

"Do you ever visit them, Catherine," his wife asked, "or do you merely hand over the funds?"

"I visit as often as I can," the duchess said. "I've started bringing Jenny with me. When the other children are older, I'll allow them to come along, as well. I think it's important for them to understand how privileged their upbringing is and how they should do everything in their power to help others."

"The next time you go to the one I'm familiar with, please allow me to accompany you," Laurel said. "I've wanted to do something for the people in the area I grew up in."

"I'd be happy to have your company," the duchess said. "In fact, I am encouraging others to lend their patronage to various orphanages. The need is so great. Since you are familiar with the vicinity and I have only visited there twice, you might consider throwing your full support behind it and help raise funds for that particular place."

Cor, the matriarch of the St. Clair family, said, "It's good to find something you love to do, Laurel. As a duchess, you will wield great power and influence in society. Take your time. You'll find the right projects to devote yourself to."

"I certainly want to work with this particular orphanage," Laurel said. "Having grown up nearby, I feel strongly about helping those who live where I came from."

"I'm delighted to hear that, Laurel," the duchess said. "Your personal connection will make a huge difference."

Finally, Everton said, "We must be getting home. We like to spend time in the nursery before we head out for the evening. Frankly, I'm already tired of all the social events." He smiled at his wife. "I cannot wait to get back to Eversleigh so I can have you and the children all to myself." He took her hand and kissed it tenderly.

Anthony stiffened. He was unused to any kind of affection, much less blatant affection in public. It wasn't the done thing.

"Catherine tells her stories to the children," Laurel said to him, distracting him from seeing the hungry look in Everton's eyes. "Once she's practiced on them, she finally commits the story to paper."

Everton rose, pulling his wife to her feet. "Perhaps we can skip tonight's ball, Duchess. We could dance in our bedroom instead." His eyes spoke of more than dancing.

Merrick chuckled and said gruffly, "You think you love your wife more than the rest of us, don't you, Everton?" With that, the marquess pulled his wife to him and kissed her in front of all of them.

Alford turned to Anthony, shaking his head. "It's a competition between them. You'll have to learn to keep up, Linfield." He took Lady Alford's hand and turned it over, kissing her palm. "Shall we go home, love? I will put all these men to shame."

Anthony turned and saw Laurel's cheeks were bright red. He felt helpless, not knowing how to respond to the actions of these three men.

As everyone began saying their goodbyes, the dowager duchess stepped toward him and said, "I know yours wasn't a love match, Linfield, but I hope you'll learn to cherish my granddaughter."

With that, the grand dame swept from the room, followed by all the St. Clairs and their spouses. He saw mirth in Aunt Constance's eyes and wonder in Hannah's.

Laurel slipped her arm through his. "Don't worry, Anthony. I'm not asking you to change that much," she said lightly and then released him, following their guests from the drawing room in order to see them out.

He trailed after everyone at a distance. Surprisingly, he had enjoyed the teatime more than he could have expected and would gladly entertain Laurel's relatives in the future. The very closeness between the husbands and wives, though, gave him pause. Laurel had agreed that love would have nothing to do with their union. Somehow, though, Anthony felt they were both missing out. A twinge of jealousy rippled through him.

Could he ever shutter the darkness within him and find love with his wife?

CHAPTER NINETEEN

Laurel joined Catherine in the Everton ducal carriage.

"I'm so glad you could come with me today," her sister-in-law said. She indicated a large stack of boxes on the coach floor. "I stopped by Evie's and picked up scones for the children."

Laurel had eaten scones a few days ago when she and Anthony had attended Catherine's reading.

"Having tried Mrs. Stinch's and Mrs. Baker's baked goods recently, I can vouch that the children will be delighted with these treats." She chuckled. "And I saw Luke took several with him."

Her brother had come in to London for the day to support Catherine and make sure everything ran smoothly at the bookstore reading. Everyone had eagerly asked about Caroline's condition. Luke had told them they were enjoying the last bit of peace and quiet before the storm of the new baby's cries filled the halls.

"He does relish eating anything the two women make," Catherine agreed.

"He's going to make a wonderful father," Laurel said.

"I believe he will. Who would have guessed London's biggest rogue would make one of its best husbands and fathers?"

"Luke . . . was a rogue?" she asked, startled by the comment.

"Oh, don't get me wrong. I have always adored Luke. From the moment we met, he was charming and amiable. But yes, he left a string of broken hearts and had a bevy of mistresses." Catherine smiled. "It merely took the right woman coming along to settle him down. They do say reformed rakes make the best husbands."

"He certainly adores Caroline."

"He does. I am glad he was able to change and grow into the man we now know."

Laurel wondered if Luke could change so much, could Anthony do the same?

They arrived at the orphanage she had walked past so many times over the years. As she stood on the sidewalk, she looked at the neighborhood she'd grown up in with new eyes. It hadn't been so long since she'd left here yet it seemed ages ago. Despite its short distance from Mayfair, these streets were a different world from the one she now inhabited. She determined to use her position to do all she could for its residents, especially the children she would soon meet.

They entered, one footman carrying the boxes of scones and another loaded with something unknown to her. Laurel asked what they contained.

"Those are copies of my latest book," Catherine explained. "Books are a precious commodity. When I come to the various places and read my work to the children, I give them a copy to call their own. I've brought dolls and the like in the past wherever I go but the children seem to appreciate books most of all."

"Good morning, Your Grace."

Laurel turned and saw a woman approaching, her brown hair starting to turn to gray. She looked to be about forty years of age and had a kind face.

"Mrs. Kinnon, it's a pleasure to see you again. May I introduce to you my sister-in-law, the Duchess of Linfield."

Laurel offered the woman her hand, seeing the surprise that brought.

"It's very nice to meet you, Your Grace."

"Mrs. Kinnon runs the house," Catherine explained. "I've brought scones for the children. Perhaps you could show the duchess around while I distribute them."

"Very good, Your Grace."

Laurel was led on a tour of the building. There were separate dormitory rooms for boys and girls and a large room with numerous cribs for babies. She went to one and leaned over, seeing a baby sleeping peacefully.

"They come to you this young?" she asked.

"All ages do. The babies are found on our doorstep. Sometimes with a note revealing their name but more often not. Mothers too young or too poor and desperate to raise them."

Next, she saw the schoolrooms. Mrs. Kinnon told Laurel that it was easier to educate the children on the property. When sent to a public school, the orphans were often belittled and made fun of. Too many fights had occurred and too many never wanted to return so keeping the orphans in one place for their schooling made the most sense. She met the three teachers, all young and earnest. Two had grown up in this very orphanage. Last, she saw a large playroom.

"This space is new," Mrs. Kinnon said with pride. "Her Grace insisted that play is important for young children. All the toys, books, and puzzles you see come from the Duke and Duchess of Everton."

"I grew up in this neighborhood," Laurel revealed.

Mrs. Kinnon's eyes grew wide. "You did?"

"Yes. I last worked at Mr. Cole's chandlery. I believe it's been purchased now by Mr. Farmon."

"Then . . . how . . ." the woman's voice trailed off.

"How did I become a duchess?" Laurel smiled. "It is a long story but now that I'm in a position to help others, I will do what I can for your orphanage, Mrs. Kinnon. The Duchess of Everton has said that you are looking for a new patron. I would like me and my husband to step into that role if you'll allow us to do so."

"Thank you, Your Grace. Thank you so much. We would be delighted to have you work with us."

They returned to a dining hall, where Catherine sat with about eighty children.

"We enjoyed the scones, Your Grace," Laurel overheard a young girl tell Catherine.

"I'm very glad you did." She patted the girl's cheek and then looked out across the room. "How would you like to hear a story?"

The children cheered and clapped.

"I brought someone with me today that wanted to meet you. This is the Duchess of Linfield. She will be spending time visiting with you."

"Hello, Your Grace," echoed throughout the room.

As all eyes turned to her, Laurel felt her cheeks grow warm. A boy near her tugged on her gown and asked, "Are you going to read to us, Your Grace?"

"No, that is for the Duchess of Everton to do."

"I think that's a lovely idea," Catherine said. "How many would like to hear my sister-in-law read to you?"

More cheers erupted and someone asked, "What's a sister-in-law?"

"Her Grace is a sister to my husband. That makes her a sister-in-law to me." Catherine smiled. "Honestly, though, we feel like true sisters." She held out her hand and Laurel took it. Catherine squeezed it encouragingly and said quietly, "Go ahead. Read to them. They'll love it."

Catherine turned back to the children. "I've brought the book the duchess will read to you. Let's make sure everyone gets one and then you can follow along."

The footmen helped distribute books to all the children and then they gathered on the floor, surrounding Laurel. She remembered how Catherine had used different voices for the various characters and tried her hand at it. Although not quite as successful as the author when she read her own work, Laurel thought she did a credible job by the time she finished. She and Catherine then circulated through the crowd, talking to individual children.

Mrs. Kinnon finally appeared and said it was time for classes to begin. Though a few groans were heard, the orphans stood and began to file from the room. Each child stopped and thanked both her and Catherine for coming and for bringing the scones and books. By the time the last one left the room, Laurel was overcome with emotion.

"Thank you again so much, Your Grace," Mrs. Kinnon said. "The children enjoyed your visit today." She turned to Laurel. "I look forward to seeing you on a regular basis, Your Grace."

"I look forward to visiting often—and bringing my husband with me."

At least she hoped Anthony would want to come. Laurel had a feeling that this orphanage would become a huge part of her life. She wanted to share the experience with Anthony.

As she and Catherine left the building, a deep sense of satisfaction filled Laurel. She turned in a circle, taking in the surrounding area, knowing she would be back and that she had the means to make a difference in so many lives. A footman handed them into the carriage and they talked about the children the entire way home.

JULIUS FARMON FROZE in his tracks.

The little bitch was back.

He'd looked for Laurel Wright everywhere after she'd attacked him, putting out the word that no one was to hire her. He'd sent Braxton to the room the three Wrights lived in, tripling their rent. Julius knew if he forced her into desperation, she would be his.

Then she'd vanished. Her mother died and the next time Braxton went to carry through with his boss' threats, both Laurel and her brother had disappeared. He'd sent word through his network to find her and her brother. One man thought they were living at a boardinghouse several miles away but by the time Julius arrived, they were gone. No forwarding address. The woman who owned the place mentioned something about the pair leaving in a grand carriage but she slurred her words and was already deep into her cups by ten in the morning so he hadn't lent any credence to what she said.

But Laurel had just gotten into a fancy coach. Rage surged through him. She'd turned him down flat, saying she wasn't that kind of woman, yet here she was riding in a fine carriage. A ducal one. He saw the crest on the door as it passed by him. She was a fancy woman now. Mistress to a man with a lofty title. Wearing fine clothes. Laurel Wright had thought herself too good to be the mistress of Julius Farmon and had simply sold herself to a higher bidder.

He would make her sorry for rejecting him. Revenge was second nature to him.

Turning to Braxton, his shadow, he asked, "Did you see her? The Wright girl?"

His henchman nodded.

"Go inside that orphanage. Find out why she was there," he barked. "Whose coach she rode in. The name of her protector. I'll be back at my office."

Braxton strode toward the building as Julius walked the two blocks to a saloon he owned, a brothel on the floor above. He entered and went to the large room in the back that served as the core of his enterprises. He sat behind the desk and opened the bottom drawer, pulling out a bottle of whisky. He poured three fingers into a glass and knocked it back then poured more. This time, he sipped.

And waited.

More than four hours later, Braxton returned. He took a seat in front of the desk.

"Well?" he demanded. "Why the bloody hell did it take you so long?"

"I had other stops to make after I left the orphanage. That was the tip of the iceberg. You won't like it, Boss."

"I don't have to like it," Julius snapped. "Give me what you learned."

Braxton crossed one ankle over his knee. "She's not Laurel Wright anymore."

"I figured she had changed her name. That's what made it harder to track her," he complained.

"She changed her name because she got married."

"What?" he exclaimed.

"She's now the Duchess of Linfield," Braxton revealed. "She's also the half-sister of another duke."

Julius looked at his underling, clenching his jaw.

"Apparently, she is a St. Clair."

He knew the name. All of London did. Jeremy St. Clair, Duke of Everton, had inherited little more than a title, thanks to his father's gambling most of the family fortune away. The new duke had, through cunning and outrageous investments, not only recouped the losses but increased the family's coffers tenfold. Julius had seen the man once and suddenly realized that Laurel Wright had the same uncanny green eyes.

"She's a bastard. We all knew that," Braxton continued. "Her and her twin. Somehow, she made the connection that she was a St. Clair and the family took her in. She wed the Duke of Linfield a few weeks ago."

"That was fast work."

"Apparently, there was some hint of scandal and the duke had to marry her quickly by special license."

Julius knew the truth. Laurel Wright had seen an opportunity and spread her legs to ensnare a man with a lofty title.

"Did you learn anything about him—the husband?"

"He's a war hero. Served directly under Wellington. He's wealthy.

Very wealthy."

An idea began forming in Julius' mind. He raised his hand to keep Braxton quiet while he thought.

Laurel Wright was now a wealthy woman. He would have her snatched up and held for ransom. A duke would pay a fortune for the return of his wife, especially if Julius told him if he didn't, she would be raped repeatedly before being left on Linfield's doorstep—and that he'd make sure all of London knew she'd been sullied. This duke might not care much for a woman who'd forced him into marriage but Linfield would care for his reputation. No man of the *ton* would want Polite Society to know about the atrocities that had happened to his wife.

Of course, Julius had no intentions of returning Laurel to her duke. He would collect the hefty ransom, enough so that he'd never have to work a day in his life again. He'd also use Laurel up and then sell her to a brothel. Or kill her. It didn't matter. What was important was she would be at his mercy. He would collect the debt she owed him.

Julius smiled. "Here's what we're going to do."

CHAPTER TWENTY

ONKTON ASSESSED ANTHONY and readjusted his cravat, nodding with satisfaction.

"You are happy tonight, Your Grace?" the valet asked.

The servant's question took Anthony aback. Monkton rarely spoke, unless he was discussing members of the *ton*, and the man never asked anything personal of Anthony.

"I am," he admitted. "Very much so."

"Her Grace seems very happy these days, as well," Monkton noted.

"I hope she is."

For two weeks, he had gotten along splendidly with his duchess. They hadn't argued once. He had done small things that he thought would please her. Taken her riding every morning. Brought her flowers once. Took her to her first opera. Complimented her gowns. It was funny how making an effort to be pleasant to his wife had buoyed his own spirits. He seemed to get more accomplished regarding business and his holdings. He didn't mind going to social engagements as much. He even believed he had more energy—despite the lack of sleep. He'd made love to Laurel every night, learning more of what pleased her. Making her happy, in and out of bed, had been a goal worth setting and more easily accomplished than he could have imagined.

He also had grown protective of Hannah. Ever since he saw her for the eager, sweet girl that she was and not an extension of her father, he'd grown fonder of her. She had picked up on the difference in his attitude and was effervescent and charming with him. Anthony had even begun looking into a few of the young bachelors who seemed most interested in her, making subtle inquiries into the gentlemen and their backgrounds. Her father had left Hannah a substantial dowry, as befitted the daughter of a duke. Anthony didn't want some penniless suitor sweeping her off her feet simply to get his hands on that dowry. He wanted Hannah to find lasting happiness.

He cut through the rooms that connected his to Laurel's and entered. She sat in front of a mirror and watched as Retta styled her hair. Tonight, the black mane was swept high on her head with small tendrils floating along the sides. Her gown was a rich red, the neckline low, revealing a creamy expanse of skin. His eyes dropped to the rounded tops of her breasts.

"That will be all, Retta," she told the maid, who quickly exited the room.

Anthony went and placed a hand on her bare shoulder, sliding his thumb back and forth. She shivered. He lowered his lips to her nape and nibbled on it, causing her to giggle. He slid his hand from her shoulder to her chin, holding it and then turning her head to the side so he could feast upon her neck. Her sigh was the sweetest sound he'd heard all day.

"You haven't any jewels on yet," he noted, his gaze holding hers in the mirror.

"I couldn't decide if the diamonds or pearls would look best. Shall I try on each and let you decide?"

"I prefer these."

He pulled his other hand from where it rested behind his back and placed the case on the dressing table in front of her. Anthony had already discussed with Retta what Laurel would wear tonight and had made the appropriate choice from the safe.

"What? Another gift?"

"Open it."

She lowered her eyes and hesitated for a moment, then lifted the lid. He looked over her shoulder at the ruby necklace and earrings resting against the dark blue velvet.

Laurel shook her head. "They're too much. You give me far too much."

He placed his hands on her shoulders. "You give me more in return." His lips caressed the side of her throat. He longed to cup her breasts but that would lead to him undressing her. As it was, Hannah and Aunt Constance probably waited for them downstairs.

Reaching out, he lifted the necklace and placed the rubies about her neck. They were the exact shade of her dress, a perfect match.

"Put on the earrings," he urged. "My fingers aren't as nimble as yours."

She lifted one to her earlobe and snorted. "Your fingers are quite nimble, Your Grace. I remember them being so only last night."

He thought of where he had put his fingers and swallowed. "Maybe I can place them in the same places tonight."

Her eyes shone. "You can try," she said, grinning at him.

Anthony pulled her to her feet and kissed her hard. As he'd feared, Laurel had become a drug he was addicted to. What had changed is he no longer cared if she knew. His desire for her was too great.

He broke the kiss. "One earring won't do, Duchess. You better put on the other one. Unless you are planning to start a new trend of wearing only one earring to balls."

She laughed throatily and attached the other to her earlobe. He kissed her lightly.

"There. You are perfect now."

Escorting her downstairs, he saw Hannah waiting and asked, "Where is Aunt Constance?"

"I'm here, my darlings." The older woman hurried down the

stairs. "Oh, my. Those rubies are exquisite, Laurel. They look as if they were made for you."

The younger women turned to go. Aunt Constance touched Anthony's arm, holding him back. "Well done, Anthony. Very well done."

The carriage ride to Lord and Lady Prattford's seemed to take forever. Traffic was heavier than usual. Hannah constantly tapped her foot. At least Anthony knew why. Laurel had told him they were to meet a certain Lord Brixley tonight. Laurel had already met the viscount at tea when he'd visited—twice. Tonight, though, Brixley had to pass inspection from Anthony.

They finally arrived and joined the crush of people entering the townhouse. After interminable minutes in the receiving line, Hannah was off with her friends. He and Laurel joined Lord and Lady Alford. The two women immediately began talking about the latest novel their book club would discuss next week. He and Alford talked boxing and the latest illegal match to be held outside London in two days' time. Though women weren't supposed to attend boxing matches, they did so all the time. Because of that, Anthony was considering asking Laurel if she wished to go with him. The carriage ride would be at least two hours to get there.

A lot of kissing could occur in two hours.

"Hannah wishes for us to join her," Laurel said.

"How do you know that?" he asked. "I've kept my eyes on her the entire time Alford and I have been talking."

"It's the fan," the earl told him. "Women send messages all the time using their fans."

"They do?" Anthony asked, perplexed.

"Clearly, you're clueless, Linfield," Alford said, laughing.

"I must be. Are we to rescue Hannah?" he asked his wife as they started in his sister's direction.

"No. Quite the opposite. She wants us to meet Brixley."

They arrived and the viscount greeted Laurel, kissing her hand. "You are a vision of loveliness tonight, Your Grace."

"Thank you, Lord Brixley. May I introduce my husband, the Duke of Linfield?"

The two men eyed each other with interest as they shook hands.

"I hear you've called upon my sister," he said gruffly.

"Yes, Your Grace. Lady Hannah is a remarkable young woman."

"I agree."

Anthony noticed the pleased look on both Hannah's and Laurel's faces and said, "Do you like horses, Brixley?"

"I do, Your Grace. I have just purchased a new set to pull my curricle."

"Hmm. Why don't you bring them around tomorrow afternoon? I can see them and you may stay for tea."

Brixley beamed. "Would it be possible after tea to take Lady Hannah riding in the park?"

"I'll think about it," he said, not wanting to make things too easy for this suitor.

They spoke a few more minutes and then the musicians began tuning their instruments.

Brixley said, "I will see you for the supper dance, my lady," and bowed to Hannah.

The moment Brixley was out of earshot, Anthony asked his sister, "Do you like this one? Better than any of the others?"

Hannah's eyes shone. "I do, Anthony. Very much."

"Then you may ride with him in the park tomorrow. Only don't tell him tonight. Let him keep wondering."

"Isn't that a little cruel?" Laurel asked, though she failed to hide her mirth.

"No, Anthony is right," Hannah said. "Let Brixley work for me."

A gentleman came and claimed Hannah for the first dance and led her away.

"Has your first dance been taken?" he asked his wife.

"None have, Your Grace," she replied, her smile flirtatious now.

"Then I suppose I can have them all."

"That's not really—"

"Remember, Duchess, that I am a duke. If I want to dance with my wife once, thrice, or twenty times tonight, I will do as I please."

Laughter bubbled up from her. "Yes, Duke. Whatever you say."

He didn't take every dance, knowing it wouldn't be fair to monopolize her in such a manner. Anthony did dance several times with her, though. At one point, he watched her being twirled about on the dance floor. His aunt joined him.

"You've been quite kind to Hannah recently."

"I feel protective of my sister," he said, his eyes never leaving his wife. "I want her to make a good match. This Brixley fellow seems a decent sort."

"He is." She paused. "Family seems to be growing on you, Anthony."

He faced her. "Laurel is growing on me."

Anthony went to the card room for a while and then decided to return to the ballroom and dance again with his duchess. He spotted her and immediately knew something was wrong. She was surrounded by several older women. Two were the nosy pair who had caught them kissing on the terrace that night at Everton's. From the look on Laurel's face and the color in her cheeks, the women were on the attack.

As he reached them, his wife said, "You are cruel, vindictive women. My husband is the very best of men."

"He was forced to wed you," one said. "I'm sure he wasn't pleased being stuck with a bastard, half-sister to Everton when he could have done much better."

Fury filled him. He knew he couldn't strike a lady but he had to rescue Laurel and put an end to this attack.

"Actually, Linfield is most pleased with me," Laurel said calmly. "And I with him. You're wrong about him, Lady Chatham. My husband is not cold. He is a warm, kindhearted man. One whom I am proud to be a wife to. He is a war hero—but he's also my hero. He rescued me when I didn't know I even needed rescuing."

Anthony stepped to her and slipped his arm about her waist. "There you are, my love. Are you ready to leave?" He looked deep into her eyes, letting her know he had overheard what had been said.

"Yes," she said, her head high.

"Good. Because I cannot wait to have you in my bed."

The women in the circle audibly gasped, which is exactly the reaction he had wanted from them. Anthony tore his eyes from Laurel and gazed about the circle.

"This is the last time any of you will ever address my duchess. You are nothing more than a bunch of spiteful, malevolent, dried-up gossips, spreading your malicious rumors. I've never seen a more savage, heartless, unkind group of women in my entire life."

The women's fear was obvious from the look of terror on their faces as they absorbed his words.

"As the Duke of Linfield, I wield power you can only begin to imagine. As of this moment, I will never recognize any of you. Neither will anyone in my family, as well as the Duke of Everton's, my wife's family. You officially have received my cut direct. I warn you—never cross my path or that of my duchess. If you do, you will regret it. If I hear that even one of you have mentioned my wife's name to someone else, I will destroy not only that person and her family—but all those present here and those families."

Anthony saw the group of ruthless biddies quaked in fear.

Then calmly, he added, "I'm sorry to take my duchess away from you, ladies. I simply cannot get enough of this woman. She has my heart and soul."

Briefly, he touched his mouth to hers, knowing it would cause a flurry of gossip.

Without another word, he led her away. He signaled to his aunt and she touched Hannah's shoulder and began crossing the ballroom to join them.

"You have started a new scandal, Anthony," Laurel said quietly.

"You were defending me. Rather nobly. It was the least I could do. Lady Chatham is a horrible person. She needed to be put in her place." He grinned. "Besides, I am glad I married you." Raising her hand, he kissed it as Aunt Constance and Hannah joined them.

Anthony escorted the trio to the carriage. Hannah talked endlessly but it didn't seem to bother Anthony as it had before.

They arrived at home and he accompanied Laurel to her room.

"Fifteen minutes and I will join you," he said, raising her gloved hand and brushing a kiss upon it.

Monkton undressed him and Anthony pulled on his dressing gown, his heart beating rapidly. He made his way to Laurel's room. He'd come to a decision.

Anthony only hoped it was the right one.

Laurel was seated as Retta brushed her hair. He took the brush and said, "I'll finish."

He started at her image in the mirror and pulled the brush through the thick, dark locks. Over and over, he ran the brush through her hair. She closed her eyes and he drank her in.

"Don't stop," she murmured. "It feels too good."

Anthony placed the brush on the table. "There are things that feel even better." He came to stand so close that his body touched hers. He grasped her shoulders lightly and then ran his palms down her chest, cupping her breasts as he kissed her neck.

"Mmm. Maybe you're right."

"I'm always right, Duchess. I'm the Duke of Linfield."

He stroked and kneaded her breasts, tweaking her nipples, sending shivers through her. He slid his hands lower and untied the knot of her dressing gown, parting it and slipping it from her shoulders. He began fondling her breasts again, this time, slipping his hands inside the night rail's neckline. The smoothness of her skin felt so right under his callused fingertips. He pinched her nipples slightly and she moaned. He continued rolling them and her hips began to move.

"I believe you said something about nimble fingers," he murmured into her ear.

"Oh, yes," she sighed.

Anthony brought Laurel to her feet and turned her, kissing her deeply. He would never tire of the taste of her. He backed her up slowly until they came to the bed and she fell backwards, her legs dangling. Just how he wanted her.

He knelt, pushing the night rail up to her waist and then parted her thighs. He stroked her core, finding her already wet for him. Fighting the urge to unbutton his fall and plunge into her, he kept petting her. She began whimpering. He inserted a finger and teased her bud. It didn't take long before she writhed on the bed. Her release came quickly.

He allowed her to calm and then began stroking her again. Those little sounds in the back of her throat thrilled him. He moved between her legs, holding her thighs in place and touched his tongue to her.

"Anthony!"

He looked up. Laurel had raised up on her elbows, her eyes wide.

"My fingers aren't the only nimble thing I possess."

With that, he touched his mouth to her and began kissing and nibbling at her sex. He felt how stiff she was. Slowly, though, she began to relax. Her hips began moving. He plunged his tongue into her and she cried out. Using his mouth, teeth, and tongue, Anthony brought her to a shattering climax. He kissed his way back up to her mouth and found tears on her cheeks.

Worry filled him. "Are you all right?"

"I . . . am. That was . . ." Her voice trailed off as she panted. After a few breaths, she said, "Wicked. That was very, very wicked, Anthony." Grinning, she added, "And incredibly nimble."

"I'm glad you thought so."

He couldn't wait any longer. While she lay almost paralyzed, he doffed his clothes and swung her legs onto the bed.

"I'm going to love you, Laurel," he said. "As best I can."

He meant the words in two ways. In a physical sense, his body joining with hers.

And emotionally. Letting go and truly giving himself to her.

Anthony made love to Laurel with a renewed sense of urgency. They climaxed together and he fell atop her, burying his face in her abundant hair. She stroked his back, pressing kisses against his throat. He rolled to his side, keeping his arms around her.

"We must talk," he said quietly.

She smiled lazily. "Oh, I think your body did all the talking necessary, Duke."

He brought his hand to her face and smoothed her hair from it.

"My father gave me away when I was eight years old."

Horror filled her face. "Anthony?"

Her palm went to his cheek, caressing it. She didn't ask him anything, for which he was grateful. Gradually, words spilled from him.

"I suppose I was a difficult child. I constantly got into trouble. My mother died giving birth to me. I know Theodore blamed me for her death and I think my father did, as well. Theodore bulled me unmercifully. The duke turned a blind eye to it. He favored his heir and had no use for me."

He smoothed her hair again. "I fought a lot with other boys. I never received any attention at home. Everything was always about Theodore since he was the heir to the dukedom. It's . . . as if I never existed. I was ignored. The longer it went on, the more the anger built within me. Then I used my fists because how could I use words? How could I tell other boys while they talked about their families—and I had none?"

She placed her head against his chest, stroking it lightly. He guessed she knew how hard this was for him and it might be easier for him to speak without seeing the pity in her eyes.

"I used my fists all the time. I didn't have any friends. I was asked to leave two schools because of my violent behavior. At the third school, Ridingham Academy, I was goaded by a boy who said some awful things to me and then blackened my eye. I went berserk, attacking him with all the rage within me. It took two grown men to pull me off him. The duke came and was informed that I could no longer attend school there.

"He told me he had no use for me. That his time would be spent grooming Theodore into the perfect son and heir. He dropped me at Aunt Constance's that day. I never saw him again."

Warm tears covered his chest. Laurel lifted her head, her eyes swimming with them.

"I'm so sorry."

"He abandoned me. Never wrote to me once. The hate I had for him grew and grew until rage was the only emotion I knew. I lied to Aunt Constance as I got older and told her I was taking my holidays with friends when I had none and merely stayed at school. I cut myself off from anything that resembled family." He sighed. "On my eighteenth birthday, a solicitor came to see him. He notified me of a commission being purchased for me by the Duke of Linfield. I went into the military and never looked back."

"Anthony." Laurel kissed his cheek softly. "There are no words I can share that can comfort you." She bit her lip. "I have insisted you spend time with my family. I'm sorry. I never knew how truly awful your childhood was."

"It made me strong. Stronger than all the other men around me, especially officers who came from families who'd coddled them. I displayed no emotion to others. I bottled up the anger which surged through my blood and directed it at the enemy. I had a clear mind and was a brilliant strategist. Wellington saw that in me. He listened to me, more often than not. I was fearless on the battlefield because I didn't care if I lived or died—because I had no one to come home to."

She lay her cheek against his for a long while and then raised her head and looked him in the eye.

"You have me now. I have enough love in my heart to take care of you. I cannot change your past but I can love you now and forever."

He stilled. "You love me?"

"I do," she admitted. "I know I wasn't supposed to. Because of my own childhood and circumstances, I never believed in love. When you were forced to wed me, my head told me it was nothing more than a business arrangement." She smiled. "But somehow you slipped into my heart, Anthony. Yes, I love you. I don't expect you to love me but it doesn't matter. I have so much love for you that I hope I can heal your heart."

"I love you, Laurel."

She shook her head. "No, don't feel you have to echo my words. You desire me. I understand that. Passion doesn't equal love. It doesn't matter. You are a good man, Anthony Godwin. You have been a good husband and will make for an excellent father."

"I haven't always been a good husband."

She smiled wryly. "Well, I haven't been an ideal wife."

He cradled her face. "I am speaking from my heart, Laurel. That black, empty hole that has been there for so long. The one that I thought rendered me dead inside. It's not gone at all. You brought me back to life, sweetheart. I fought hard to push you away and hang on to my anger. Whenever I feared you grew too close to me, I distanced myself from you. I didn't think I was good enough for you. I still feel like a fake. A pretender. I was never meant to be a duke."

"I feel the same. I'm a poor girl from humble means, not some grand duchess. I've never felt good enough to be your wife."

He kissed the tip of her nose. "Oh, we are a pair. We are the Duke and Duchess of Linfield, though. Nothing is going to change that. We might as well enjoy it."

"Is that why you don't wish me to call you Linfield? Because you think of your father when you hear the name?"

He nodded. "Every day I thought of him and my hatred grew. Suddenly, after so many years of my heart and soul being twisted, *I* was Linfield."

"It's true. You are Linfield now but you can be the Linfield you want to be. When others speak of Linfield in society, it will be the kind, generous, wonderful, loving man that you are."

"How did I ever deserve you, my love?" he asked, overcome with emotion.

Laurel smiled. "You comforted a sad young woman with a kiss, never knowing the price you would pay."

"I would pay it ten thousand times over. I love you, Laurel. More than I ever imagined. The emptiness within me has filled with love and light—all because of you."

Anthony made love to his wife tenderly, savoring her. When he finished, he rolled her on her side and nestled her against him, his arms keeping her close.

"Go to sleep, Duchess," he said softly. "When you wake up, I will be here. I will always be here for you."

CHAPTER TWENTY-ONE

L AUREL WOKE.
Anthony was still here . . .

She hadn't dreamed last night. He'd had stayed. All night. He'd told her he loved her. Joy filled her. She never knew such happiness could be possible.

At least she understood him better now. Her childhood may have been difficult but she'd always had her mother's unconditional love. Hudson's, too. Poor Anthony had no one. Even when Aunt Constance had taken him in, he hadn't allowed her to get close to him. He'd held himself apart, thinking he wasn't good enough because his bastard of a father had tossed him aside like rubbish.

Still, he had grown into a good man.

Her man.

He began to stir, his arm tightening about her possessively. His chest pressed into her back. She could feel his manhood beginning to stir as his lips caressed her neck. His hand stroked her belly and went lower. Lower.

"Oh," she murmured.

Her husband made love to her very thoroughly. When he finished, he gathered her against him, his hand absently stroking her back.

"This is a very nice way to start our day," she said.

"Perhaps the Duke and Duchess of Everton have the right idea after all."

Laurel remembered she had told him Jeremy and Catherine slept together in one chamber.

"Would you like to follow their pattern?" he asked. "Turn your bedchamber in a dressing room and storage for your gowns? Then you could share my bed every night." He kissed her. "That would make me happy. Very, very happy."

"I know it is a wife's job to make her husband happy," Laurel teased. "How can I say no?"

He kissed her again. "You can't."

"I would like to redecorate some. It's very dark and gloomy. Don't worry. I won't make it all full of feminine frills. It will still retain a manly look."

"I don't care. I won't be looking at the room. I'll only have eyes for the woman I love."

They kissed again for long minutes and Laurel thought marriage couldn't get any better than this. Her stomach gurgled noisily and his joined in. They laughed and rose.

"We definitely need some breakfast."

She played valet to him and helped him dress and he returned the favor. They went to the breakfast room, their fingers entwined, and she was surprised to see Hannah there. Usually, the girl slept until noon and like Aunt Constance, had a tray in her room for her first meal of the day.

Immediately, Laurel saw Hannah noticed them holding hands because a smile spread across her face.

Anthony seated Laurel and said, "You're up awfully early. Thinking about Brixley?"

"Yes," Hannah admitted. "I couldn't sleep any longer. I don't know how I'll pass all the hours until teatime."

"Why don't you accompany me to the orphanage?" Laurel suggested. "Catherine and I are going this morning at eleven o'clock. I wanted her to see some of the changes we've made."

"You don't think she'd mind?"

"Not at all. I'd like you to see it." She looked to her husband. "You, too, Anthony."

"I can't today, love. Let me know the next time you're going, though. I'll be happy to see the place with you."

They finished breakfast and Anthony excused himself. He bent and kissed her cheek and took a few steps away. Then he returned and kissed her on the mouth, a lovely, sweet kiss.

"I will see you both at tea with this vexing viscount."

As he left the room, Hannah called out, "Brixley is not vexing at all!"

Laurel laughed. "He doesn't think that. He's teasing you."

"I know," Hannah said with wonder. "I quite like this new Anthony. You were holding hands when you came in, Laurel. And he came back and kissed you. Really kissed you. Does he love you?"

"Yes," she said with confidence. "I also love him. It's the most wonderful, marvelous, amazing feeling in the world."

"I wonder if Brixley might make me that happy," Hannah mused.

"Give him a chance," Laurel said. "If he doesn't, there are many more bachelors available."

They met downstairs at the appointed time and climbed into the carriage that Anthony had thoughtfully left behind for their use. When they arrived at the Everton townhome, Barton admitted them.

"It's wonderful to see you, Your Grace. Lady Hannah. I'm afraid Her Grace will not be available today for your trip to see the orphans. Lady Delia has come down with a fever."

"I'm sorry to hear that," Laurel said. "May we go up to the nursery and see her?"

"She is in Her Grace's sitting room."

"Come along, Hannah," she said.

They went upstairs and found Catherine rocking her daughter. The usually rambunctious Delia was curled up in her mother's arms, sucking on her thumb. Her face was flushed.

"We heard Delia is unwell and just wanted to pop up and see how she is."

Catherine kissed her daughter's forehead. "It's only a slight fever. It's made her grumpy and sluggish. I thought it best to keep her out of the nursery so the others wouldn't be struck with fever, too. I'm sorry I can't go with you to the orphanage today."

"It's quite all right. Hannah will accompany me." Laurel bent and kissed her niece's cheek. "I hope you feel better soon."

She and Hannah returned downstairs and informed the driver of the address. The footman assisted them into the carriage and, before long, they'd arrived. Laurel had told Hannah the orphanage was located in her former neighborhood. She could tell by the look on her friend's face how surprised Hannah was as she took in the surroundings.

"You were very poor, weren't you?"

"We were. But Mama loved Hudson and me so very much."

Seeing her sister-in-law's thoughtful expression, Laurel decided to describe her childhood in greater detail, hoping to educate Hannah and help her understand more why this work was so important.

"I only owned two gowns when I came to the St. Clairs a few months ago, Hannah. Both threadbare. And I only had two because I worked more than one job. When I was younger, I possessed only one. There was no money for more than that. I didn't even own a pair of shoes until I was almost fifteen."

Hannah gasped. "Oh, Laurel, how awful. I've already worn one dress to breakfast and changed into another to come here. I'll wear a third for tea once we arrive home and then don my fourth for tonight's social event. I had no idea how hard your childhood must have been."

"It was quite difficult. Food was hard to come by because our rent claimed so much of what Mama, Hudson, and I earned. If we each had one meal a day, it was considered a luxury. Most days, we took turns eating and even then, there was little of it to be had. I've gone to bed hungry more often than not. At least I had a roof over my head and family who loved me. Many others in this neighborhood are not so fortunate.

"That's why supporting this orphanage is something I care so much about. I know of children who've lived on the streets all their lives. Eating from mounds of garbage. Sleeping huddled against the walls of an alleyway as rats bit them. Selling their bodies to strangers, their innocence bought for a few shillings."

Hannah's eyes welled with tears. "I have never heard of such things, Laurel. I didn't see anything like you speak of in the country. Even coming to London, I've never been exposed to such a wretched side of life."

"I know." Laurel took Hannah's hand and squeezed it. "The orphanage is a refuge to so many children and the need is so great. The workers keep both it and the children neat and clean. My hope is you will take to these orphans as much as I have." She smiled. "Are you still willing to come inside?"

Hannah nodded. "I want to learn all I can about the place and its orphans. I feel I have been quite naïve. It's time I learned something about the real world."

Mrs. Kinnon greeted them and Laurel introduced her to Hannah. Laurel explained how Catherine wouldn't be able to come today, due to Delia's fever.

"That's quite all right, Your Grace. The children will be happy to see you." The woman looked to Hannah. "Would you like to have a look at our facilities, Lady Hannah?"

"I would."

Laurel accompanied them on the tour. Most of the children were in the classrooms so they stood and viewed those from the hall. A few spotted her and waved. She waved back, warmth spreading through her.

After they'd toured the entire building, they went to Mrs. Kinnon's office, where Laurel asked what the most pertinent needs were.

"Clothing and shoes are what come to mind first, Your Grace. Children grow so quickly. Of course, we pass down the clothes numerous times through as many children as we can but new clothing and unworn shoes would be something we'd all be grateful for."

"I wonder," Laurel mused. "Linfield and I haven't hosted any kind of social event. What if we had a ball and the admittance was predicated upon donating something the children could use?"

"That is very unique, Laurel," Hannah said. "It would also raise awareness among the *ton*. You might gain monetary donations, as well as clothing items."

"I will speak to my husband about it. What else?"

Mrs. Kinnon hesitated and then said, "Our teachers could use a consistent salary. Though we provide room and board here for the three of them, often there is nothing left with which to pay them."

She thought how crowded the schoolrooms were and how many pupils those teachers were responsible for.

"I will guarantee a salary for them for the rest of the year," she declared. "And a fourth should be hired."

"Oh, my! Your Grace, that would be wonderful," Mrs. Kinnon said.

"I noticed the empty lot next to the orphanage. I had an idea. What if we purchased that land and built schoolrooms there? Then you could take in more children here."

"But . . . that would cost a great deal of money," Mrs. Kinnon protested.

"My husband is a wealthy man. He also knows of my interest in the orphanage, especially since I grew up in the area. Do you know who owns the lot?"

A look of distaste came across the woman's face. "A Mr. Farmon. He has bought quite a few places in the surrounding area."

The pit of Laurel's stomach went ice cold. She had never thought she would hear that name again. She told herself it didn't matter. Anthony had a solicitor. The sale could go through him. She need never see Julius Farmon's face again.

"I know of this man. He purchased the chandlery where I used to be employed. If we offer him the right amount, I'm sure he will sell the parcel of land. Would you like me to carry through with this?"

Tears formed in the woman's eyes. "Please. To have so much room for the children, both for their education and taking in other orphans. It would be a blessing. Thank you, Your Grace. Thank you so much."

"Go ahead and look for a new teacher then," she suggested. "I will see that Linfield makes an offer on the property next door. Could we meet any day next week and discuss how to move forward? Hopefully, by then the property will have traded hands."

"Yes. Come whenever. And bring His Grace. Oh, this is so wonderful."

Mrs. Kinnon told them it was time for the children to have their bread and milk so she and Hannah joined them in the dining hall. Laurel saw Hannah seemed a bit standoffish at first but she soon warmed to the children. When they begged for Laurel to read to them, she readily agreed. A boy went to fetch a book and she had them gather around as they had on her first visit. With more confidence this time, Laurel read the story, another one written by Catherine, with enthusiasm.

When it came time to leave, the children hugged both her and Hannah. By now, her sister-in-law had opened up and embraced the orphans, promising to return soon.

"I see why you have grown so fond of them," Hannah said. "They are so sweet, despite having no parents and so little in material goods. Anthony will be happy to help. I believe he would do anything to put a smile on your face."

They told Mrs. Kinnon goodbye and left through the front door. They had almost reached the carriage when a man stepped out in front of them, blocking their path. She recognized him immediately as the one who had informed her that her and Hudson's rent would be tripled. He held a gun in his hands and pointed it at Hannah.

"We're going to get in your carriage. You won't call out for help. If you do, I'll shoot your friend here."

Laurel knew it was no idle threat and nodded. Hannah clutched her arm.

"Do as he says." She placed her hand over Hannah's and led her to the carriage.

The footman was gone. No driver sat atop the vehicle. Fear filled her. The man unlatched the door and opened it wide. He nodded and another large man joined them. That one grabbed Laurel roughly by the waist and hoisted her into the coach. Hannah joined her and the man with the pistol climbed in after them.

By now, she saw her driver and footman bound and gagged, lying on the floor of the vehicle. At least they hadn't been killed.

Yet.

Hannah scooted close to her and Laurel could feel the girl's body trembling. She took Hannah's hands in hers, feeling how cold they were. The carriage took off, throwing them against the cushions. The man sat opposite them, his weapon still trained on Hannah.

"Who is she?" he asked.

"Lady Hannah Godwin. My sister-in-law," Laurel said stiffly.

A gleam appeared in his eyes. "Good. Very good. A bonus."

She didn't understand what he meant. She only knew the danger to her and Hannah—and the servants—was very real. They drove a short distance and the carriage stopped. She glanced out the window and saw nothing but a brick wall very close to the vehicle. The door opened and the other man reached in and grabbed the folds of Hannah's dress. He yanked her away from Laurel and Hannah cried out as he hauled her from the carriage.

The other one merely motioned her with his gun. She rose and stepped to the open doorway, where she was also grabbed and brought to the ground.

Once the man with the weapon joined them, she asked, "What are you going to do with my driver and footman?"

"I may kill them. It depends upon whether you cooperate or not."

Her eyes flew to the inside of the carriage at the bound, helpless men. A sick feeling washed over her as the door slammed, knowing she might never see them again.

She looked around and saw they were in a narrow alley. The ducal carriage barely fit into the space. The first man climbed atop it and took up the reins and the vehicle pulled away.

"Walk inside. Don't say a word," the man said as he opened the door.

He shoved Laurel through and motioned for the weeping Hannah to follow. Hannah ran to Laurel and clung to her. They shuffled through the dark passageway until he called, "Stop."

Opening a door, she and Hannah walked through it. Laurel already knew who would be waiting.

Julius Farmon.

He sat behind a desk, his gloating, black eyes roaming over her from head to foot. He glanced toward Hannah and licked his lips. Both women shuddered.

"Sit," he ordered.

They did as commanded. Hannah continued to weep copiously but Laurel remained dry-eyed.

"I'm the one you want. Let her go."

Farmon's eyes narrowed. "I'll issue the orders around here," he snapped. He steepled his fat fingers and studied Hannah. "Who is she?"

When Laurel didn't reply, he turned to the man who'd brought them here. "Braxton?"

"Lady Hannah Godwin. The sister-in-law."

"Ah." Farmon looked pleased. "An extra, unexpected prize. You are the sister to the Duke of Linfield?" he asked.

Hannah nodded, her hand tightening on Laurel's.

"I only thought I would be ransoming Linfield's wife to him. Now, I'll receive twice what I ask for."

His words caused Hannah to wail. Farmon nodded and the man he'd called Braxton moved quickly, slapping Hannah hard. It stunned her and then she buried her head against Laurel's shoulder.

She stroked her friend's hair. "Hush, Hannah. Quiet now."

Hannah quivered against her.

"My husband will pay you. Just don't touch her again."

What Laurel didn't say was that once Anthony saw his sister's face, it would fuel his rage. He would kill these men for what they had dared to do.

Farmon nodded again and she wrapped both arms around Hannah, trying to protect her. Instead, she found herself ripped away from her friend. Braxton struck Laurel even harder than he had Hannah. Instead of a slap, he hit her with his fist. Pain shot through her as if a lightning bolt had struck her cheekbone. He'd also clipped her eye and she knew it would turn black.

"I said I am in charge here, Laurel." Farmon pursed his lips. "Don't tell me what to do. Don't even speak again. Is that understood?"

She wavered, dizzy, but nodded, letting this monster know she would not cause further trouble. Her face throbbed painfully. Nausea grew in her belly and not only because of having been hit so hard. Her gut told her Farmon would demand a hefty ransom from Anthony— but he had no intention of returning them. He wasn't a man anyone stood up to. Laurel had not only refused to become his mistress, she had physically attacked him. Embarrassed him. Julius Farmon was a man whose revenge would be complete.

Would it mean he would rape her? Or kill her?

Perhaps both. She—and Hannah—would pay the price for her actions. Laurel knew their lives were in danger. They had to find a way to escape.

"Bind their wrists," Farmon instructed his minion.

Braxton had come prepared. He removed a cord from his coat pocket and wrapped it around her wrists, knotting it securely. He pulled another length from the other pocket and did the same to Hannah.

"Take them upstairs."

The henchman opened the door and grasped both women by their elbows. He led them along the narrow passageway. They passed a man, who averted his eyes, keeping them on the ground. When they reached a back staircase, Braxton ordered them up it. Opening the first door on the right once they reached the upper floor, he shoved them inside and followed, closing the door behind him.

"You're in a brothel. Save your voices because screams are ignored. If you give me any trouble, I'll gag you and tie you to the bed and let every customer here take a turn with both of you." He looked to Hannah. "Virgins are especially prized."

Hannah gagged. She turned and retched into a nearby chamber pot. The man laughed and exited the room. Laurel heard the lock turn.

She went to Hannah and held her elbow. The vomiting finally ceased. Hannah looked at her, misery filling her face.

"What are we going to do, Laurel?"

With determination, she said, "We are going to find a way out of here."

CHAPTER TWENTY-TWO

ANTHONY STOOD, STRETCHING his arms high above his head. Satisfaction filled him. After several interviews over the past few weeks, he'd finally hired a business manager today. His army days had taught him to trust his gut when evaluating others and the man he'd spoken with today was both knowledgeable and trustworthy. He would report tomorrow morning so Anthony had worked on organizing his desk this afternoon, placing items in different stacks so that things would be prioritized.

He knew it must be close to teatime and glanced out the window. Sure enough, Viscount Brixley pulled up in front of the house in his curricle, his matched bays definitely worth whatever he'd paid for them. Anthony moved a few more documents around, giving Brixley time to be escorted to the drawing room. He wanted to enter after and observe how the suitor interacted with the three female Godwins. Anthony had made subtle inquiries regarding the viscount at White's and had learned Brixley was known for his keen intelligence and devotion to his parents. That boded well, considering Anthony's interest in family now. He wanted Hannah to be as happy as he was with Laurel. Brixley seemed to fit the bill.

He left his study and approached the drawing room, eager to see Laurel again. She and Hannah must have stayed a good while at the orphanage because she hadn't stopped by for a quick kiss upon her return. Most likely, his sister had dragged Laurel to her rooms and made her watch as Hannah tried on gown after gown, trying to find the most suitable one for today's tea.

Entering the room, it surprised him to find only Aunt Constance and Brixley. The viscount rose.

"Good afternoon, Your Grace," he greeted.

Anthony went and shook hands with him. He supposed Hannah wanted to make a grand entrance, especially after her remark last night saying that Brixley would have to work for her.

"Did you bring your curricle?" he asked.

"Yes. Would you like to see my pair since Her Grace and Lady Hannah are not here yet?"

"Certainly."

The two men went downstairs and Anthony admired the beauties, learning they'd been purchased at Tattersall's last week. Brixley convinced him to take the vehicle for a quick spin. Anthony climbed up and took the reins, finding the horses handled well.

Once he'd returned, they went back inside to the drawing room. Concern filled him since Laurel and Hannah still weren't present. The tea cart was already there so his aunt offered them both a cup.

The door opened and all eyes turned in that direction. A footman entered, carrying a small silver tray with a note upon it. He delivered it to Anthony, who opened it and scanned the few words. A winter chilled filled him as he masked his emotions. Calmly, he looked to the others.

"It seems Laurel and Hannah have been unavoidably detained at the orphanage. I'm afraid we'll have to do tea another time, Brixley."

The viscount stood. "Of course, Your Grace. Would you please give Lady Hannah and Her Grace my best?"

"Of course."

Brixley took his leave and Aunt Constance asked, "Whatever could have delayed them? Hannah was so looking forward to seeing Brixley."

He gave her a tight smile. "I think I will go and see if I can smooth things over."

He kissed her cheek and left, his rage boiling now. Fortunately, he had years of experience in keeping it hidden. Pocketing the note, he found his butler.

"Have my wife and sister returned yet?" he asked, the slim chance of the note being a cruel joke making him stop and check.

"No, Your Grace."

Anthony quickly left the house. He didn't take time to have his horse saddled because he was only going a few blocks. Each step, though, fed his fury and by the time he arrived at the Everton townhouse, Anthony was ready to explode.

Barton, the butler, admitted him. "Good afternoon, Your Grace. I hope Her Grace is doing well."

"She is," he lied. "Is His Grace available?" he asked, thinking Everton would be at tea with his duchess.

"His Grace is in the library. I'll show you there now."

As the butler led Anthony upstairs, he wished the man would move faster. Everything inside him wanted to scream to the heavens. It took all he had to rein in his fear and anger.

Barton announced him and as Anthony walked in, he saw Everton had company. Lord Merrick and Lord Alford were there, as was Laurel's brother. Thank God no females were present. He waited for the servant to close the door and strode toward where the men sat.

"Laurel and Hannah have been taken."

To their credit, all four men shot to their feet. Everton said, "Tell us everything."

Anthony pulled the note from his pocket and handed it to the duke. "They went to the orphanage this morning with your wife. They never returned home."

"Catherine did not go with them today," Everton revealed. "Delia was running a fever so she stayed home." He unfolded the page and read it aloud. *"I have your wife and sister. A ransom demand will follow."* The duke looked up, anger sparking in his eyes. "Have you made any enemies, Linfield?"

"None that I know of," he said truthfully.

"I know who is responsible."

All eyes turned to Hudson, Laurel's twin.

"Julius Farmon has taken her. Them." He pushed a hand through his dark hair. "I worried when Laurel told me where the orphanage was located. It's in the neighborhood where we grew up."

"Who is this Farmon?" demanded Anthony. "Why in God's name would he kidnap them?"

"Farmon owns several saloons and brothels. That's where he made his money. In the past few years, he's begun buying up chunks of land and buildings, including Mr. Cole's chandlery, where Laurel worked." Hudson's hands balled into fists. "He told her she could keep her day job only if she took on one at night. As his mistress."

Anthony felt as if someone had punched him in the gut.

"You know Laurel," Hudson continued. "She gave him a tongue lashing—and worse. Boxed his ears and kneed him in the balls. Farmon was out for blood after that. He tripled our rent since he owned the tenement where we lived. Threatened to bring me up on charges and have me transported to Australia. We fled to a boardinghouse miles away but lived in constant fear."

Hudson looked to Everton. "That's when she was desperate enough to come to you. If you hadn't taken us in, I don't know what would have happened. Farmon's network of thugs runs deep. I don't know how I would have protected her if they'd found us."

Anthony rushed to Hudson, gripping him by the lapels. "Why didn't you tell me this?" he shouted, shaking the young man. "I never would have let her return to that neighborhood if I would have known of the danger."

Merrick peeled him away. "Turning on one another and casting blame is pointless. We have to think how to get them back."

He knew Merrick had been an officer in the Peninsular Wars and would know how to keep a cool head during a crisis.

"What do we do?" he asked. "I'll pay anything. Everything. I can't lose her. Them."

"We return to your house," Merrick said. "The ransom note could come tonight or even tomorrow. This Farmon may wish to drive you to your breaking point before he makes known how much he wants for their return."

"It won't matter," Hudson said dully. "You can pay him a king's ransom. He won't release Laurel. He'll keep her for himself. She humiliated him. He's a vengeful bastard. He'll never let her go."

Blind rage struck Anthony. He turned wildly, not knowing what to do. All rational thought fled as he thought of another man touching Laurel. A primal scream erupted, its piercing wail sounding inhuman. He fell to his knees, a wave of helplessness overcoming him.

Everton helped bring him to his feet. Their gazes met. Determination flooded Anthony as a calm descended upon him. Years of honing his rage and directing it elsewhere finally took over.

"I will fight to Hell and back—but I will bring them home," he said.

"We will return to your house," Everton said. "Merrick will go and retrieve a few Bow Street Runners. We will wait together for the ransom demand."

"Merrick and I will follow whoever delivers it," Lord Alford said. "We can be on opposite sides of the streets and trade off tracking the messenger. See if he goes back to this Farmon. Or learn if someone else is behind this scheme."

The men left the library without a word. Merrick peeled off from the others to make his way to the Runners' headquarters in Covent Garden while the rest returned to the Linfield townhouse.

When they arrived, Alford motioned to Hudson. Anthony knew

they would wait outside at a distance in case the ransom note arrived before Merrick returned. Everton accompanied him inside.

"Where is your aunt? Does she know anything?"

"No. I merely told her Laurel and Hannah were delayed at the orphanage."

"It would be best to keep her in the dark," the duke advised. "Think of something."

"I'll go see her now."

He found Aunt Constance reading in her sitting room. She smiled. "There you are, Anthony. How are the girls?"

"They are involved in a special project of the Duchess of Everton's making," he lied smoothly. "They are with her and several other important society matrons and will still be tied up for several hours."

"They won't be attending tonight's rout?"

"No, Aunt Constance. I fear Her Grace will keep them busy well into the night."

"Oh, well. I have grown rather weary of attending so many society events in a row. I think I will take my book and read in bed all night."

"I may do the same. I see no point in attending the rout without Laurel or Hannah."

She smiled. "I'm so glad you and Laurel seemed to have come to an understanding, Anthony. She's just lovely."

"She's more than lovely, Aunt. She is the woman I love," he said earnestly, his heart twisting, knowing that it was possible he might never see her again.

Her eyes widened at his remark, a radiant smile lighting her face. "Oh, Anthony. I'm so happy for you." She embraced him for a long moment. "It's what I've always wished for you. To find happiness. Love. You'll create a family all of your own."

"You are a part of that family, Aunt," he said, his voice breaking.

There would be no family—no children—nothing. Unless he got Laurel back.

He left her and returned to Everton. "Aunt Constance won't be a problem. At least for tonight."

"We should wait close to the front door."

"In here," he said, leading them to a small parlor for visitors just off the foyer.

The men sat in silence for some minutes before Everton spoke.

"You seem a different man in recent weeks," he noted.

"I am. Now that I have Laurel in my life."

"I saw you kiss her at the Prattfords' ball."

That kiss seemed a lifetime ago.

"I did. Laurel thought a public kiss might start a bit of a scandal."

Everton smiled. "Kissing your wife in public is exactly the right kind of scandal." He paused. "Do you love her?"

"Desperately. If I don't get her back . . ." He shook his head.

"We will. I know of this Julius Farmon and some of his business dealings. Together, we will see Laurel and Hannah returned and squash him like a bug."

"I want more than that," Anthony said fervently. "I want him dead. If he's touched Laurel—or Hannah—I will see him in Hell."

They sat again in silence until Merrick arrived, three Bow Street Runners in tow.

"They've been informed of the situation and will take up a post outside," the marquess said. "I'll summon the others."

Before Merrick could leave, though, a maid entered. Anthony saw the note in her hand and snatched it. He read it and turned to her.

"When did this come?" he asked, his voice calm though emotion rocked through him.

"Some lad came to the back door and gave it to a scullery maid. She gave it to Cook. Cook gave it to me, Your Grace."

"Thank you," he said, dismissing her. He knew by now the messenger would be long gone. He read aloud, *"Five o'clock in the morning. The day after tomorrow. Twenty thousand pounds. Rotten Row. Come alone on foot. We'll be watching."*

It struck Anthony that the ducal carriage Laurel and Hannah had departed in had never returned. He wondered what had happened to the servants who accompanied them.

The Runners introduced themselves quickly and then two departed with Merrick. Within minutes, the family members had returned.

Waxby, the Runner in charge, said, "The others will keep watch on the house tonight, both the front and back doors. They will be replaced during the day and another shift will come on tomorrow night. Those will be rotated until we bring home your wife and sister, Your Grace. Lord Merrick shared your suspicions regarding Julius Farmon and I've sent two more Runners to keep watch on where he keeps an office. It's likely he's holding his hostages nearby. By reputation, Farmon is a careful man. He would not want them far from him."

Continuing, the Runner said, "I already have someone in place who will visit Farmon's establishment and ascertain its layout for us. If he can, he'll not only scout the location but try to glean any information he can. See if the women were sighted. Get into the upper story and basement if possible." Pausing, he asked, "Are you willing to pay the ransom?"

"Yes," Anthony hissed. "I will go to my bank first thing tomorrow and make arrangements."

"It's a good deal of money, Linfield," Everton said. "I doubt a bank would have that sum on hand, much less be willing to part with it all in a single transaction. Requesting to withdraw so much might prove difficult—and arouse suspicion. It's also my sister being held. Let me at least share in the cost. I can withdraw half."

Merrick and Alford said, "I'm in," at the same time, and Merrick added, "A smaller sum will be easier for all of us to withdraw. Put together, we can make the ransom easily."

A wave of emotion rippled through Anthony. "You don't have to do this."

Everton gripped his shoulder. "Of course, we do. We are family."

The support—and love—Anthony was being shown nearly brought him to his knees.

"An excellent idea, Your Grace," Waxby praised. "You can all go at separate times to make your withdrawals. Use different branches. One or two of you might even mention a business opportunity in which you're interested in investing a large amount of capital." The Runner looked to Anthony. "We'll do our best to follow the money and see it returned."

"I don't care about the money," he said. "I will reimburse every man here if a farthing goes missing. I only want Laurel and Hannah back." He swallowed. "And hopefully, the driver and footman that were with them."

"Now that we know the place the exchange will occur, I will scout it now and again tomorrow. I want to see the best areas to place agents. We'll also have several men on horseback who will follow the carriage. We won't let Farmon get away, Your Grace."

"I want him brought to me," Anthony said firmly. "I will deal with him."

He wasn't going to openly talk murder in front of these men.

But he had no intention of letting Julius Farmon live.

And every man in the room knew it.

CHAPTER TWENTY-THREE

ANTHONY FINALLY ROSE. Staying in bed would be a waste of time. He'd only dozed a bit, not truly getting any real sleep. Hopefully, he would be able to sleep after all the arrangements had been finalized with Waxby later today. He needed his mind to be sharp and clear by tomorrow morning at this time.

He shaved and dressed on his own and slipped down the stairs, knowing at some point today he would have to tell Aunt Constance something. What, he hadn't the foggiest notion. He cut through the kitchen and left the townhouse using a rear door. Waxby had scheduled a meeting of all the men at Everton's residence for six this morning. The Bow Street Runner thought it wise for them to meet somewhere different in case Anthony's house was being watched. The less Farmon knew of their activities, the better.

He set out for his brother-in-law's on foot, walking for less than five minutes before arriving. He entered by a back gate and froze in his tracks.

His carriage sat in the yard behind the house.

Anthony ran to it and flung open the door. No one was inside the vehicle. The slim ray of hope vanished. It had been foolish to believe Laurel and Hannah would be inside. Grimly, he went to the back entrance and stepped inside, moving through the kitchen and heading straight to the library. Though he was still half an hour early, the entire room was already filled with family members and Waxby.

Another man, unknown to him, stood in a far corner, warily watching the group.

Everyone greeted him with firm handshakes and reassuring grips to his shoulder. Anthony took a seat, looking to Waxby.

"I have much to report, Your Grace," the man in charge began. "First, your abandoned coach was found in Hampstead Heath yesterday. I had it brought here. Inside it were your driver and a footman."

"Alive?" he asked.

"Yes. They were brought to headquarters and questioned. The footman remembers nothing. He was struck on the head from behind and knocked unconscious. The driver was ordered down from his seat at gunpoint. He gave a good description of the two men involved in the kidnapping. One is Braxton, who serves as Julius Farmon's right-hand man. He's known to be savvy—and brutal. The other one is Sims. He's used strictly for his muscle. Not a brain in his head. Both servants were bound hand and foot and left in the coach the entire time. The driver was able to tell us that both Her Grace and Lady Hannah had been placed in the vehicle once they left the orphanage, and the coach only traveled a short distance. Your driver thought they parked in an alley since the brick building was so close to the carriage that it was hard to get the door open the entire way. The women were removed and taken inside."

"Where are my servants now?" Anthony asked.

"They are at one of the safe houses we use from time to time," Waxby said. "I thought it best not to return them to your household. Too many questions. We don't want word of the ladies' abduction to get out and cause a fly in the ointment."

"What about Rotten Row?" Hudson asked. "You said you would look it over and decide where to station your agents."

"I did that personally," Waxby confirmed. "We will have two Runners there and another three on horseback at a greater distance.

They will move into position at midnight tonight, so they'll be there well before the five o'clock exchange. We also sent two men into Farmon's saloon last night."

Anthony's gut tightened.

"One was able to slip downstairs into the basement and found nothing. He did, however, meet Mr. Johnson." Waxby turned and motioned over the stranger.

He saw the man was younger than he'd first thought, probably not even twenty years of age. He had brown hair and a lean, wiry frame.

"This is Mr. Johnson," the Runner said. "He works for Farmon."

A wave of rage surged through Anthony. It took him a moment to control it. He wanted to jerk the man off his feet and throttle him simply for being associated with Julius Farmon.

Johnson looked at Anthony. "I'm a good man, Your Grace. I took the only job I could find as a barkeep for Farmon. I seen too many things I don't like the six months I've been employed there but I have a younger sister I need to feed."

"Mr. Johnson has cooperated with the Runners, Your Grace, in the hopes that you will find him and his sister employment elsewhere. I told him we couldn't guarantee it but that you owned many properties and would be grateful for his assistance in getting your wife and sister back."

"Whatever you want," Anthony promised. "You may stay in London at my townhouse. Go to one of many country estates. Work in any capacity you choose. Just tell us what you know."

Waxby nodded and Johnson said, "I seen your wife and sister when they were brought in yesterday afternoon. I'd just come on duty and was out dumping rubbish. Sims drove the carriage away while Braxton took the women inside to Farmon's office. I followed at a distance. I knew something wasn't right. The way they were dressed. They weren't sporting girls for upstairs."

Johnson paused and took a deep breath. "I waited down the corridor until Braxton brought them out. Their wrists were tied. He led them upstairs."

"Do you know where they are? What room?"

"No, Your Grace. I returned to the bar and went back to work. It weren't right, though. They were ladies. I felt bad for them. So when the Runner came around, asking a few questions, I knew I had to help. Farmon'll slice my throat, though, if'n he figures out I've talked."

"Mr. Johnson has already provided us with a diagram of the entire layout of the building," continued Waxby. "If we attempt to rescue the ladies, we wouldn't be going in blind."

"Is that a possibility?" Everton asked. "Or too great a risk?"

"It will be up to His Grace to decide what action we take," the Runner said. "I believe we need to prepare as if the ransom is to be paid. Have the four of you go to the bank and withdraw the funds. Have my men in place at Rotten Row."

"How many do you think Farmon might bring tomorrow morning?" Anthony asked. "If several men accompany him, it might be a good time to strike at the brothel. Especially at that time of the morning, the clients will have gone home. The whores would have gone to bed. There'd be no customers in the saloon. It would be the perfect time to attempt a rescue."

"It would," Waxby agreed. "If Farmon doesn't move the women. I seriously doubt he'll be involved in the ransom drop."

Hudson spoke up. "I've already told you, Farmon has no intention of bringing Laurel or Hannah to the park. He'll want the money and keep the women, whether at his brothel or somewhere else."

"Some kidnappers demand the exchange of money and don't bring their prisoner to the meet. Instead, they share where the abductee can be found. Sometimes they are there. Sometimes they aren't," Waxby said, his voice deliberately neutral.

"If Hudson is right and Farmon has no plans to relinquish them, then he might move them while the exchange of money takes place,"

Anthony pointed out. "He would think we believed Laurel and Hannah would be at Rotten Row to be traded. If he planned to move them anywhere, that would be the perfect time to do so, especially with no traffic on the streets. Either we could wait outside for a bit and catch them being transferred, or it would be the perfect time to enter his property and save them."

"There can be no *we*, Linfield," Merrick said. "You need to be at Rotten Row. Leave it to the rest of us to—"

"Wait," Alford interrupted. "This Farmon doesn't move in society. He's never seen Linfield. Even if he had, I doubt Farmon will be at the exchange. Let me go in Linfield's place. We're approximately the same height and build. We both have blond hair. *I* can play Linfield and deliver the ransom so he can go to the brothel with the rest of you."

"You would do that?" Anthony asked. "It could be dangerous. The kidnappers could take the money—and kill you."

"You must be there when Laurel and Hannah are found. They'll need you after the trauma they've faced," Alford said. "There'll be Runners about who can protect me." He paused and confessed, "Besides, if it had been Leah and Catherine taken, I would be out of my mind. I would want to be there when they were found. I know any man here feels the same and would gladly take your place. I just happen to resemble you the most from a distance."

No one spoke for a moment. Anthony realized just how united this family was. How close their ties and loyalty lay with one another.

And he was a part of it now.

He offered Alford his hand. "Thank you." He looked around the circle. "Thank you all. I now understand the deep connection and strong bond we have, linked by blood or marriage. Together, we are stronger, better men. For ourselves and our families."

"We will go forward with our plans then," Waxby said. "Lord Alford will take His Grace's place tomorrow morning, with the funds in hand that the four of you will withdraw sometime today. I'll have men stationed in and near Rotten Row. I'll also arrange a separate mission at Farmon's saloon." He looked to the barkeep. "Johnson, you need to remain behind after closing tonight. Be our eyes and ears inside. You'll also unlock the door and allow us to gain entry in case the women aren't brought out."

"You won't need to spare any men at Farmon's," Everton said, a steely resolve in his eyes. "I've already sent for Luke. This will be a family affair. We will render justice to Julius Farmon."

Anthony looked around and saw Merrick and Hudson nodding in agreement. If Lord Mayfield joined them tomorrow morning, they would be five men strong. The emotion that moved through him was unlike any he'd ever known. He was a part of a family who would stand together. Not only did he now understand the importance of family from being around these St. Clairs, but Anthony wanted to protect his own in the same way. That included anyone under his care, including his servants and tenants. It meant seeing that Johnson and his sister would be safe, as well.

"I'll leave you to it then, Your Grace," Waxby said. "Johnson, be sure you report on time today. Keep your head down and your mouth closed." The Runner left.

Anthony went to Johnson and took him aside. "I know the risk you are taking. I cannot thank you enough. Would it ease your mind if I sent for your sister? She could stay here while we free my wife and sister. You wouldn't have to worry about her. She will be safe."

The barkeep's face filled with relief. "You would do that, Your Grace? She's only fourteen and I'm all she's got since our parents passed away."

He nodded. "I understand how important family is. If this goes as planned, you and your sister not only have a position for life with my family, but you will receive a healthy bonus."

"Thank you, Your Grace," the younger man said. "I'm willing to do anything to get out from under Farmon's thumb."

Johnson provided Anthony with the address of the boardinghouse where his sister worked. He promised to have the girl brought here for the duration. Johnson asked that they be sent from London to any estate in the country, stating he wanted to be as far from Farmon's reach as possible. With that now taken care of, Johnson took his leave.

"I'll send for Luke now," Everton said. "The rest of us need to go about our business as usual today."

Anthony left with the rest, heading back to his townhouse. By this time tomorrow, he hoped to God that he had Laurel back in his arms.

LAUREL LAY ON the bed and watched the room gradually grow lighter as the sun rose. No one had come to the room since they'd been left here yesterday afternoon. She'd looked around, trying to see if she could find anything to use to help her break the restraints around their wrists. Other than the dilapidated bed and a chamber pot, though, the room was empty. She'd even poked her head under the bed and found nothing but cobwebs.

Her face ached from where Braxton had punched her. She knew far worse would befall her—and Hannah—if they couldn't escape. By now, Farmon would have sent his ransom demand to Anthony. She knew her husband must be out of his mind with worry. She didn't doubt that he would pay whatever Farmon demanded and only wished she could tell him to save his money.

Farmon would never release them. They would disappear and never be seen again.

Laurel wondered if Anthony would tell Hudson—or any of the St. Clairs—that she and Hannah had been abducted. She'd always had her twin to turn to no matter what happened and now all her new St. Clair siblings and their spouses. Anthony, though, was used to being on his own and would never think to share his troubles with her family. She only prayed they would be there for him when, after he paid the ransom, she and Hannah never returned. He would blame himself for not protecting them. Sink into an abyss she doubted he would ever emerge from. Laurel prayed fervently that her siblings would rally around Anthony and try to keep him sane.

Hannah began stirring on the bed next to her. Laurel had tried to keep up Hannah's spirits but her friend had dissolved into tears again and turned away, refusing to speak. Laurel couldn't blame her. Their situation was beyond hopeless.

"Are you awake?" Hannah asked quietly.

"I am. How are you?"

"Hungry," Hannah admitted. "But you know about that, don't you? You've lived through all sorts of dreadful things."

"Yes," she said, her voice a whisper. "There wasn't always enough to eat even though all three of us worked long hours. Mama would take turns giving us some of her food, saying she wasn't hungry. Hudson and I didn't know any better when we were young and so we would eat whatever she pushed toward us. Later, I understood. Then we all played that game, trying to give one another something and go without ourselves."

"You told that man to let me go. That you were who he wanted." Hannah paused. "Who is he, Laurel? Why does he want you?"

She wasn't sure how much she should tell Hannah, knowing what evils lay in store for them. Her friend was so innocent—but wouldn't be for long.

"His name is Julius Farmon," she began. "He is a man that many are afraid of. He owns several businesses and has bought up many more in this neighborhood, including the chandlery where I worked. He also owned the tenement where I lived with Hudson and Mama."

When she didn't speak for several minutes, Hannah prompted, "Tell me. I would rather know and prepare myself than be left in the dark."

"Farmon is a very evil man, Hannah. He wanted me to become his mistress. He made that the condition of keeping my job at the chandlery once he bought it. I . . . couldn't." Her voice broke and she waited again, afraid she would start sobbing and totally lose control. Hannah was already frightened enough. She didn't need to witness Laurel falling apart.

"I refused him. He is not a man anyone refuses."

"You think he still wants to make you his mistress?"

She thought Farmon wanted much more than that. He wanted to break her. "I do."

Laurel couldn't continue. Her aching face was nothing compared to her aching heart, knowing she would never see Anthony again. Never know his arms about her or share in his kiss. They'd never create the family they both longed for. Then fear struck her.

What if she already carried their child? What would Farmon to do her—and the baby?

"Laurel, I'm frightened," Hannah said, her voice small.

Laurel moved her hands to where her numbed fingers rested against her friend's.

"I am, too."

CHAPTER TWENTY-FOUR

ANTHONY CAME HOME and found his new man of business had reported for work. The last thing he'd wanted was to talk business with Mr. Chase. Still, he took the man to his office and described each pile of documents and what had priority. He instructed Chase to become familiar with everything in the documents and write detailed reports of his impressions of each one. He also tasked Chase to make a list of a dozen businesses or industries that were showing prosperity and why Anthony should consider investing in them. He gave Chase a week in which to complete everything, hoping it would keep the man busy.

He'd also gone to Aunt Constance's sitting room and spoken to her at length, revealing what had happened to Laurel and Hannah and promising her things had been set in motion that would see them soon returned. Despite what he'd thought, she didn't shed a single tear, only nodded stoically. She told him she would keep to her rooms today and not say a word to any of the servants.

After that conversation, he'd gone to the bank, spending close to two hours before he secured the funds. He'd assured the bank manager countless times that he knew it was a large transaction and that he urgently needed it for a remarkable business opportunity which might never present itself again. Once he revealed it presented the chance to triple the amount he withdrew if things panned out, the bank manager had grown more amenable. Anthony also promised that he would return the funds—and profits—to his account as soon as possible. As if any of that mattered. It was his money and the bank manager could really do nothing to stop him from withdrawing his own funds. It was a miracle that he hadn't crushed the bank manager's skull into dust.

After that, he forced himself to eat something and then slept for a few hours. When he awoke, he was given a note which had arrived from Everton. It informed him that Lord Mayfield had come to town and would be here for a few days and that he hoped Linfield and his duchess might be able to come for dinner the next evening. Anthony knew Everton had worded the note tersely in case it had been intercepted by any of Farmon's minions. He was grateful for the earl coming. Anthony knew how much Laurel liked this brother and his wife and how she'd mentioned visiting them in the country once their baby came. At the time, he hadn't cared one way or another. It took this crisis—and falling in love—for Anthony to understand how much family was to be treasured.

What if Laurel were already pregnant? What if this trauma caused her to lose the child?

What if he lost her?

If he did, life would no longer be worth living.

Around midnight, Lord Alford appeared in the library.

"I slipped in the back," the earl assured Anthony. "I have the case." He held it up. "My portion of the ransom is already inside."

"Everton and Merrick sent their shares to me," he revealed. "I have mine, as well."

The two took the additional money and placed it inside the large satchel. Alford declined a brandy and the two sat in the dimly lit room without speaking for a short time.

"Waxby came to see me this afternoon," Alford finally said. "He wanted me to know that he left two Runners positioned where they will be able to see me leave your townhouse on the off-chance that

Farmon might send men here to seize the ransom before I arrive in the park. They will follow me to Rotten Row at a distance to make sure I'm not attacked along the way."

"Waxby seems to think of everything," Anthony murmured.

The clock chimed and he stood. Alford did the same and they shook hands.

"Thank you," he said, his throat thick with unshed tears.

"We'll get them back, Linfield," the earl said. "And see that vermin Farmon dead."

Anthony left the library and moved quietly down the carpeted stairs. He made his way carefully through the darkened kitchen until his heard his name called out softly.

"Aunt Constance?"

She came toward him and wrapped her arms tightly about him. When she released him, she said, "Get our girls back. Whatever it takes. I know you were a soldier, Anthony, and no stranger to death. I will rest better—as will Laurel and Hannah—if we know the threat is ended."

"I will take care of Farmon myself, Aunt," he promised.

With that, he slipped through the door. The night air was cool. He saw no one on his way to Everton's. As before, he went to the back door and found it unlocked. As he pushed open the library door, he heard the clock sound three.

Everton, Merrick, and Hudson were all seated. Only Mayfield paced restlessly about the room. He spied Anthony and came to him.

Wrapping him in a bearhug, Mayfield said, "We just found Laurel. We won't lose her now."

"Thank you for coming," Anthony said, overcome with emotion.

Mayfield released him. "Once we have Laurel back, plan to come visit us once the baby is born."

He could only nod, knowing Laurel's brother tried to bolster Anthony's spirits, making plans for the future.

Everton asked, "Are you ready?"

He nodded. All the men wore black from head to toe. The duke led them outside to a waiting carriage. A man stood beside it.

"This is Strong," Everton said. "He will take us all but a few blocks to Farmon's. He is our most trusted servant. If not for Strong, I would not be wed to Catherine today."

Anthony offered the driver his hand. The man took it. "We'll get them back, Your Grace," Strong said. "You can count on it."

As they boarded the carriage, he noticed it was plain black, no ducal coat of arms on its doors. They rode without speaking until the vehicle slowed and they disembarked.

"Someone will come when we're ready for you, Strong," Everton said.

The driver nodded and the five men moved down the block, turning left. Farmon's saloon and brothel stood a block away. They stopped and discussed the best places for them to observe when a lone man approached. Conversation ceased.

As he drew near, he said, "Waxby sent me."

They all relaxed as the Runner joined them.

"Waxby had me to watch the place in case Farmon moved Her Grace and Lady Hannah. I haven't seen any sign of them. By my count, there's still a handful—no more than three—customers still in the place. They should be leaving shortly. I'll show you where you can stand watch."

"After that, you're dismissed," Anthony said. "This is a family affair."

The Runner grinned. "Waxby said you'd say that. I want to ask if I can stay, though. I only know Farmon by reputation but I would love to be part of seeing him put down."

"We would appreciate your help—but don't stop us," he warned. "What must be done will be done."

"I understand," the Runner said. "Follow me."

They took places in the shadows, watching the last of the paying clients exit the building. Ten minutes later, just before four o'clock, four men came out the front door. Anthony assumed one was Braxton, Farmon's top lieutenant. It shocked him when he recognized Johnson. Had the barkeep betrayed them?

The man he believed to be Braxton did all the talking. Two men peeled away, one of them Johnson. The pair returned a few minutes later with three horses. Everyone but Johnson mounted and rode off. Johnson stood watching them go. After the men turned the corner and were out of sight, he looked furtively into the dark and motioned.

"I'll go," Everton volunteered.

Though fearful of a trap, Anthony said, "I will, too."

They crossed the street and he asked Johnson, "Why are you still here? Waxby told you to stay out of sight."

"Farmon told me to stay," the barkeep replied. "You don't question an order from Farmon. He said I'd be helping Braxton tonight but Braxton's never taken to me. He said I wasn't needed and told me to go home."

Anthony took a deep breath, relieved that Johnson hadn't betrayed them.

"I did overhear Farmon tell Sims he'd need to help move the two women once Braxton left. I saw Sims readying a coach when I went to saddle the horses just now. He'll probably pull into the alley behind the saloon."

"Leave now," Everton said. "Farmon thinks you're gone anyway. The door is unlocked?"

The barkeep nodded.

"Wait," Anthony said. "Are there any men besides Farmon and Sims inside?"

"No," Johnson said. "The whores have all gone to their rooms. The last client left a quarter of an hour ago. The others left with Braxton. You'll only have Farmon and Sims to deal with." He paused.

"They'll both be armed. Be careful."

"Go," Everton urged and the young barkeep hurried down the street.

Anthony waved his hand and Merrick, Mayfield, Hudson, and the Runner all hurried to them. Quickly, he recounted what Johnson had said.

Merrick said, "Half of us should go around to the back. The others go through the front door." He moved away and Hudson and the Runner followed.

Anthony took the lead, entering the darkened saloon.

LAUREL ROSE FROM the bed, unable to sleep. She and Hannah had dozed off and on throughout the day since they'd had nothing to do. She massaged her sore wrists, grateful that Braxton had finally cut the restraints. He had showed up with two bowls of cold, congealed stew this afternoon, the first food they'd had in over a day. Instinct told her begging wouldn't work so she'd calmly requested that he remove the cords, telling him they weren't a threat and had nowhere to go, especially since she'd seen the hulking brute standing guard outside their door when Braxton had entered. He'd set the bowls on the floor and removed a knife from his boot, slicing through the ropes and pocketing it before leaving.

Hannah had turned her nose up at the food until Laurel began to eat it, using her fingers since no utensil had been brought. If she'd had a spoon, she certainly would have turned it into a weapon. Finally, hunger got the best of her friend and Hannah had followed Laurel's lead, though she gagged several times as she swallowed. Laurel knew she would need strength for whatever lay ahead and so wasn't picky, even licking her bowl clean.

She continued rubbing her wrists as she stood in the dark. They were raw from her pulling on the restraints. Listening, she realized the brothel had quietened. Something told her Farmon would be coming for them soon.

Going to the bed, she shook Hannah awake and had her sit up.

"I think they will try and move us soon," she said. "The customers are gone. The streets will be deserted." She gripped Hannah's shoulders. "When they do, I want you to run if you have the chance. Don't look back. Don't wait for me. Just get away. Do you understand?"

The Hannah who had entered this room would never have agreed to leave Laurel behind. The new Hannah merely whispered, "Yes."

Suddenly, she heard footsteps and released Hannah, taking her hand and sitting on the bed next to her. "Wait until we're outside. There's a better chance of escape outdoors. I'll do what I can to distract them."

The key turned in the lock and the door swung open, revealing Julius Farmon. His feral smile brought terror to her but Laurel knew she had to stay strong—even if it meant sacrificing herself so Hannah might go free. Laurel had known complete happiness for a short while with Anthony. It was her fault Hannah had been dragged into this situation. If she had to relinquish her own freedom in order for Hannah to earn hers, Laurel was willing to do so in order to give Hannah the opportunity to find love as Laurel had with Anthony.

Since over a day had passed since their abduction, she guessed Farmon had given Anthony a day to raise the requested ransom. By the time they hadn't returned from the orphanage and her husband received the demand, the banks would have already been closed. That had given yesterday to pull together the sum Farmon would have required. She decided to take a chance and see if she was right.

"Are you taking us to my husband now? Has he agreed to pay for our return?"

The slight hesitation told her all she needed to know. Farmon wouldn't be delivering them back to Anthony.

"Of course. That's why I'm here. We're taking you to Linfield now."

Laurel made a show of things. "Thank God!" she exclaimed, throwing her arms about Hannah. Then she whispered in her friend's ear. "He's lying. When you get the chance, run."

She pulled Hannah to her feet, noting that neither man held a gun on them. Farmon must have thought them broken in spirit by now and posing no threat, especially since they supposedly believed they would soon be freed.

"Come along," he ordered.

She clasped Hannah's elbow, knowing the girl might be a little unsteady. The large man set off and they followed him. Farmon brought up the rear. They were led back down the staircase and along the same long, dark corridor they'd traveled before. When they reached the door to the outside, the man pushed it open and held it while they exited the building. She spied a small coach in the alley. No driver was present so she assumed this man would drive and Farmon would ride inside with them.

The henchman turned away to open the vehicle's door, presenting the best chance they would ever get. She knew if she got into the carriage, she would never be free. Nudging Hannah, she hissed, "Run."

Immediately, Laurel wheeled and jammed her knee into Farmon's bollocks. He gasped, moving his hands to his groin. She'd gone over and over in her mind what came next. Balling her hand into a fist as Gentleman Jack had taught her, she drew back her arm and smashed it into his nose. She didn't know if the loud crunch came from his nose or her fingers breaking as pain lit her hand on fire.

She was grabbed from behind and knew it was the large man. Before she could react, she heard her name called out.

By Anthony.

He spun her around. Laurel recognized him but couldn't compre-hend him being here. Rage distorted his handsome features. He pushed her aside, raising a pistol and aiming it at Farmon.

"Wait!" she cried, latching on to his forearm and forcing it down.

She knew he had killed many times during war. He was a different man now. If he murdered Farmon in cold blood—even to keep her safe—it would haunt him. Eat away at him. She couldn't allow Farmon this last victory and enable him to be the ghost between them in their marriage.

"Killing him isn't good enough," she said. "Have this monster rot for the rest of his life in prison. Take everything from him, including his freedom. Let him know every day that he is suffering because you put him there."

Laurel held her breath, not knowing if through his fury, Anthony understood what she said.

He nodded and suddenly Jeremy and Luke latched on to Farmon. She turned and saw Hudson and Merrick pummeling Farmon's minion into submission. A stranger appeared. He produced handcuffs and tossed them to Luke, who caught them and snapped them around Farmon's wrists. The stranger pulled out another pair and Hudson and Merrick restrained the man they held so he, too, could be controlled.

Anthony's arms enveloped her. "You're safe, my love."

He kissed her and all her fears melted away. She entwined her arms about his neck, pressing as close as she could. Then she jerked her head away.

"Hannah!" she cried, looking for her friend.

Hannah flung herself at Laurel and the two clung to one another. Then she was pulled away, enfolded in Luke's arms. She found herself being passed from him to Hudson to Jeremy, as Merrick and Anthony watched, smiles on their faces.

"We need to get you home," her husband said, returning to her side and slipping his arm about her waist.

The stranger introduced himself as a Bow Street Runner and told them, "I'll see these two back to headquarters. They'll be charged by the magistrate."

"You'll need help getting them there," Merrick said. "Toss them into this coach. I'll drive you to Covent Garden."

"I'll ride with you," Hudson said. "I want to watch Farmon every moment until he is led away."

Merrick climbed onto the driver's seat as the Runner hoisted a cursing Farmon into the vehicle. Hudson pushed the other man and he, too, was brought into the carriage. Hudson climbed inside after the Runner and closed the door.

Merrick took off, calling out, "Tell Rachel I'm fine."

"I'll fetch Strong," Jeremy said, hurrying away.

Luke put an arm about Hannah to steady her and then he released her. Peeling his coat off, her wrapped it around her.

"You'll be fine, Lady Hannah," Luke reassured. "Jeremy has arranged for a doctor to be waiting, just to look you and Laurel over."

By now, the carriage pulled up. Anthony assisted her and Hannah into it. He pulled Laurel into his lap, his strong arms holding her, keeping her safe.

"I'll never let you go," he promised.

As Strong drove them through the empty streets of London, Jeremy said, "We are going to my townhome first. A doctor is waiting, as well as Catherine, Rachel, Cor, and Leah. They are eager to see you. Hopefully, Alford will arrive with good news."

Laurel frowned. "What do you mean?"

Her husband said, "Alford offered to take my place and bring the ransom to the kidnappers. He knew I wanted to be with you."

"How did you know Farmon would be moving us at the same time the ransom meet occurred?"

Anthony shrugged. "Hudson told us Farmon would never return you. While his thugs were collecting the money, it made sense he would move you. We'd already learned where you were, thanks to the Bow Street Runners and a young barkeep who'd seen you and Hannah brought in. He gave us valuable information. We'll be taking on him and his younger sister to help them find a better life."

All this information overwhelmed her. Laurel rested her head against her husband's shoulder, inhaling the familiar scents of his soap and cologne.

They arrived at the Everton townhome and went inside, where she and Hannah were swarmed by all her female relatives. Hugs and tears were plentiful. The waiting doctor spoke to them briefly and they assured him, beyond their chafed wrists, that no harm had come to them.

Then Leah shouted, "Alex!"

Lord Alford sauntered into the room, carrying a large satchel. He lit up as his wife flung herself into his arms and kissed him over and over. Laurel totally understood how Leah felt.

The couple joined the group and Alford said, "Everything went as planned. They called me Linfield and took the case with all the money inside. The Runners gave chase and took them into custody." He raised the case in his hand. "All the money is here so we can head to our banks later today and deposit the funds into our accounts once more."

Laurel realized that not only had all of these men risked their lives to save her and Hannah but they'd also helped in paying the ransom.

"Thank you," she said. "All of you. No matter what role you played in seeing Hannah and me safely returned, we are grateful from the bottom of our hearts."

Anthony wrapped his arms about her. "It was your relatives, Laurel. They are who saved you. In my darkest hour, I turned to them—and found just how important family can be."

He kissed her, a kiss that told her just how much she was loved. It spoke of the unbreakable bond between them and the years to come, ones in which their love would see them through whatever life brought their way.

Anthony broke the kiss. "Shall we go home, my love?"

"Home is wherever you are," Laurel said.

EPILOGUE

Three months later . . .

"WHERE DID I put them?" Laurel asked herself aloud, looking for her gloves. "I know they were here just a moment ago."

"Are you looking for these?" Anthony asked.

She looked at her husband, who seemed to grow more handsome by the day. It seemed impossible but she fell more in love with him with each passing week. She had loved him before her abduction but ever since they'd been reunited, Laurel treated each day as the only day they might have together. She had known great happiness and love and appreciated it all the more after her experience, knowing how fast it could be snatched away. They lived and loved and laughed richly and deeply, never taking a moment for granted.

Today marked a very special day—for two reasons. The dedication ceremony for the new school built on the property Anthony had purchased would take place. Not only had Mrs. Kinnon hired an additional teacher as Laurel had recommended, but two others had been added to the staff. Anthony had poured all his efforts into seeing the school completed quickly, wanting the children to begin the upcoming school year in the new space.

She would also tell him today why she had turned so absentminded recently. Laurel smiled, deciding to keep her secret a little longer. If she told him now, they would never make it to the dedication ceremony.

Her husband handed her the gloves and she slipped them on. Anthony pulled her into his arms and gave her a lovely, lingering kiss.

"I'm so proud of you and all your hard work," he said.

"I merely worked with Rachel and Mrs. Kinnon to come up with the design. You are the one who badgered everyone so construction would be completed quickly."

He nuzzled her neck. "I do everything for you, love."

She kissed him. "I do the same. We need to go downstairs," she reminded him.

"I know we are celebrating the opening of the school today. Promise me we'll have our own celebration tonight, Duchess."

Laurel grinned. *If he only knew.* "I'll hold you to that, Duke."

They went to the foyer and found Aunt Constance smiling at Hannah and Brixley. The couple had been inseparable and he'd come to Anthony last week, asking for Hannah's hand in marriage. Laurel was pleased to see the two engaged. It would be a love match from the start.

"Brixley," Anthony said in greeting. Turning to the butler, he asked, "Is the carriage waiting?"

The butler assured him it was ready and they went outside. For ten o'clock, traffic moved briskly and they arrived at the orphanage in less than half an hour. As Anthony handed her down, Laurel's gaze roamed over her old neighborhood. It was changing, thanks to the Duke of Linfield. Her husband had picked up where Julius Farmon had left off and had begun buying various properties in the area. The difference was Anthony considered his purchases not only an investment for himself but in the very people who lived here. Already, the quality of life had begun to improve as he'd started renovations at several tenements he'd purchased. Those had led to additional jobs, putting more people to work. Anthony worked closely with Mr. Chase, his business manager, and Laurel could see the neighborhood starting to flourish. It was cleaner. Safer. Friendlier.

Many locals had gathered for the dedication, interested in meeting the Duke and Duchess of Linfield. Along with them were several of her family members. She went to Luke first, who held his two-month-old daughter.

"Let me see her," she said.

Teasingly, he replied, "I don't think so. You might steal her away," before laughing and handing her over.

Laurel cooed at the baby, remembering how she and Anthony had been the first family members to visit Luke and Caroline after the baby's birth. Her husband, who continued to grow and change, was now close to all her brothers and brothers-in-law and he played uncle to all the children when they visited relatives.

She handed the baby back to Luke and embraced Caroline, telling her, "You are already regaining your figure."

"Nursing seems to help." She eyed her husband. "And running as Luke chases me."

"You make sure I catch you every time," Luke said, his emerald St. Clair eyes twinkling.

Rachel waved her over and Laurel greeted her and Seth, who wriggled in his mother's arms.

"Take him, Evan. I must speak to Laurel." She handed her son to his father and pulled Laurel aside. "I've told Evan. And Caroline when she and Luke arrived in town last night. Wait. There's Catherine and Leah."

Rachel motioned the pair over. They came and greeted Laurel and Rachel and then Rachel said, "I'm bursting with good news. Seth is going to have a new brother or sister come early next March."

All the women squealed with excitement, kissing Rachel's cheek and wishing her well. Laurel did the same. From what she figured, she would also give birth in March, probably the middle of the month. Not only did she not want to steal attention away from Rachel and the good news her sister had just shared, but Laurel wanted Anthony to be the first to know. She would tell him today and the others after a couple of weeks had passed.

Anthony joined them. "Mrs. Kinnon has need of you. She's ready to start the program."

Laurel excused herself and the next hour flew by. Mrs. Kinnon spoke, praising the work begun by the Duke and Duchess of Everton and now taken in a new direction by the Duke and Duchess of Linfield. Anthony made a few, brief remarks and then indicated for Laurel to join him.

"My wife wishes to say a few words," he told the crowd.

Panic filled her. "What do I say?"

Her husband cradled her cheek. "What's in your heart, love."

She stepped forward as he moved aside, allowing all the attention to be focused on her.

"I was born in this neighborhood, along with my twin brother, Hudson," she began. "My mother, Dinah Wright, raised us two blocks from here. The three of us worked tirelessly and never seemed to get ahead, despite all our efforts. I always dreamed of a better life. That dream came true with my marriage to the Duke of Linfield. He has made it his personal crusade to improve the lives of the citizens in this area. He is bringing new businesses and jobs and has especially taken an interest in the children at this orphanage."

Laurel took a deep breath. "Many children will attend this school, built and paid for by my husband. He provides the salaries for its teachers and has purchased the books and slates. The orphans who attend this school will receive a stellar education, with his promise to help find them jobs when they complete their education. Because of that, I would like to dedicate this school in my husband's name, to honor his work in this community. Ladies and gentlemen, boys and girls—I give you Linfield School."

The applause was deafening. She turned and held out a hand and

Anthony took it. He kissed her cheek.

"The name Linfield stands for good now, Anthony. You need never be ashamed of it again."

Happiness radiated on his face. Laurel knew she couldn't have made him any happier.

At least, for now.

They were surrounded by many of the residents in the community and made sure to speak to all of them. Various family members waved to her and took their leave, seeing she would be busy for the next hour or so. Finally, the crowd abated, leaving only them and Mrs. Kinnon, who thanked them heartily for all their efforts.

Anthony led Laurel to their carriage and said, "Merrick signaled to me that he was seeing Aunt Constance, Hannah, and Brixley home." One eyebrow arched. "You do realize that means we have the carriage all to ourselves."

She laughed. "I'm sure you and Evan planned it that way."

"Let's just say it's convenient to have a brother-in-law. Or two. Or more."

He saw her inside and climbed in after her, the footman closing the door behind them. Immediately, her husband lifted her into his lap.

"Perfect," he said as the vehicle took off.

His palm cradled her cheek, stroking it, then it slid to her nape as his arm went around her waist. Slowly, he lowered her until his lips met hers, brushing tenderly back and forth. Desire rippled through her and she slid her tongue lazily along his bottom lip, tracing it. He growled and urged her mouth to open to him, his tongue seeking hers. They kissed several minutes until she broke away, breathless.

Heat filled his blue eyes. "I want you," he said, his voice low and rough.

"Now?" she squeaked.

"Always," he replied, kissing her again deeply.

Laurel lifted her head. "I'd like to tell you something first."

"Tell me whatever you wish, Duchess. I am yours to command, ready to do your bidding."

She flattened her palms against his chest, one above his heart. It beat steadily.

"I wanted to tell a secret. It won't be one to keep for long. We'll want to share it with others."

He smiled lazily. "What kind of secret?"

"We're going to have a baby come March."

Beneath her fingertips, his heart began to thump wildly. His smile and eyes widened. Joy filled his face.

"A baby? Ours? In March?"

"Yes," she managed to say before he covered her face in kisses. Between each kiss, he murmured a single word.

Baby . . .

Finally, he stopped. "You have made me the happiest man in the entire world, Laurel." He lowered his hand and placed it atop her belly. "I already love this little one more than words can say." Tears glimmered in his eyes. "And I love you, Laurel. With all my heart. You took a cold, broken man and made him whole for the first time in his life."

Anthony kissed her again. Laurel decided it was the best kiss of their marriage.

Until the next kiss.

THE END

About the Author

Award-winning and international bestselling author Alexa Aston's historical romances use history as a backdrop to place her characters in extraordinary circumstances, where their intense desire for one another grows into the treasured gift of love.

She is the author of Medieval and Regency romance, including *The Knights of Honor, The King's Cousins, The St Clairs,* and *The de Wolfes of Esterley Castle.*

A native Texan, Alexa lives with her husband in a Dallas suburb, where she eats her fair share of dark chocolate and plots out stories while she walks every morning. She enjoys reading, Netflix binge-watching, and can't get enough of *Survivor, The Crown,* or *Game of Thrones.*

Made in the USA
Lexington, KY
24 October 2019